SPECIAL THANKS

I want to give a special thanks to the people that made this book possible, from those who read each chapter as I wrote it and offered feedback, to those who helped build the world and the lore, not only for this book, but any sequels to follow.

Putting this together has been hard work, as not only have I focused on a conclusive story to be told here, but the stories that would then lead on from it. This was only meant to be a single book and has turned into something else entirely, every second of writing it as fun as the last.

So without further ado, thank you to:

Kunal - For reading the first copy, providing feedback and helping me create this alternate universe.

Heloise - For providing useful info pertaining to immunisation that would serve to make the book and the lore more believable.

My dearest brother - For supporting me in this, providing feedback and helping me develop a lore packed world.

You three have truly been pillars of support, both for me and for this, so again, all my thanks.

To those reading for the first time, I hope you enjoy the read and thank you too for all the support.

Knowledge is power... knowledge is and always has been the very foundation to which our world was built upon, the key to our survival. The sharing of knowledge has served to not only advance our understandings of that which exists around us, but build for the future. Knowledge has not been without flaw, no one could ever say we attained greatness without obstacle and conflict, but it has often been with the ambition of uncovering the great unknowns. In our thirst for knowledge however, we so quickly abandoned our sense of duty to one another, to our survival as a species in order to selfishly harbour knowledge for our own gain or to hide away our illegitimate or immoral methods for obtaining it and its purpose.

Knowledge is indeed power... but to those without access to it, what is it?

If the repeated mistakes of mankind have taught me anything, it's that we should fear not what we have yet to learn, for we have no control over that, but what we already know and have chosen not to share.

Fear the unknown.

CHAPTER 1 - TERRY

August 20th, 6:45am - 5 Hours until outbreak

. . .

"The oldest and strongest emotion of mankind is fear, and the oldest and strongest kind of fear is fear of the unknown"

— *H.P. Lovecraft*

. . .

It was the sound of the buzzing alarm clock that roused Terry Burnham from his deep slumber, a sound that had become less frequent to him over the course of the last few years. His once thriving business collapsing and subsequently filing for bankruptcy could both be attributed to that, but since that was the unfortunate case, there was little reason for him to wake up so early.

Groaning, he shuffled to the other side of the bed, as far away from it as possible and attempted to drown out the sound with the pillow.

His attempts to ignore the unpleasant sound consisted of burying his face further into his pillow, but it became abundantly apparent that that was doing him no favours, so conceding, he outstretched his arm, masterfully searching for it without looking and before long, found what he was looking for, that damned button to turn it off.

Chuffed with his achievement, he drifted back to sleep... for all of fifteen minutes, before the nefarious little bastard went off again. Typical, what he had honestly expected after pressing the *snooze* button was beyond all conceivable logic.

He accepted defeat and pushed himself up from the bed, groaning and slowly opening his eyes, allowing them to adjust to the surrounding light.

He felt like a mess and he could barely remember the events of the night prior. What time was it?

Glancing over at the alarm clock, he stared at it blankly until his eyesight had focused enough to register what was displayed.

7:01, he had already overslept, but he was still good for time. He had at least an hour still to play with.

Swinging his legs over the edge of the bed, he sat there rubbing his stubbled face, yawning and stretching.

He could just about remember the events that took place yesterday, a great deal of pathetic self-pity, angry calls to his solicitor, pleading calls to his bank, the usual austerity bullshit, oh and he couldn't forget the comforting embrace of a bottle of Daviduke Whiskey, the same bottle that now lay on the floor empty besides his feet.

The overwhelming urge to piss compelled him to stand up, turn off the alarm - *seriously* off this time - and make his way over to the bog, leaving the bathroom door wide open.

He flicked on the bathroom light, stood before the toilet and basked in the sweet release of opening the floodgates and letting that water flow. If there was ever one advantage to living alone, it was that he could leave the toilet seat up and the bathroom door open without the constant yattering about it, a small win perched upon a mountain of problems.

He glanced over towards the mirror besides him, his grisly reflection staring back at him.

Fuck, he was a mess. He was in desperate need of a shave and something needed to be done about this ginger mop on his head, he looked like a drugged-up version of Santa Claus and those red eyes weren't helping matters.

Moving his jaw in a circular fashion to relieve himself of an ache, he left the toilet seat open once again and stepped closer to the mirror. Beneath the blanket of hair that he had allowed to accumulate, mostly due to stress and lack of self-care, was a fairly handsome looking white man, a little paler than he would have liked, but you couldn't be everything. He wasn't tall, but he could safely say he was above average.

Not that he was some prince charming before, but he certainly didn't look homeless, that went without saying. He was neither muscular or fat, average build he'd say; finding the time to hit the gym had simply never been easy, but he had plenty of that now, so maybe it was about time he stopped making excuses and just do it. A man in his early forties, such as himself, ought to be taking better care of himself.

He sighed and picked up the shaver, might as well start with that.

Stepping out of the bathroom fresh faced and beardless, he drew the curtains, allowing the sunlight to pour into his little box apartment. Grabbing a comb, he straightened his mess of a hair.

Would there be time to get a haircut? He could just about fit it in if he hurried.

He put his glasses on and checked the time again, before scampering into the kitchen, 7:21, there was still time to grab some breakfast.

"Good morning, Cindy", he said, to which his artificial personal assistant, a Soba-tech product that had become exceedingly popular over the past five years, recognised his voice and replied.

"Good morning, Terry. Would you like morning updates?" A soft spoken, British female accent.

"I would".

"Understood. Today is August the twentieth, the temperature in your local area is twenty-one degrees Celsius. Due to a crash, traffic has built up specifically around and between Holborn and Tottenham Court Road. All underground trains are running normally. On breaking news today, Prime Minister Andrew Parlow has taken a hard stance against NOMA operatives after a series of terror attacks across the globe days before the national election, stating that *terror will not and never will be tolerated, the people will not fear the oppressors and those responsible will be stomped down hard upon with justice*, this comes right after a string of attacks across Europe, including the Home Office shootings and the festival bombing, to name two, both of which NOMA proudly took responsibility for. Some have accused the prime minister of pushing an agenda before the elections in order to sway voters. Cypher, responsible for leaking confidential and incriminating information about large corporations and government institutions, has once again struck, this time targeting Aradin, placing them at the epicentre of a scandal implicating them in deliberately overpaying certain members of staff and underpaying others, this comes after their new A88 models had to be recalled for faulty scanners, resulting in fifteen deaths within just a few short days of its launch. Aradin refuses to comment on the matter, but it is expected they will make a full disclosure in due course. In other news, David Hallinan, a famous comedian and influencer in the seventies, passed away in his bed last night, his wife stated that his passing is a tragic blow to not only her, but the world that loved him. Lugo Neil, suspected leader of the three accused in the Walters Foundation massacre investigation, a horrific tragedy that left twenty-four dead and six critically injured, was released on technicalities yesterday after the three accused committed suicide. Dr Marlen, the founder of the Walters Soldier Re-assimilation Foundation was last quoted as stating that *he has never known such pain, his thoughts also go out to all those who lost, those responsible will face justice and serve their time, it will never heal the pain we are now forced to endure, but at least we have comfort in knowing they will no longer be able to do harm to others*. Since the recent developments however, Dr Marlen hasn't been available for comment, but the move has been the cause of controversy, sparking protests outside the court where Lugo stood trial...".

"That's enough misery for one morning I think, Cindy.

"Understood".

"Geez, I suddenly feel compelled to drown myself in the bathtub. This is why people don't listen to the news. Cindy, why is the world so shit?"

"I don't understand your question, could you try asking it in a different way?"

"Why do bad things happen all the time?"

"Bad things happen, good things happen, from good, bad can manifest, but from bad, good can also shine through, that's the balance of life".

"Should have expected a philosophical reply", Terry groaned.

Terry didn't consider himself a religious man by any means, but if a God really did exist, why didn't he intervene and prevent all the cruelty in the world? How could humans be so barbaric? How could monsters be allowed to co-exist amongst everyday normal innocent folk?

He opened the drawers and took out a bowl for himself, pouring cornflakes into it, but upon checking the fridge, he realised he had no milk.

"Shit! I was supposed to buy some on the way home yesterday". How had it slipped his mind? It looked as though he had no other option.

Leaving the bowl on the counter as it was, he took out two slices of bread and stuck them in the toaster, grabbing two eggs while he was at it. Keeping an eye on the time displayed on the digital clock, he fried the eggs, making himself a brief egg and butter sandwich.

The quick snack took no more than 25 minutes, so after brushing his teeth, changing into something warm - because you could never be too sure with British weather -, grabbing his keys, wallet and mobile, he was out of the apartment, locking it behind him.

The apartment block was far from special, but it was dirt cheap, a luxury in this age. His landlord was a hero for doing him this solid whilst he was temporarily living off of job seekers allowance.

He waited for the elevator to come up and descended to the bottom floor, to be greeted by the bitter chill of British autumn weather, as expected.

There was no car for him to drive, that luxury had been taken from him over three months ago, so getting used to the whole idea of using public transport, was now something he had to live with. This whole clam card thing for one, wasn't so bad once you got used to it, but what was with those ridiculous prices for a single journey? When did travel become so expensive? He didn't recall it being anything like this as a child.

He crossed the road and ventured over to the barbers, Joe's, contemplating whether or not it was the best decision to make. Surely it wouldn't take any more than 15 to 20 minutes, right?

CHAPTER 2 - TERRY

8:35am - 3 Hours, 10 Minutes until outbreak

. . .

OUT NOW!

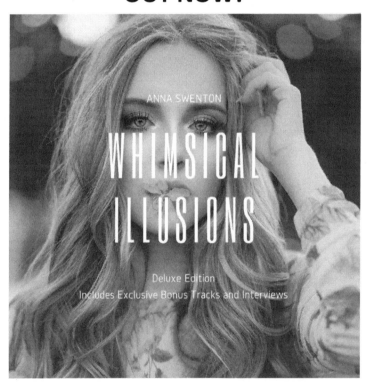

. . .

Terry stepped out of Joe's an extra 10 to 15 minutes late, cursing his lacklustre decision-making abilities. He was late, he was stupidly late. Who would have expected the barbers to be *that* busy this early in the fucking morning?

He was supposed to be in Ilford by 8:45 and had his haircut not taken so long, he would have certainly made it in time. There was no way he would make it there in the next 10 minutes. Waiting for the number 25 bus soaked up another precious 5 minutes he couldn't afford to lose.

She would definitely be pissed at him and in the interest of avoiding the pronoun game, *she* being his ex-wife.

No more than 5 minutes into his journey and the vibrations of his tPhone 4 - he really needed to upgrade this phone, he was already 4 generations behind - in his pocket, had him bracing himself for the worst.

He dug through his pockets to reach it before the vibrations ceased, pulling it out to face him. There on the screen was a picture of his ex-wife, a beautiful black curly haired woman, with light brown eyes to compliment her gracious curls. Beneath the picture was her name, Natasha Burnham, a constant reminder of what once was.

Why had he never changed or at the very least removed the surname? Why was he hanging on to the past? Somehow the minor action of changing her surname on his phone was a brutal reminder that it was all over, there was no hope and when a part of him still clung on to that glimmer of hope she would return to him one day, he simply couldn't muster up the courage to do it.

There was still that small matter of the new man in her life he had to contend with, and by small he meant gigantic, epic proportions even.

He slid his finger across the screen, putting an abrupt end to the funky - albeit a little embarrassing for a grown man such as himself - pop sound of Anna Swenton, a ringtone his daughter had put on his phone two whole years ago and taking a breath before lifting it to his ear.

"Natasha..."

There was an uneasy silence before he heard her exasperated sigh.

"Where the hell are you?"

"Something came up, I'll be there shortly".

"You were supposed to be here now, you promised".

"Yeah, I'm sorry, I just..."

"Spare me the bullshit excuses", she snapped, "Some of us are working, I can't afford to get to work late, you did this shit to me last time, I'm not going to end up like you".

"Come on, that's just uncalled for, I'm not doing this deliberately".

"Are you behaving this way because of Daniel and I?" Her new fiancé, though why she thought to mention him was another question. Just his name alone was enough to irritate Terry, like the scratch of long nails against a chalkboard.

"The kids are waiting for you, it's for their sake alone that I still bother, don't fucking ruin that".

"Natasha, you know I'm not trying to".

"Then make the bloody effort, stop being an ass".

"I'm doing my best".

"Well do better, this isn't good enough! If you still want the privilege of seeing your kids as often, try frigging harder!"

"Natasha, I'm..." Terry was silenced by the sound of the dial tone. She had hung up on him. *That* certainly caught him by surprise, he couldn't quite tell or not, but he was fairly certain she was angry.

After 17 years of their marriage, she left him not because of his situation, but because of the little faith he had in himself and her. After he lost his job, she was tremendously supportive of his efforts to get back on his feet, but she wasn't willing to join him on his self-destructive path, it was something she had already endured in a previous relationship and needless to say, that didn't fare well. She insisted he get help and his stupid pride obstructed that opportunity to maintain his marriage. So here he was living alone, comforted only by his regrets.

Maybe he could argue that she had given up on him too easily, but that wasn't going to change a damn thing now and he still had to face his own exceeding contributions to the problems.

Maybe it was paranoia getting the better of him, but it just seemed like she met and started dating Daniel awfully quickly, was there a possibility they knew each other beforehand?

Wasn't there usually a cooldown period with these sorts of things? Sensitivities to keep in mind and more.

The morning was plagued with the usual public transport nightmares, inside the bus was the rowdy kids on their summer holidays with seemingly poor upbringing, little old ladies asking 21 questions of the bus driver and of course you couldn't leave out the hoodlums at the back blasting some rap or grime, Terry didn't really know the difference. Outside the bus was another story, congestion meant they were getting nowhere quickly.

Needless to say, strolling up to the apartment his ex-wife was now living in with Daniel, at 9:05 certainly wasn't a good look.

He dialled number 35 and waited, within seconds there was a buzz and the main door to the building clicked open. It was a swish building, understated wasn't welcome here, everything was made to scream look at me in adoration and wallow in that pitiful delusion that one day you'll be able to afford anything remotely as nice as this, you peasant.

The only thing more painful than knowing another man took the woman of his life away from him was knowing it was a man he could probably never match up to. There was no denying that, Daniel lived good and if there was one thing out of all of this that eased his mind, it was that his kids weren't living rough and his eldest daughter could still attend her private school. Though it was tremendously frustrating to have some other man ensuring that, Terry's *replacement.*

The floor was marble, the elevator had a theme tune. Really? A theme tune? Not even standard hotels had that.

He got off at the top floor and stepped out into a lush corridor, decorated with the finest art, ornaments and furnishings. It wasn't like he hadn't been here before, but every time he came here, it was a reminder of what he had never been able to afford. A reminder that even when he *was* working, he earned nothing compared to *this* guy.

Lawyers were paid very well it seemed, especially senior partners. It felt like a privilege just to be able to step into the building, far less approach the door of someone living in the building.

Daniel's front door swung open before Terry had even reached it and there stood his fuming ex-wife glaring him down. She was in that navy-blue pencil skirt she used to wear, with her leather handbag at her arm, black stilettos and her hair tied back. The sweet fragrance of Venelisse Eau de Parfum tantalizing his nostrils as he passed her by, the perfume that Daniel had bought for her.

"What the fuck are you playing at?" She snapped.

"Look, I got held up", Terry lied. Somehow, he knew that telling her the truth wouldn't go down well.

"What the fuck could have been so important you were late to pick up your own children?" Before he could reply, she raised her hand. "You know what? I don't care to know. You're just going to make up some more bullshit".

Terry stepped past her into the apartment, a massive open-plan apartment with a stunning view of London. Though there wasn't a great deal to see on a miserable day like today.

"Daddy!" Came the voice of his 8-year-old son, running out from one of the bedrooms. A shaggy ginger haired kid, with a freckled baby face his mother always saw the innocence in. He wore a grey and green sports shirt with long beige trousers and white trainers. He even had on his coat, just to tell how ready he was for the day.

"George!" Terry replied, kneeling down to embrace him. "How was your match?"

"If you bothered to show up, you would have realised they lost the match. Fullwood came third overall in the league", Natasha replied, as she stood over him with her hands on her waist in a condescending manner.

"Third ey? Not bad. I bet you were a right little star. Might have to see if we can get you into a club", Terry said to his son.

"That's the least of your concern, in case you hadn't noticed, your son has secondary school to think about and your daughter has her GCSE's to think about. Has any of that crossed your mind?" Natasha intervened.

Having left where they used to live, George had begun attending Fullwood primary while Ria, his 16-year-old daughter had begun attending Stratford Girls' Grammar School. George was born for sports and lived for anything that involved running and kicking a ball, his daughter on the other hand was academic, very sharp and independent. Their different personalities in some ways reflected that of their parents, with George's happy-go spirit and Ria's attention to the little details.

George had always been easy to get on with, never having given any trouble whatsoever, Ria had been a daddy's little girl up until a few years ago. Since then, her desire to be seen as a respectable adult led her to respect her father less, a man she often considered to be the most useless man in her life. She didn't have to say it, Terry could always see it in her eyes and cold attitude towards him, an aura of bitter resentment.

Terry knew he could only blame this on himself, she was a smart girl and she was able to see and understand everything that went on around her, but he knew not how to earn her respect again, aided no further by his lack of a job and Daniel wriggling his way into their lives.

"I haven't forgotten", Terry replied, without looking up at her.

"Good, I just have to remind you about your priorities, because every now and then you seem to neglect your duties as a father". As she said that, who should step out from the kitchen with a sandwich in his hands? None other than Daniel, the smug, self-assured son of a bitch who derailed Terry's entire life. There he stood in his grey suit, slick gelled hair and polished shiny black shoes as though he owned the world, looking down on Terry both metaphorically and literally.

He was a middle-aged white man, pompous looking with perfect white teeth, perfect skin, chiselled jawline and a broad muscular stature. He embodied manliness and that was infuriating. Ria liked him, Natasha was in love with him and only George didn't like him. Good lad George was, a supporter of his real father all the way.

"Terry..." Daniel greeted him in a monotone manner, with a simple nod. He didn't need to say anything more for Terry to know that he was laughing inside. Laughing at Terry's failures as a father, laughing at Terry's inability to satisfy his former wife, emotionally, financially, mentally and sexually. The very thought of them in bed together churned Terry's stomach.

Believe it or not, but Terry had already *attempted* to punch the guy in an earlier instance, due attention to *attempted*, simply because he failed at even that. Daniel partook in boxing as an extracurricular activity, little to Terry's knowledge at the time, of course until he ended up himself with a broken nose, black eye and a wife who hated his fucking guts.

If Terry had planned to win her back, any possible hope he had was dashed when faced with this man, the very quintessence of perfection and success.

"Daniel..." Terry replied, standing up to gain some height and not feel so emasculated. They need not say anything further to each other. The silent sparks between the men was as far as a *conversation* would ever go.

"Where is... where is Ria?" Terry asked Natasha, merely glancing at her as though taking his eyes off Daniel for even so much as a second could potentially dent his pride as a man. Natasha sighed and looked around as though trying to escape the question.

"The kitchen. Though it'll take some serious persuasion to get her to come with you now, I spent the best part of yesterday convincing her to give you the benefit of the doubt and it's taken you just the morning to mess things up. As per usual, you never fail to disappoint".

"I'm here now".

"Yes, and I'm late, so whatever you plan to do, do it quickly". Terry stood up and Daniel stepped aside to let him by, all the while maintaining that smug look on his goddamn face.

The kitchen was grand and modern, spacious and light, the perfect example of what a modern-day cook wanted from their kitchen and another reminder of what Terry could never afford. In the middle was an island counter with stools propped up against it and pots and pans hanging above it.

Ria sat leaning over the counter with her head propped up on one arm and turned away from him. She wore a pretty flowery dress with shorts and her favourite brown boots.

"Ria", Terry called out to her, but she didn't hear him. Convinced that she was simply too pissed off to talk to him, he tried a few more times, all the while approaching her, but she didn't respond. It was only when he reached her side did he realise that she had her headphones in her ears, flicking through a magazine. Terry tapped her on the shoulder and she turned to face him, his pretty, brown curly haired daughter with the splitting image of her mother.

"Hey there, kiddo", he greeted her, not before she had noticed him and removed the headphones from her ears.

"Oh, it's you. Hey, I guess", she replied. She wasn't exactly ecstatic to see him and that was no surprise if what Natasha said was true.

"You don't seem happy to see me".

"I'm over the moon, can't you tell?" She replied, forcing a sarcastic smile to go with her sarcastic reply.

"How are you?"

"Fine, not that you care". She returned to her magazine.

"Don't say that, you know I do. I'm sorry for getting here late. I just... got held up is all".

"Don't mention it, it's not as if I ever believed you'd be here on time or anything. I'm surprised you even showed up".

"I made a promise, I just want to spend time with you two today".

"Don't force yourself".

"It's not like that".

"Then what is it like?"

"Like I said, I want to spend some quality time with you both, just us against the world, like we used to be".

"What, so you can feel less guilty about being a shit father?"

"Watch your language and no, it's because I love you kids, more than you both know".

"Whatever, words don't mean much without action, Terry". Terry didn't like the fact she had begun referring to him by his first name rather than *dad,* but at the same time he didn't feel as though he deserved the title given how little of it he had been recently.

"That's why I'm determined to prove myself. Give me a chance, Ria, we'll have a good day, the best day, I promise".

"Whenever you promise something, the opposite happens".

"Well I'll make sure nothing interferes with our day out together".

"Mum, can't I just stay home?" She shouted pass Terry, disregarding her father completely.

"Go with your father, I can't leave you home on your own".

"Why not, I'm old enough now, Lacey's parents let her stay home alone".

"It's not about legalities, it's about trust and before you answer, no, I don't trust you in the slightest".

"Aww come on, mum, what's going to happen? We're on the top floor of a building with more security than a police station".

"You are going with your father, we are not arguing about this, Ria. My patience has already been thinned, don't test me any further". Ria sighed.

"Fine…" She stormed past her father into the hallway of the apartment and Terry couldn't help but feel hurt by her words and actions.

Following her through to the hallway, he waited for the kids to gather their things before finally escorting them out of the door.

"Christ, I'm so late", Natasha grumbled as she rummaged through her handbag.

"I'll give you a lift, sugarcake", Daniel suggested and locked the door to the apartment behind them.

Sugarcake? Cringe inducing, also another man calling his ex-wife, sugarcake? Anger inducing.

"But then *you'll* be late", Natasha replied. There was something incredibly uncomfortable about having two people talking indirectly about you. It was clear that their frustrations were directed at Terry and that only aided to further his guilt.

"I'll be fine, the client can wait, if he wants the best, he won't mind waiting a few more minutes for it", Daniel replied as they all made their way into the elevator and he pressed the ground and basement floor buttons.

"Are you sure? It won't be too much trouble?"

"Stop panicking, I'll have you at work in no time". He kissed her in front of Terry deliberately, knowing full well what emotions and thoughts the action would induce in Terry and even though she pulled away to lessen the blow, the damage had already been done.

Terry's stomach tightened and holding back his fury was unbearable, he literally wanted to strangle this man. How much of a fucking arrogant tool could a person be? To kiss someone's ex-wife right in front of them when you know full well that they are still in love with her is a whole different world of cockiness.

"Thank you", Natasha replied.

As they arrived at the ground floor, Terry stepped out with the kids, with Daniel remaining in the elevator holding the door open for Natasha to part ways with her offspring. Natasha kissed them both and warned them to be on their best behaviour before standing upright to face Terry. Her expression changed, becoming more serious.

"Have them home by six thirty at the latest", she warned.

"Aren't they on half term, I was hoping to take them..." Terry begun but was cut short.

"Six thirty, Terry. I don't really give a sh... crap about what your intentions were. You lost that opportunity when you arrived late this morning. Don't push it, otherwise I'll make life difficult for you, I promise you that. You are treading on thin ice at the moment, *really* thin ice". Why was she treating him like a child? Was this an attempt to embarrass him in front of Daniel?

"... Six thirty it is then".

"Good. No later, I'm warning you".

"I heard you". She gazed back at the kids.

"I love you both, stay close your father, he's idle minded, so you both need to be extra perceptive and aware".

"We're not kids anymore, mum. We get the message... well at least I'm not", Ria protested.

"I know, I know. But you can't blame me for being worried, it's only because I care".

"Go, go! Haven't you got work?" Ria insisted.

"Yes, yes I do, have fun you two", Natasha replied, kissing them both on the forehead and running back into the elevator.

"We'll try", Ria muttered.

CHAPTER 3 - TERRY

9:39am - 2 Hours, 36 Minutes until outbreak

. . .

Venelisse Eau de Parfum

. . .

Ria had barely uttered a word since they left that apartment block. The extent to which she appeared willing to communicate consisted of short grunts and the slight shake or nod of her head. It was fairly evident she had no intention of making any effort whatsoever today, despite Terry's persistent efforts.

Eventually she stuck her headphones into her ears, begun babbadooing her friend - a free messaging app all the kids used these days - and refused to partake in any of the bonding session between her brother and her father.

In the interest of keeping the calm, Terry chose against pulling the headphones from her ears and encouraging her to at least try to be a little less antisocial, at least for now. He couldn't deny that the urge to confiscate her phone and possibly break it was overwhelming.

Passing by a quaint little bakery, the aroma drifting out of the open doors was quite enticing. They were in no particular rush now that he had picked them up, they had the whole day and to be entirely honest, rushing here had pretty much negated any effects eating the toast and fried eggs he had had this morning had done to benefit him.

"Should we get something to eat first? Have you two had breakfast?" Terry asked.

"We had cereals", George replied. Ria didn't answer and to be honest Terry wasn't expecting an answer from her, not with those headphones in her ears and her eyes pasted to that screen.

"How do you feel about hot chocolate and scones?"

"Yay! I love scones!" George yelped, waving his arms in the air, "Can I have a gingerbread man too?" Terry sighed.

"Just this once, but don't tell your mother". Deciding to play Ria's game, knowing it was probably the only way he would get a response from her, Terry texted her asking her what she wanted, knowing how silly it felt, considering the fact she was standing right beside him.

Having read the text, she pulled out a headphone and said "Nothing".

"Are you sure?"

"I'm fine. Where are we going anyway?"

"It's a surprise", Terry replied.

"I bet it's lame".

"It'll be an enlightening experience".

"Another way of saying *boring*?"

"Not at all".

"Whatever". Her attitude was beginning to bug Terry, it took a tremendous amount of willpower to remain level headed at this point.

"Not hungry anyway, you two eat what you want. I also have my own money, you don't need to buy anything for me". Where did that come from? This was a girl who used to always want pocket money

They stepped into the little shop and Terry instructed the two children to find a seat whilst he made his selection. The pretty little blonde girl standing behind the till was most pleasant, whipping up his order of a double cappuccino, hot chocolate, gingerbread man, single scone and croissant.

Whilst paying, Terry made small talk, anything to get Natasha and Daniel kissing off of his mind.

"Crap morning isn't it". The girl laughed.

"On most days I'd probably agree, but today doesn't seem so bad. I feel good about it, maybe something good will happen. We tend to get our share of assholes...oops". She covered her mouth and apologised. It was Terry's turn to laugh.

"Ah, don't worry about it, I spend the majority of the day cursing people".

"That was unprofessional of me". Terry waved his hand.

"Forget about it. Why are days usually crap... if you don't mind me asking. I would have thought working in a bakery with delicious bread, biscuits and what have you, would be somewhat enjoyable".

"Yeah, none of which you can eat, so it's like tantalising torture. To top it off, customers in the mornings are right... so and sos. We had a customer yesterday complain about me making small talk and showing", she air-quoted, *"false politeness like a robot.* We don't always get jerks like him, but it really dampens the day, yaknow?" She was certainly the chatty one once you got her started.

"Well, keep that false politeness up, I'm sure most people appreciate it".

"Especially the little old ladies", she laughed.

"Especially them".

"That will be three pounds and forty pence", she informed, returning to the till after having placed Terry's orders on a tray. "Are those your children?" She asked as Terry dug through his pockets for the right change, he was never one for wallets, one of the many things that used to agitate Natasha.

"They are indeed", Terry replied, glancing towards them.

"They look adorable".

"Thank you, both a handful though".

"Going through that stage I guess, better now than later I guess".

"Any idea how long that lasts?" Terry asked as he paid up. She laughed.

"No, sorry. Different personalities and stages of maturity and all that".

"Thank you anyway, I guess it's just one of the many things I'll never understand. Have a nice day".

"You too", she replied, handing him his receipt.

Terry left her there and returned to his kids at the table to find the two of them bickering.

"What's this about?"

"George, just being an idiot", Ria groaned.

"Don't call me an idiot!" George replied.

"Then don't be an idiot".

"I'm not!"

"Okay, okay, calm down you two, what happened?" Terry asked, attempting to quell the anger.

"He won't sit still and almost knocked down my fucking phone", Ria replied. Two old ladies looked over in shock. Terry apologised and returned his attention to Ria.

"Language, Ria, do you swear like this in front of your mother?"

"No, because I respect mum". That reply stung and shook Terry's hopes of rekindling his relationship with her, but he wasn't about to give up just yet.

"Please respect me as well".

"Well do something that deserves it and stop being a jerk". Terry sat down next to George facing her.

"Do you hate me, Ria?"

"Well that's a dumb question, of course I do, after all, the only reason I'm here is because mum made me come". Terry couldn't believe the words spilling from his daughter's mouth, they were like acid, burning the very skin from his bones.

"I don't believe that's true, or at least I don't want to believe it".

"I don't much care what you believe, just control George, if you can even do that. You don't need to worry about me", she replied with the shrug of her shoulders.

"Of course I do, you're the fruit of my loins, whether you like that or not". She screwed up her face and shuddered.

"I really don't want to think about you and mum having sex or any of the fruits and loins that went into it".

Terry turned and apologised to the old women behind him again, who appeared utterly disgusted by the conversation. George's ears perked up as well.

"What's sex?" He asked. Ria burst out laughing.

"See what you've gone and done, it's not funny", Terry replied, most unamused by the turn of events, "Please watch your mouth. When did you pick up such a filthy tongue? This is not the Ria I knew".

"The Ria *you* knew grew up without you".

"I can see that, I want to make it up to you if you'd at least offer me that chance".

"You're just going to say that and mess up again, like as if you haven't messed up enough already, *dad*".

"I know that. My life has been a mess lately, I want to get back on track and be there for all of you again, I want you all back in my life. We can be a family again, a real family".

"Even with mum?" George asked excitedly.

"Her too", Terry replied. Ria laughed.

"Now I know you're dreaming. If you think for a second you'll be able to snatch mum from Daniel, you've got another thing coming, besides, I like Daniel and I prefer him a whole lot more than you at the moment". The hurtful words just kept coming. When had his daughter become so malicious and uncaring. She was right when she said she was a new person, Terry was having trouble understanding who she had become.

"I still love your mum".

"If you did dad, you'd make more effort, you wouldn't keep disappointing us. You're always such a fucking disappointment". The old women behind them had had enough and turned to them.

"Excuse me, could you control your daughter, this is a respectful establishment. We don't want to hear that kind of language, especially not from someone so young".

"I'm sorry about..." Terry was about to apologise, but Ria cut in.

"Oh, shut up and mind your own business", she snapped, rolling her eyes.

"Ria!" Terry scolded her as the old women gasped.

"Parents and children these days!" The two old ladies got up and stormed out of the cafe, but not without Ria laughing and mocking them.

"Do you find that funny?" Terry asked, unamused by Ria's behaviour.

"Yeah, kinda", Ria replied between laughter.

"I'm glad you feel proud of yourself".

"Thanks".

"That was sarcasm".

"Oh really? I thought you were genuinely proud of me about something for once in your pathetic life", she replied sarcastically.

"What's that meant to mean? I've always been proud of you".

"You certainly don't show it, even before the whole financial issue. Remember that play you promised you would be there to watch and support me when I told you how nervous I was? Remember how you let me down? Mum was there and I was so nerve racked I went silent and couldn't move. I felt humiliated, dad".

"I told you that I got held up that day".

"Yeah, you did, but you always conveniently get held up when I need you, when *we* need you".

"That's not entirely true".

"It is, dad! What about George, how many times have you let him down? It's only because he's young and naive that she still looks up to you, he wants a dad, *his* dad. But how long do you think it'll be before he too gives you the cold shoulder? Then you'll *really* have no one". Terry went quiet for a few moments, realising the detrimental impact his behaviour had had on his family, how his period of self-destructive tendencies had created rifts between he and the ones he loved. Ria was right, he failed them.

"I won't let that happen. Like I said, I'm prepared to make amends and I honestly love all of you with all my heart. I know I don't say it very often, Ria, but I am tremendously proud of you, not so much the new attitude, but the fine and beautiful young woman you have become".

"Whatever..." Ria replied and plugged her headphones back into her ears.

Terry wasn't entirely sure if that was her way of avoiding any further conversation. Ria was never quite sure how to handle compliments, so being given one she really didn't want to hear was probably a serious struggle to deal with.

Feeling rather flustered by the whole debacle and her strong words, Terry wasn't entirely sure what to do next, how could he possibly turn this day around for the better? Ria had closed herself off from the world and it was clear that she was prepared to remain like this for the rest of the day. If she kept this up, she wouldn't be able to appreciate any of the surprises he had in store for them.

Distracted by her complete lack of interest in the two and his probing concerns, Terry couldn't help but miss most of the questions George had about topics Ria had inconveniently brought up in front of him.

They sat in that cafe for the best part of an hour and twenty minutes before deciding to make a move. Terry had made no progress with swaying Ria's mind around to his way of thinking and he wasn't entirely sure if he was going to be able to do that at all today. Still, it was a start and Rome wasn't built in a day.

Terry couldn't help but think about her words. Though she was 16 and 16-year olds often said a great deal of things they didn't mean or frankly quite fully understand, but those words had the stinger of a scorpion behind them, potent and heart wrenching.

Terry glanced at his watch, 11:00 exactly, perfect timing, for he needed a mere hour or so to get into central London. See, despite the morning having gotten off on the wrong foot, things were shaping up a great deal better than expected. Terry wasn't about to give up hope on Ria just yet, he had the whole day ahead of him to prove to her his worth and he was about to damn well do that no matter what it took.

Arriving at Ilford station, Terry took to the queue to buy travel tickets for the two kids and top up his clam card. An old woman asking a seemingly endless spree of questions about the senior citizen's pass, held up the queue for a while, but eventually they managed to get to the ticket booth window.

Supplied with his and the kids' tickets, finally, they made their way down to the platform to wait for their train. The Shenfield to London Liverpool Street arrived no more than two minutes later, they appeared to be good for time, a vast contrast from the debacle that occurred that morning.

Terry still couldn't erase the thought of Daniel and Natasha kissing from his head, every time he thought he was free of the memory, something only moments later would remind him of it and spike his irritation.

Why was it when you most wanted to forget something, subliminal messages start popping up all over the place?

The train pulled into the station in timely manner and the doors slid open for them to board. For a half term and post peak time rush, it seemed to be unusually busy. Terry let the kids sit and took a spot standing next to them, half tempted to confiscate Ria's headphones again as she took a seat and completely disregarded him. Maybe it was wise to wait until they arrived at Liverpool Street before taking it, he couldn't have her swearing and creating a scene on a busy train like this.

Spacing out as he gazed out of the train window, he considered his life and how similar it was to this scenario, racing past faster than he could imagine and he was missing every stop. Maybe it was time to slow down and focus on the little things, the things that would redefine this life he led, if it could even be referred to as a *life* anymore.

CHAPTER 4 - RIA

11:25am - **20 Minutes until outbreak**

. . .

. . .

Simply attempting to get off the train and walk down the platform towards the ticket barriers was an unpleasant reminder of just how crowded London could get, thank heavens it wasn't peak period. If it wasn't the forgetful or idle-minded holding things up, it was the slow walkers and wayward suitcases.

On top of that all, there were those people who would wait until they reached the barriers to pull out their clam cards and those who despite it not working, would try persistently, as if half expecting the machine to realise the error of its ways, holding everyone else up in the process.

No sooner had he thought that, Ria did exactly the same thing whilst attempting to multitask her texting habit and find her ticket. That was the last straw, time for Terry to switch to dad mode, so without thinking, he grabbed her phone from her hands along with the headphones plugged into her ears and shoved it into his inside coat pocket.

Ria almost immediately protested.

"What the hell are you doing, Terry?"

"Dad, I'm dad to you".

"You're no dad of mine! Give it back!"

"No, we are going to have fun today as a family, whether you like that or not". It was a good thing the noise of the crowds drowned them out, because their raised voices were already enough to pique the interest of any nosey bystander.

"Fun? You call this fun? It's more like torture! Every minute I have to spend with you is a challenge just to prevent being sick!"

"You don't mean that".

"I mean it! Give it back!"

"Fine, have it back", Terry replied, surprising her, but she knew all too well that it was too good to be true, for no sooner had he taken the phone out of his pocket, he removed the battery and gave her the shell.

"Give my fucking battery back!"

"Ria! I told you to mind your tongue. You're not getting this back until the end of the day".

"What! You can't boss me around!"

"Well I am, get used to it".

"Ugh! I hate you!" She yelped and threw a strop. "I didn't even want to go on this stupid trip! I could have stayed with Lacey! I would have *actually* had fun unlike this... crap".

"You'll enjoy yourself, we've only just begun".

"Yeah right, whatever! I wish you'd just disappear! I'm not going to talk to either of you!" She snapped, crossing her arms and pouting her lips.

"I'm sure you eventually will, but until then, I'll happily wait until you do".

"You'll be waiting a long time. Give back my battery!"

"You might get it back earlier if you at least try to enjoy the day". She shot him a sarcastic smile before completely disregarding him once again.

"You could do better, but I suppose that's enough to ask for now. Should we make a move then?"

"Yay!" George yelped with glee. Terry took him by the hand and led the way towards the underground, Ria following reluctantly behind in silence.

As they passed through the barrier, at least there was one thing Terry could be satisfied with, it was her new-found ability to focus on one thing, the most important thing at the given time. Hopefully now she would no longer hold up the queues and boy were there queues. The crowds were stressful just to look at, let alone travel amongst. Had he not held George's hand so tight, he would surely lose him. Was there some kind of event going on?

A platform attendant answered the question.

"Customer information, we apologise for the congestion this morning, we have severe delays on Metropolitan, Hammersmith and City and Circle lines due to engineering work. Again, we apologise for the inconvenience and any disruptions this may cause to your journey. Thank you for your patience".

The slow trail to the trains was mind-numbing, only to have to fight to get to the front of the platform in order to get on the trains at all.

Who would believe at the time that just a little impatience could turn the tides of their fates so drastically and the same could be applied to just about everyone here.

No sooner did the train doors open, people flooded in, some even disregarding those attempting to get out. Ria, who stood just a little ahead of Terry and George was forced by the crowd onto the train, but before Terry and George could join her, another man pushed in without regard for the fact that they were ahead of him and took the remaining spot

"Fucking idiot, don't just push in! We were ahead of you!" Terry snapped.

The man, headphones over his ears and seemingly oblivious to the world around him, completely disregarded Terry.

"Ria, can you get off?" Terry shouted over the man.

"I'll be fine, Terry. Where am I getting off? I'll just wait for you both there, you don't have to make an issue out of nothing, I can look after myself".

"Okay, we'll get on the next train, meet us at South Kensington".

"Fine…" She replied simply and said nothing more. If anything, this to her was probably a blessing, a chance in a lifetime to escape her so called father.

"Don't wander off", Terry instructed as the doors shut, but he was fairly certain she didn't hear a word of it. The train left the station as George waved to his sister and it took some time before the next one would arrive.

Terry and George managed to wriggle their way onto the next train and there they waited for the doors to close, not realising what lay in store for them.

Ria stood in the train ahead of them as it pulled into Aldgate, brooding over her confiscated battery. She glanced down at her dead phone and just looking at it stirred her irritation even more. Why did Terry have to be such an asshole? Were the imps of bad luck - a reference to a concept she and her best friends had conjured up to make sense of unfortunate situations - looming over her again? Was she the only one with an incompetent chimp for a father? Bearing in mind that the thoughtless comparison was probably more offensive to the chimp.

He was supposed to be supportive like that of her friends' fathers, instead he was a constant burden, a constant disappointment. It wasn't that she genuinely hated him, she just hated the fact that she *wanted* to hate him so much. What was it about his half-hearted attitude that irritated her so much?

Ria could recall a time when he was her favourite person in the world, so maybe it was just the fact that it was more painful for those you loved the most to let you down.

What hurt her most wasn't that she was ashamed of him for not having a job or anything like that, in fact that was pretty miniscule in the grand scheme of things. It was that he made little to no effort to return to the person he used to be. The business loss shouldn't have been the be all and end all, but it sapped every last bit of zest for life he had remaining and in return he constantly let her down,

She didn't want to admit it, but she only swore at him because this man posing as her father didn't deserve her respect and it was the only time he seemed to *react* to anything anymore. Did things really have to get to the extreme before he acted like a father should? Then if swearing and acting up in front of him was the only thing to spark any reaction out of him, at least enough to prove he wasn't just a zombie, then she would keep on doing that, because as things currently stood, the dire reality was that Daniel was more of a father figure to her than he could ever be.

In the interest of keeping up appearances, she neither ignored nor disrespected Daniel or her mother for that matter, in any way. That didn't mean that by any measure she liked Daniel, but it was just frustrating that he was a great deal more attentive, responsible, proactive and useful, not to mention a lot easier to introduce to and brag about to her friends, the ones who hadn't had the misfortune of meeting her real father already that is.

It was true, her life was a sham, a massive cancerous sham, but there wasn't exactly a fountain of choice. She was embarrassed to even be with her real father. He always looked scruffy, rarely showered - today was a surprise, evidence that he had made some effort - and always looked lazy and spaced out, it was pathetic. The least he could do was care about his presentation a little more, maybe then he'd be presented with more job opportunities.

She sighed and fanned herself with her hands. She hated underground trains, they were always hot and filled with smelly people crammed together like sardines, it was truly an unpleasant experience. At least if she had her music she would be able to drown out the anguish. Her taste in music had transitioned drastically over the years, from cheesy pop to indie rock, that was part and parcel due to the change in trends and maturity having kicked in, it simply wasn't cool to listen to pop any more. Even if there were some guilty pleasures, her friends wouldn't find out she liked them.

On the thought of friends, she only had three that she could genuinely call friends and they were the same and only ones that knew about her family situation, she would fabricate most of the rest to the other more materialistic girls at her school.

Pompous daddy's girls playing big shit, the lot of them. Honestly, her school was absolutely plagued with competitive, status obsessed, materialistic girls. Maybe that seemed a little hypocritical given that here she was doing just that.

She sighed again, she was doing a lot of that today. Lacey, a friend she had known since nursery, probably wasn't going to get a reply until Ria got her battery back. Before Terry had taken her battery hostage she was in the process of sending a text regarding a boy she had a crush on. Lacey, being Lacey, mocked her taste in boys usually, but she was particularly brutal with this one. It probably had something to do with the fact he was a bit of an airhead, but he was also tremendously cool, he smoked after school and had a tattoo his parents didn't know about, also he was really cute, with his long rocker hair, his tall stature and those brown puppy dog eyes that left her in a trance every time they locked gazes. Had her father simply not shown up and dragged her on this stupid trip, she could have gone to Lacey's house and invited him over.

On top of his good looks, he was a bass guitarist and loved the artists she did about as much as she did.

What she didn't know was whether or not he liked her back. He kept sending all these mixed signals, total mind fuck, like put his arms around her to say hello. Who did that to someone they didn't know all that well? Why were boys so infuriatingly ambiguous and why did she get so irritatingly nervous and immature whenever he was around?

Just thinking about it now was kind of embarrassing and the only one she felt she could ever genuinely talk to about it was Lacey, despite her mockery. It trumped talking to her mother who would no doubt go into an awkwardly drawn out lecture about the birds and the bees, a lecture she certainly didn't need at this age.

The last few days had been spent sending childish Snapee photos to one another, it was probably she and her friends' best way of communicating their feelings towards matters such as these, for sometimes words just weren't enough to express how you felt.

The train pulled into London Blackfriars, having already passed Tower Hill and Monument. For every few people that got off, a wave of others got on. The crowd and heat were becoming unbearable, how many stops did she have left? She wriggled herself into a position to look up at the tube map. Seven more? It already felt like she had been in here forever, did she really have to endure seven more stops worth of this?

Ria decided to distract herself with other thoughts before her predicament overwhelmed her, but her thoughts kept returning to her phone, which in turn made her think about her father.

When did she start to feel this resentment towards her father she wondered. He had never been all there even during the times he had a job, he was always busy and when he was home, he still looked distant. Maybe the reason Ria wasn't too bothered initially about him losing his job was because she naively believed it would give him more free time to spend with the three of them as a family. What a disappointment *that* was. He was probably more distant now than ever before.

Maybe it was the combination of his distant attitude and lack of enthusiasm towards anything in particular that frustrated her, or maybe it was the fact that he simply allowed Daniel to step into their lives without fighting for mum the way he should have and by fighting, she didn't mean physically, they all knew how well that turned out last time.

Even taking that particular altercation into account, it wasn't so much the fact that he lost that irritated her, what could she really expect her passive, mostly docile father to do against someone who participated in one of the most violent popular pastimes for a hobby, it was the fact that he completely gave up following that. Men were supposed to fight for their woman, even when pummelled to an inch of their lives, they were supposed to attempt any means necessary to win her back, they were supposed to scale cliffs and traverse lava fields in order to win her heart back, but he just gave up and receded into his shell like a scared turtle, basically handing mum over to Daniel and that was the story of his entire existence , half-heartedly attempt to do something and then give up the moment that hill starts to look a little more like a mountain.

Even hearing him talk about mum now is somewhat aggravating. He can barely get his act together, any thoughts of getting them all back together as a family again and winning mum's heart was delusional at best.

There was also the time he was so distracted with something else, he forgot George in a store. Anything could have happened to her kid brother and his idle-mindedness could have resulted in a sour situation he would forever regret, so it was a good thing they kept it from mum. Could she imagine if they did? She'd probably never see her father again. Why was he such an idiot?

She gazed up again, they were just passing embankment and on their way to Westminster, five stops left to go.

Honestly, most of the time she was with her father, you would think she was the adult, of course today he was trying to prove something, though what that was, was beyond her. It so wasn't his personality to behave like a responsible adult for a change. There was that time he was involved in a minor car crash and he wasn't even the one responsible, yet still, he was the one apologising to the guy who was. Why couldn't he just be more of a man for a change?

Thinking about it now, it was an accumulation of various factors that created this resentment towards her pathetic father and she didn't believe he would change anytime soon. It was any wonder how he managed to get through the daily grind of life. Mind you, she hadn't visited her father's flat in well over a year, it probably looked a dump now that mum had stopped cleaning it and thinking about it, the only reason she even used to was probably out of guilt, the guilt of going off with Daniel and leaving him a complete wreck, it was probably the least she could do.

As the train passed St James's Park, her thoughts trailed on to her mother, brother and Daniel. George was a pest to say the least, he loved rough play and never knew when enough was enough. If he wasn't football it was wrestling, that fake crap with men rolling around in their underwear, who could like that? Still, he was harmless in a manner of speaking and if he had his ways, it was only because he strived to be like his father so much, someone Ria would have preferred he didn't try to replicate. There wasn't much else to think about regarding George to be entirely honest, he was her kid brother, a pain but no more than to be expected from any male. She had grown more than accustomed to the headache that males brought with them, but the least she could hope for was that her kid brother grew up to be nothing like his father.

On the thought of men, there was also Daniel, a man that took himself a little too seriously. His drive to be the best at everything was almost nauseating, from the best looking, the best at tennis, the best at golf to the best at mundane things like flipping pancakes, who gets competitive over pancakes for God sake?

He'd wake up early just to perfect his slick hair and gleaming white teeth, it was almost creepy how much he admired himself. There wasn't anyone he loved more than himself and even her mother spent less time in front of the mirror. But at the very least he was an affluent man, there was no doubt about that. He had earned his keep from the ground up, so it was understandable that he was so obsessed with presentation, but Ria knew that he simply wasn't compatible with her mother. It wasn't that he didn't love her or couldn't protect and support her, because he was more than capable of all, but he would never replace the love he had for himself with anyone else, his house always had to be immaculate, something that irritated Ria and his mood would fluctuate more than British weather.

If she and her brother even so much as moved a cushion out of place, he'd be on their backs faster than a man on a horse. He was an utter nightmare to live with and even worse to cross. Still, maybe living with him was enough to spur her father into action, maybe it was the wakeup call her father needed, though whether or not her mother felt the same way was another question.

Ria was fairly certain that her mother was madly in love with that man. Her mother often reassured she and her brother that she would always love their father, for feelings were no simple thing to get rid of, but she simply wasn't *in* love with him anymore.

Who knew what her mother was thinking half the time, she was such an unpredictable woman, so it was never easy to tell if her intentions were calculated to stir some kind of reaction from her father or otherwise. As the thought of her mother lingered in her mind, she was jolted back to reality by a sudden and shocking screech of the train coming to a stop halfway between Sloane Square and last stop South Kensington.

"What the hell?"

CHAPTER 5 - RIA

11:45am - Outbreak

. . .

FACT FILE #1:

NOMA, the name coined by the terrorist group formally originated in Eastern Europe and since spread its influence across the western regions of Europe, stands for **N**ationalist **O**perative **M**ovement **A**llegiance. Its specific origins within Eastern Europe are not known and the name was initially, whether intentionally or not, associated with the gangrenous bacterial infection. It has now somewhat ironically adopted the definition. Rumours are awry that some European politicians are secretly enabling NOMA with funding and resources. NOMA's humble beginnings derive from the impeachment of European states former leader and avid fundamentalist, **Benedicte Spades**, who was ousted because of his ties to the New Soviets. Conspiracy theorists speculate that he one of the founders of a New World Order secret elitist group with substantial power over politics, finance and more, the **Honourary Masons**.

. . .

By the time the train had completely slowed down to a standstill, everyone on board had already been flung towards the front direction of the train. Naturally, irritation set in as everyone on board composed themselves, some having falling over on to others.

As people began to chatter, most speculating the cause of such a drastic halt, the intercom clicked on.

"Customer information, sorry about that, the train ahead pulled to a stop just before the platform. I have no information yet, but I'll be sure to provide it as soon as I know. Sorry for the delay that this will cause to your journey and we'll be on our way as soon as we get the go ahead". A soft click and the intercom cut.

"Ah, for fuck sake", a man not too far away from Ria grumbled and followed it up with a tut, a common expression of irritation for Brits.

Ria composed herself and looked around, it was clear that irritation had settled in, people made that obvious with their facial expressions alone. No one wanted to admit it, but as time ticked away and the hot and cramped conditions failed to improve, they were all, including Ria, beginning to understand and relate to that angry man.

Ria sighed, today just wasn't going her way. Ten minutes passed and the intercom clicked on again.

"Erm... sorry about this, folks, hopefully we should be on our way soon. Something is happening at the station ahead, but I have yet to receive any information, until then, we'll be waiting here a little longer for the signal. Once again, sorry for the disruption this will cause to your journey". The intercom clicked off once again.

"See, it's this kind of shit that gets me angry, how the hell could you not know what's happening? Who are the incompetent pillocks in charge? Typical, and this is the public transport we pay increasing fares for every year, everyone, a bunch of chimps running the show and charging us more for less!" The same angry man snapped, but this time there was a crowd of angry commuters less reserved about agreeing with him.

Like a scene straight from a TV show, everyone begun contributing towards his point with other unpleasant experiences they had had using public transport and mentioning how ridiculous this situation was.

A lady turned to Ria and asked if she was okay, Ria smiled and nodded. She wasn't, but the lady didn't need to hear her further complaints about the heat and cramped conditions, there wasn't as though there was anything either of them could do about it.

Another ten minutes passed and anger had set in before any further announcement was made and when it did finally come, it certainly wasn't what anyone wanted to hear.

"Customer information, I err..." There was a drawn-out silence before he continued. "I'm going to begin leading you all off from the back. Please do not panic. I will lead us back to Sloane Square. The current running through the tracks has been switched off, but that doesn't mean we shouldn't still take precautions, it is dark in some spots and the emergency lights haven't been switched on. I only have one torchlight, so if any of you have flashlights on your phone or at the very least a bright screen, please make use of them when we enter the tunnels. Stay close to everyone else, it's easy to fall behind. I'll make my way around to the back and we can make our way from there". For the third and final time, the intercom clicked off, but this time the passengers on board didn't know what to make of it.

There was no shortage of concerned chatter, but there was no doubt that things were a great deal more serious than they had all first anticipated, even that angry man had few words to say.

Fortunately, there were at least a few open parts of the tunnel on the journey back that that allowed the outside light to pour in from above, so the journey back to Sloane Square wouldn't be entirely dark and treacherous.

Ria was beginning to get more frustrated, as if she wasn't enough already. This was the perfect scenario to chirp or write a status about, but guess what? She didn't have her battery! She couldn't call her mum to let her know of the debacle and she couldn't call Terry to let him know of what was going on either. Even if they walked back to Sloane Square, what was she going to do? Just stand there and wait like an idiot?

It wasn't long before the crowd of people on the train began making their way towards the back of the train in an orderly fashion, they had nothing yet to panic about after all, even if an aura of concern loomed over them all.

Ria couldn't help but wonder what the cause of the holdup had been, then she began to ponder if it was something she even wanted to know.

Upon reaching the back of the train, she was helped down to the grotty space between the tracks, a surprisingly high drop from carriage to the ground that she would have had a tough time managing.

It felt strange standing on the tracks, she usually associated it with death. Growing up, she had honestly believed that any contact with any track at any time was more than enough to instantly kill her, not much different from how the notion of standing on the road meant instant death, regardless of whether or not there were cars on it. It was her overprotective mother that had instilled that irrational sense of fear she upheld to this day. It was that very same irrational thinking that irked her now.

As others remained behind to help the remaining half off the train, Ria proceeded ahead.

The journey back was treacherous and despite the open areas, it was still very possible to buckle over or twist an ankle, if not between the tracks, then the rough ground besides it. Ria was just glad she wasn't wearing heels like some of the other women, this couldn't have been a pleasant experience for them. She herself had decided to wear her converses over her heeled boots today and even though they were getting scuffed on this gravelled mucky surface, it beat twisting an ankle.

Ria glanced back when she got the chance and saw an entire line of people following behind, further proof that the train was ridiculously crowded.

It was interesting how events like this brought people together, they could grumble about their mutual displeasure to their heart's content, but completely ignore each other when things progressed normally in their lives, usually absorbed by a book, phone, music, tablet, handheld games device, whatever it took to avoid eye contact with other commuters.

After what felt like an eternity, she reached Sloane Square and was helped up onto the platform by platform attendants. The crowds were still ridiculous and there besides the platform was the very reason why the train they were on couldn't have just returned the station, another train, completely empty with another not far behind it. It appeared that whatever had occurred at South Kensington had subsequently stalled the entire circle line.

Ria could barely move on the platform as people blocked the way, listening for news, waiting for friends and loved ones and making calls, despite platform attendants' best efforts to disperse the crowds.

Given that the train at the platform was a district line train, assuming the one behind it was another circle line and that Terry and her kid brother had managed to board it, they ought to be here somewhere, but as crowded as it was and without a phone, there was no telling where they might be.

The intercom clicked on and there came a voice, "Ladies and gentlemen, could you please leave the platform and exit the station via the stairs in a calm orderly fashion, we still have more people trying to get onto the platform and if you block their way, it will only make the process of getting everyone off the trains slower and more difficult. If you could kindly wait for family members and friends outside without blocking the roads, this would be greatly appreciated. To those planning to make their way to South Kensington and other stations beyond, we have been told to inform you that those stations have been cordoned off due to an incident which occurred. We have no further information at present". The intercom clicked off and the mass of people began making their way up the escalators.

Where the hell were Terry and her kid brother? This was exactly this reason why taking her phone battery was counterproductive.

As Ria silently fumed, the entire crowd of noisy people were silenced by the screams of people emerging from the tunnels that Ria herself had only just a moment ago come from.

Unable to see over the crowds, Ria no other choice but to sit tight and listen.

"Help!" A woman screamed and faced with looming threat, the crowds erupted into a state of panic, the polar opposite of what the person on the intercom instructed.

More people began screaming and it was only but a matter of time before frantic panicked pushing and shoving, pushing and shoving the likes of which she had never experienced before, as desperate people made for the escalators. If Ria wasn't panicking before, she certainly was now.

Terrified she would be crushed, she focused on keeping her head up so as to not get distracted by her feet, whilst at the same time managing her footing and her footing so as to no topple over. Every step was potentially fatal in this surging crowd of terrified people, so if micromanaging her every action seemed excessive, it was all just as justified.

She pushed forward, trying to make her way towards the escalators, her heart thumping in her chest. She didn't believe she had ever been this frightened, what the hell had spooked everyone like this?

Confused platform attendants tried to calm everyone down, but were shoved out of the way by people who probably didn't even know what was going on themselves.

The next thing Ria heard was enough to make her all the more desperate to get out of this station. A shrill shriek and the loud smash of something behind, sent the crowd into mass hysteria, as though they weren't panicked enough. They went from pushing without any consideration to *move or get crushed* levels of aggression and Ria was beginning to find it a difficult just being able to breathe.

She could do naught but watch in horror as an old woman before her, was shoved without regard for her wellbeing and despite her desperate terrified pleas for them all to stop.

The ascending steps would become their next obstacle, as though the challenges weren't stacked against them enough as it was.

As compelling as the idea was to turn and look behind her as the steps gave her visibility of the on goings behind, it was taking just about all of her focus just ascending these steps without stumbling.

As though having scaled Mount Everest, she finally reached the top of the steps and the crowds loosened up a little, as people stepped free of the narrow confines of the escalator and quickly made for all available exits.

Ria ran out into the open and inhaled as though it were the last gasp of air she was entitled to, relieved to finally be free of that crushing crowd. After a moment spent catching her breath, she glanced around Sloane Square with hopes of spotting Terry or her kid brother, but neither were anywhere to be found.

Maybe it a good idea to put some distance between her and the station, she certainly didn't want to be around to witness what had started all of this commotion and several police cars racing past traffic towards South Kensington was enough to convince her that that was definitely not the direction she wanted to head in.

She wandered aimlessly down the road, people running past her on either side, unsure of what to do next. She kept glancing nervously back towards the station hoping that Terry and her brother would make an appearance and it was upon glancing that she spotted police cars pull up and surround Sloane Square station. She darted across the square and turned into Lower Sloane Street just in time to hear the unmistakable sound of gunfire. If *that* wasn't compelling enough reason to run, nothing was.

She didn't stop running until she came to Chelsea Bridge, where she stopped to catch her breath. Traffic had grounded to a complete halt all along Chelsea Bridge Road and those in their vehicles on the adjacent side of the road appeared irritable, completely oblivious to the events occurring ahead of them.

"What the fuck?" Ria repeated hysterically once she had caught her breath. She had every good reason to panic the way she was, why would police officers start firing unless they had just cause to? Officers almost never held weapons, let alone fired them in the UK.

Terrorists? It had to be, this was another terrorist attack! But by who? NOMA? Was it an acid attack? Bombing? Gas? Were they shooting people?

"Ohmygod, oh my god! I can't believe this is happening!" She shrieked, running her fingers through her hair.

She glanced out towards the river and spotted what used to be Battersea Power Station, now a renovated luxury resort that only the super-rich could afford, surely there had to be someplace she could get another battery because she couldn't remember a single number on her phone.

She grabbed the attention of a woman passing by with hopes that maybe she would know where the nearest stores were.

"There's nothing around here love, you'll probably need to head up to Victoria or Sloane Square for anything li…" The woman begun, but Ria interrupted her.

"I Just came from that direction, I can't go back there, is there any phone shops around the power station over there?" Ria pointed towards the power station.

"No, just small corner shops, those types and they won't let you into the station unless you're a guest. There are phone shops in Clapham Junction though".

"How far away is that from here?"

"About ten to fifteen minutes by bus, hop on the 344, or you could take the train at Battersea Park Station, takes about 3 minutes, the station is just past the park on the other side of the bridge, go directly across the roundabout and turn left, you'll find it just beyond the bridge".

Ria thanked the woman, warned her not to continue walking towards Sloane Square and broke into a sprint towards the station.

She stopped before the station at 12:39, all the while praying that it wasn't closed like the underground and found that it hadn't been, at least not entirely, trains were coming *from* London, just not going *into* London.

Panting, she ran up the train station steps onto the platform and hopped onto the next train heading towards Clapham Junction. The train was relatively empty and only one stop long, so the journey took no more than a few minutes before she was stepping off at Clapham Junction.

She hopped off the train and made her way onto the high street, asking anyone who would stop to listen for directions to the nearest phone shop, which with time and help she would eventually find on St John's Road and she couldn't have been more elated to see it.

She walked back out ten minutes later with a brand-new battery in hand. Finally, she had another battery! How on Earth had she managed to survive this long without her phone? It was like her very pride and joy.

She popped the battery in and switched it on, only to be bombarded with several notifications she had missed during the spell it was off.

Several were from Lacey and one from Terry, including a missed call from her mother. Had her father forgotten that he had taken her phone battery? She read his text.

'They detrained us at St James's Park, so we took the bus to South Kensington, if you get this, wait there, we'll find you'. This text was sent at 11:58, so a substantial amount of time had already passed since then.

"No Terry! Don't do that! That's where the terrorists are!" She wasted no time calling him back and was relieved to hear his voice, but he didn't sound relaxed, if anything, he sounded panicked, frightened.

"Ria! You're okay! Thank god! Where are you?"

"Clapham Junction, where are *you*?"

"Clapham Junction? What the heck are you doing all the way there? No, never mind, at least you are safe. I wouldn't have wanted you anywhere near South Kensington, it's…" He went silent.

"It's what, Terry?"

"Don't worry, stay exactly where you are and keep your phone on, we'll try to get to you, we're on King's Road".

"Okay, I'll wait here. Did you hear anything about the terrorists?"

"What terrorists?"

"NOMA! This has to be them, right?"

"Is that speculation or was that confirmed?"

"It's… I mean… I heard gunshots. The police were shooting at someone or something".

"Where? When? Did you see who they shot?"

"Erm… no, I ran before they started shooting, I just heard the shots behind me. We had to leave the train and return on foot along the tracks to Sloane Square, then everyone started screaming and running and everything".

"Okay, well I'm glad you are safe. I tried calling your mother, but it went to her voicemail. Just stay where you are, I'm coming. Promise me you won't move".

Something about Terry's tone made her believe he might know something.

"Did you see something?"

"I'll explain when I get there. Promise me you won't move!"

"What did you…?" She began.

"Dammit! Promise me, Ria!"

"Okay, okay, I promise".

"I have to go now". Just like that, the line cut as he put down the phone. She stared at it in disbelief for a minute, before deciding to put her ordeal on Chirper, a social network -

@ria_riley<3 OMG! Something crazy is happening at #sloanesquare

And not a single opportunity to make it all known did she miss, as well as on Myface, another social network -

Ria Riley: Day from hell!!! Something happened at South Kensington, think it was a terrorist attack, probably NOMA again!! Heard gunshots!

CHAPTER 6 - GEORGE

11:45am - Outbreak

. . .

Chirp all day, Chirp all night

. . .

An hour prior, George clung unto his father's hand as they stood on the packed underground train. For a boy as small as he, this was a nightmare, but at least he was with his dad. Just being with his dad was more than enough to make George happy, because they spent less time together these days.

They were coming into St James's Park now and soon they would reach South Kensington where they would find Ria, so not much more of these stuffy conditions.

Ria was quite the moody one today, what was her problem and why was she always directing it at dad? This was a mystery George could not solve, for she had once loved him unconditionally and now loathed him more than loathing would allow. What could have made her change so drastically like that?

Dad was by no means perfect, he made his fair share of mistakes and he would sometimes miss or be late to things, but he had always doted on them, always tried his best to make up for his flaws. After all, mum *did* get with that Daniel man, so it was only natural dad would be upset and make more mistakes.

George didn't like Daniel much, he often tried too hard to take his dad's place and would make condescending remarks about his father. Nobody could speak badly about his father and expect to liked, regardless of how many fancy things they bought him. This warm and comfortable feeling right here towards his real dad was worth more than any material possession.

George suddenly noticed they had been sitting at St James's Park for a while now with the doors remaining open. Passengers had already gotten off and on, so what was the hold up?

The man on the intercom answered that question mere minutes later.

"Customer information, we are being held here momentarily, hopefully we should be on our way shortly. Something is happening at South Kensington, so all trains before us have been called to a stop. I have no details as of yet, but as soon as I hear anything I'll let you know. Thank you for your patience and apologies for the delay this will cause to your journey".

So that was it, something had happened and all the trains could go no further. Terry looked down to George.

"You okay, kiddo?" He asked, to which George nodded.

"Did all the trains stop?"

"They sure did, we should be moving again once they sort out the problem".

"Will Ria be there?"

"I sure hope so, otherwise I won't be pleased". George smiled up at his father and asked no further questions. However, the situation did not improve and before long the intercom clicked back on.

"Customer information, sorry but it appears that the situation at South Kensington is more severe than I thought, we have been told not to let any further trains enter the station until the situation has been resolved. As such this train will be de-trained, I repeat, this train will be de-trained. Please exit the train calmly and make your way off of the platform, thank you".

"What?" George's father grumbled as people began exiting the train. He tightened his grip around George's wrist a little and led him off the train.

"Come, we need to find out what happened to Ria". His father led the way towards one of the platform attendants.

"Excuse me, what exactly is going on? Care to explain?"

"We know not much more than you, sir. All we can say is that something happened at South Kensington and is likely still happening, though they can't give us any details themselves".

"What do you mean they can't give you any details? How difficult is it to just assess a situation and return to tell someone briefly what is going on?"

"Sir, I understand your frustration, but we have to assume that if the situation was severe enough to suspend all trains so suddenly, then there's the chance it might be more difficult to do something even as miniscule as that as you might believe. We are simply doing what we deem most fit for the situation and right now that is to get you all off the train for your own wellbeing".

"But my daughter is on one of the trains in front, what are you going to do about that?"

"Sir, don't panic, there are procedures in place for that too. I suggest you step outside and try to reach her, you might find she has undergone a similar situation. It is dangerous with overcrowding on the platform and we have another train just behind full of people".

"So, I just wait then?"

"That's the only thing I can advise, sir".

"For fuck sake", George's father grumbled, grabbing his wrist and leading him towards the escalators amongst the crowd.

"Sorry about that, son", he said, glancing down towards George, "Looks like we're going to have to take the bus". They made their way up the escalator and outside to wait for a bus.

Before long, the bus had arrived. They boarded and sat down. Given the circumstances and how crowded the bus now was, it wasn't likely they would reach South Kensington any time soon.

George stared out of the window, he was suddenly reminded of a prior trip he and his father had taken to Highbury Stadium to watch his favourite football team play off against their biggest rivals in the season finale. It was his first attended and the most important game of the season. The atmosphere was electric and thousands of fans chanting in unison was unlike anything he had ever experienced. George couldn't have been more exciting if he tried and it was moments like that that made his father's recent woes irrelevant. That day they laughed, jumped and cheered until their voices ran dry, both dressed to support their team. Even after that they sat down to a cheeseburger each. It was such a perfect day and George could only wish to have more days like that.

The two of them never used to miss a match on television, it was really the only time his mother allowed him to have snacks and his favourites were toffee popcorn and fizzy snakes. Daniel didn't like football, he called it the game of ruffians, so any bonding potential was immediately dashed with that remark.

Why did football suddenly pop to mind now though? Maybe it had something to do with the fact that they were rushing to get to that on time too because that bus broke down.

George turned to his father and found him texting someone. Noticing his glances, his father explained himself.

"I'm texting your sister, I have a feeling she'll wander off somewhere".

George was silent for a minute, before hitting his father with a realisation.

"But didn't you take Ria's battery?"

"Oh yes! Good call, I did, didn't I. Well I already sent the text, so there's not much I can do about that. I'm idle minded today, bear with me, son. I better call your mother, you know how she worries".

His father dialled in his mother's number and put the phone to his ear. A few seconds later, he put it down and hung up.

"Voicemail. She's probably in a meeting. I'll send her a text instead". He proceeded to text George's mother, but no sooner had he finished, they were distracted by the sirens of police cars whizzing by and driving on the pavements in order to bypass the traffic. As a seemingly endless stream of police cars drove by towards South Kensington, the situation became growingly disconcerting.

George's father leaned over him to peer out of the window, but neither of them could see anything from this angle and it appeared that they weren't the only curious ones, for other bus commuters and even those outside took notice.

What could be drastic enough to draw this much attention?

"Sorry everyone, it appears that there is a bit of drama up ahead, so we may be stuck here for a while, I can't say how long unfortunately", the lady bus driver announced.

George's father tutted and muttered something under his breath.

"We'd be better off walking at this rate", his father grumbled. It was clear that he was anxious.

They were stuck there for a few minutes longer, possibly waiting for a miracle, before what sounded like gunfire erupted ahead. Initially, the sound could have been mistaken for the crackle of something, but it soon became distinctive and it was more than enough to put everyone on board in edge.

People standing on the roads ducked and some began running in the opposite direction. The ruckus drew the attention of those sitting in their cars, as they stepped out to investigate the commotion, but soon enough they too were ducking.

"Get down!" A man on the bus shouted and everyone ducked, but George's curiosity got the better of him and he peeped out of the windows again, but what he saw made him wish he hadn't. People were running, policemen were backing off and shooting at something, some were injured and being dragged or carried, before being abandoned. This was like something from an action movie, although George had never seen anything quite like this

As if that wasn't enough, window screens shattered as recoil and stray bullets hit vehicles and people in the process. Parked car alarms went off, people on the bus started screaming, the gunfire grew louder and the entire scene erupted into further anarchy as though anarchy weren't enough as it was.

Some of the bus passengers started banging on the doors to the bus demanding to be let off, others took cover in the aisle between the seats.

Suddenly George's father pulled George's head back down, preventing him from seeing anything further.

As the passengers managed to open the bus doors, George's father grabbed George's wrist and led him off the bus.

"Don't lose me! Keep your eyes on me, don't look at anything else! Do you hear me, George!"

"Yes daddy", George replied meekly, terror in his voice.

They stepped over people cowering on the floor and made their way out of the door and on to the warzone Pelham Street.

His heart racing, George's father ordered him to keep his head down and follow. Even despite spotting from the corner of his eyes human sized objects lying in the middle of the road between cars, George resisted the urge to look and kept his eyes transfixed on his father, at least until a tremendous explosion from somewhere behind them tore his attention away.

People screamed, blood was everywhere, bullets were whizzing back and forth, it was like a battlefield and George couldn't see what they were shooting at during all this commotion.

The loud smash of glass attracted their attention to the bus they were just in and a few minutes later blood splattered across the rear window.

"George! Focus on me!" His father snapped, with more assertion in his tone than George had ever seen in his life. They ran without looking back, but soon found themselves blocked by a woman and man just standing there in front of them. The question of why quickly became apparent when they gazed upwards to see a man standing atop a car bonnet twitching erratically as though having an epileptic fit. Behind his eyes was stark emptiness, he foamed at the mouth and his behaviour was somewhat hostile. Why was he standing there and what was wrong with him?

Without warning he began screaming and holding his head as though in pain.

"Amanda! You fucking bitch! This is all your motherfucking fault! You'll never be happy without me, you fucking twisted motherfucking bitch! I'll kill the bastard! I'll make sure you fucking regret leaving me!" The snarl was like that of a dog and George's father didn't even have the time to cover his ears to prevent him hearing the vile language spewing forth from this man's mouth.

Seconds after the man had begun his furious unexplained rant, he leapt from the car bonnet down onto the man in front and began ripping into his face, digging into his eye sockets with his fingers, tearing at his skin like a wild animal.

The woman accompanying the man being assaulted, rushed to his aid, pouncing on the assailant and hitting him with her handbag, but she was cast aside as though she meant nothing, slamming her into a car.

George's father wasted no further time and pulled George away from the scene before they saw anything else they wouldn't be able to un-see.

What was that? Who was that?

George's heart pounded in his little chest, overwhelmed with unbelievable fear. Never had he witnessed anything like that, never! Not even in his most violent games.

They ran into Pelham Place and turned onto Pelham Crescent, a usually quiet area not known for trouble and now filled with confused and curious people who had heard the explosion and gunfire.

George and his father had no time to stop and explain to them what was going on, they had to move and they had to move fast.

They rounded a corner to the right and found themselves on a busy Fulham Road. The sound of gunshots and sirens seemed everlasting, almost surrounding them. It was difficult to determine where and where not to run with the sounds echoing everywhere.

It was just as they were coming to the road leading into Onslow Square Road that George's father spotted another bus. It really didn't matter at this point which bus they took, so long as it could offer a means of refuge and escape from this chaos.

George's father stopped at the doors to the bus and began thumping at the door with his fists for the driver to let them in. They shouldn't have been surprised at the fact that they were rewarded with the dirtiest look possible and completely ignored, they were attempting to board at a time when the bus couldn't be further away from a bus stop. It was only as George's father attempted to prise the door open did the driver open it.

As the door opened, George's father grabbed his wrist and ushered him up onto the bus.

"What the fuck, man? Have you lost your shit? There are cameras all over the bus!" The bus driver snapped.

"You have to get out of here, drive!" George's father replied. The look of bewilderment that the driver gave him said everything that needed to be said.

"Drive where? Did you miss the long fucking line of traffic ahead? You *have* lost your shit! Get off my damn bus!"

"Please, you have to drive to safety, for our sake and the sake of all your passengers. I can't explain entirely because I don't know the full details, but there may have been..."

"Get off of my fucking bus! No one wants to hear your bullshit, man!"

"For fuck sake!" George's father turned to the curious passengers on the bus.

"Something serious is going on up the road! If we don't get moving, your bus driver could be risking your lives!"

His statement was met with startled gasps and yelps from some of the passengers.

"It's a war zone up at South Kensington, if we don't make a move we'll end up caught in the crossfire!"

"Get off, you nutter!" One teenaged girl shouted and an old man immediately agreed.

"I'm not crazy! My son and I just ran from Pelham Road where gunfire was going off and people were attacking each other!"

"Oh my God", an old lady replied.

"Who do you think you are fooling, you drunkard? Anyone can see you're just trying to get free rides, but what's more disgraceful is that you've brought an innocent kid into this!" Another man shouted.

George wished these people would take his father seriously, what he had witnessed couldn't be further from a joke, his heart was still racing.

He would need to do no further explaining or convincing, for no sooner did they doubt his credibility and sanity, a surge of panicked people running towards the bus caught their eyes. Some of those panicked individuals leapt onto the bus, forcing the bus driver to shut the doors to prevent any others taking advantage.

"What the fuck? What's going on? Are you guys taking the piss?" His attention averted to people outside clambering over the bonnets of vehicles, to which the irritable or confused owners of said vehicles stepped out to investigate or vent their disapproval, but as they stepped out, they were attacked by other people, much to the horror of the ignorant.

Attempting to differentiate the fleeing from the assailants proved impossible a feat, since it appeared as though just about anyone could be considered an assailant, from a man wearing business attire to an old lady. It was as though people had simply lost their minds, making this much more than just a simple black and white situation.

Curious onlookers had the wind knocked out of them as they were tackled to the ground without warning by crazed people, before being beaten and mauled until they moved no more.

The assailants too had certainly seen better days, some of them were bleeding heavily and missing eyes and limbs amongst other things, yet seemed unperturbed by their horrific injuries and more intent on unleashing a torrent of unyielding hell upon anyone they could lay their hands upon

"Don't look", George's father ordered, covering George's eyes, but what George had seen already was more than enough to traumatise.

"What the fuck!" The bus driver shouted and mere seconds after he said that, there was a vibrating slam from the side of the bus, as though someone had run straight into it, followed by the startling shatter of glass coming from right behind George.

George's father reacted quickly and moved him out of the way before he even had the chance to spin around and find out what created the noise and a good thing too, for by the time George did turn around, a woman leaned right the way through a shattered hole in the bus door of which she had seemingly created with just her head, if the blood streaming down her face and glass shards protruding from her head were any indication. She didn't look particularly dressed to be a harbinger of terror, but her crazed behaviour told a different tale. She screamed, hurled obscenities and outstretched her arms to grab them, all whilst disregarding the glass cutting into her stomach, the mindset and actions of no sane person.

"Dad!" George screamed, panicking.

"Stay where you are!" His father instructed. Then came the sound of another glass pane shattering from the back of the bus, followed by the shrill screams of a girl.

George turned to see what was happening. A blonde girl who had been sitting beside one of the windows towards the back of the bus had had her hair grabbed through the shattered window by one of those crazed people. Helplessly, she clung onto the man next to her and screamed out for help, but instead, all those within her vicinity very quickly separated themselves from her.

The man she clung to, began hitting her and demanding she let go.

"Get the fuck off me!" He shouted, becoming alarmingly and increasingly aggressive towards her instead of helpful and then without warning or just cause, he began thumping at her in unrestrained anger, *that* even despite others screaming at him to stop. Where had this burst of aggression come from? Fear? Needless to say, his unrelenting violence rendered her stunned and unable to defend herself in her daze, freeing him, but ultimately submitting her to a grisly fate. Her head was pulled through the glass window, the protruding shards cutting into her throat as she gurgled and choked on her own blood. Try as she might to pull away, more crazed people grabbed at her hair, making for a battle she could not possibly win. She could even scream in pain before her head was severed from her shoulders and her headless corpse dropped down between the seats.

Everyone on board erupted into mass hysteria.

Two women began crying, one man began shouting erratically and others begun holding hands and praying.

The crazed people attacked drivers, smashing through their car windows and pulling them out or climbing in. Some drivers, realising the danger of the situation and impossibility of escaping the traffic in time, attempted to flee their vehicles, others managed to mount the curb, running over anyone that happened to be in the way, crazed or not.

This was humanity, *these* were the real human instincts, selfishness and lack of remorse.

"Do you fucking believe me now? Put your damn foot down! I have a son and daughter to protect!" George's father snapped at the bus driver.

The driver didn't have to be told twice, he slammed his foot on the accelerator, ramming the bus into the back of a car and throwing all passengers on board forward like ragdolls.

Parting the cars stuck in traffic like Noah an ocean and mowing down any and all posing an obstacle, the bus driver was determined to get as far away from the scene as possible.

George clung unto the handle pole for dear life, praying that wherever they ended up was safer than here. They were coming to Sumner Place road on the right and George's father then ordered the driver to turn right.

"What the hell for?" The driver snapped.

"I have to rescue my little girl, she's at South Kensington".

"Them *things* were coming from that direction! Fuck that!"

"I have to save her!" George's father shouted, banging on the door as they passed right on by the road towards South Kensington.

"No offence, but seriously, fuck you and fuck your daughter! I ain't putting my life at risk for you!"

"Bastard! Stop this bus! Stop this fucking bus now!"

"Fuck you!"

George's father tried pulling at the door to the driver's seat and when he had failed at that, he tried his luck with the main doors, but before he could press the emergency button, the reckless bus driver swerved sharply left into Old Church Street, throwing everyone violently to one side.

They pelted down that road, forcing drivers who knew nothing of the commotion they left behind, off the road, whilst colliding with others with enough force to flip their cars upside down.

George was almost certain that this bus driver had single-handedly killed or injured more people in this short journey than those crazed people had. Blood, likely from that girl's headless corpse had trickled along the bus floor towards the front, almost reaching him and given the driver's recklessness, moving away to avoid it wasn't an option.

George didn't even have the time to reflect on what he had witnessed, to be sickened by his memories of the horrific events that had occurred today, he didn't even have the time to be traumatised, everything seemed to be in a constant state of fast forward since that train came to a stop, this was all far too real and he wasn't mentally prepared for it, he couldn't process any of the complexities of what was happening, it seemed his role to simply accept his perpetual state of mixed feelings and confusion.

They swung on to King's Road and just as George's father was about to try for the emergency lever to release the door locking mechanism, his mobile rang.

George couldn't see who it was but he suspected it was probably his mother. They had lost Ria and there was all this chaos, what was his dad going to tell her?

"Ria! You're okay! Thank god! Where are you?" His father asked, having answered the phone.

Ria? But how? Did she borrow someone else's phone? George thought.

"Clapham Junction? What the heck are you doing all the way there? No, never mind, at least you are safe. I wouldn't have wanted you anywhere near South Kensington, it's…" He stopped as the bus jerked again, narrowly missing a woman and her daughter stepping onto the road at a zebra crossing.

"Don't worry, stay exactly where you are and keep your phone on, we'll try to get to you, we're on King's Road", he continued. "What terrorists?"

Terrorists? Was this the work of terrorists?

"Is that speculation or was that confirmed?" He asked. "Where? When? Did you see who they shot?" He went silent for a moment as he listened.

"Okay, well I'm glad you are safe. I tried calling your mother, but it went to her voicemail. Just stay where you are, I'm coming. Promise me you won't move".

George began to ponder whether or not having Ria with them would have had different results. They wouldn't have needed to take that bus to end up in the middle of a shootout, that's for sure.

"I'll explain when I get there. Promise me you won't move!" His father demanded. "Dammit! Promise me, Ria!"

Suddenly they came to a roadblock, the Metropolitan police had already started to cordon the roads ahead in attempt to regain control over the situation, but at the speed they were going towards it, both George and his father had every reason to fret.

"I have to go now", George's father informed his sister, as they raced towards the blockade of police vans. He put down the phone abruptly and returned to slamming on the driver's door.

"Slow down! We're going to crash!"

"I'm going right fucking through them!" The driver replied.

"What! You'll kill us all, you fucking lunatic!"

"I'm willing to take that chance! I'm not letting them get to me like they did that girl and those other people!"

"You'll kill yourself before that happens!"

"Shut the fuck up!" The driver yelled at him.

Seconds before impact, George's father turned and dived to shield his son, as the police and civilians on the road leapt out of the way, before it smashed into the van.

The impact was so powerful that glass shattered everywhere, the bus lost traction and flipped onto its side, sliding several meters down the road, before coming to a stop. There it would remain, silent and still.

CHAPTER 7 - NATASHA

11:45am - Outbreak

. . .

FACT FILE #2:

Pogo Incorporated is an international communications organisation that provides internet service provisions, search systems, cloud base systems, mobile networking and multimedia services through its global mobile telecommunications network. Pogo INC is the largest mobile telecommunications corporation by market capitalization, and also the world's largest mobile phone operator by total number of subscribers, with over 971 million subscribers as of August 20█████.

The core subsidiary of the group, "Pogo Mobile Limited", is listed on both the New York Stock Exchange and the Chinese Stock Exchange.

Pogo owns the brand, **Chirper**.

The company was founded in 1992 and is the fastest developing company in history. A buyout by Soba-Tech was turned down in 1999, and since then the company has gone from strength to strength.

. . .

Natasha Riley, once having shared the surname of her ex, sat towards the back end of a meeting table surrounded by her colleagues and staring up at the screen the chairman of the company based in California spoke from. Communicating over Babbadoo video messaging, they were *supposed to be* discussing changes made to terms and conditioning, changes that would significantly impact their clientele and business processes overall, emphasis put on *supposed to be* because somehow they had deviated onto topics of contractors and pilot schemes, giving Natasha ample private time to resume her irritation at her ex-husband.

She knew all too well that Terry would let the kids down *again,* just as he had a habit of doing in recent years, but she had hoped that for a change he would surprise her, instead he met her expectations.

He'd been using his business collapse as a pathetic excuse to give up on just about anything meaningful. His enthusiasm for life had nosedived and he showed no signs of wanting to get back on his feet. Businesses collapsed every single fucking day, it was nothing new and he certainly wasn't the end of it. If everyone who lost a business was to wallow in self-pity as much as he, what would the world be?

Honestly, she didn't want to hate him, but he made it so difficult not to. This was the man she used to be unconditionally head over heels in love with, a man she still loved, but could no longer stand to watch destroying himself and share his rapidly sinking ship.

Take today as prime example, six thirty she was up and by seven fifteen she was ready and waiting for the kids to finish getting ready. By seven thirty-seven, they too were ready and waiting. How fucking hard was it to organise just yourself?

Even after their divorce she found herself still mothering him, she already had two children and she certainly didn't want another big kid on her hands. If it wasn't problems with his solicitor or someone else, it was money, she was always loaning money to him. She swore, if he wasn't the father of her children she probably wouldn't have anything more to do with him.

What went so drastically wrong? They were once hopelessly in love. They met in secondary school and had been together ever since, she had never had eyes for another until this point. Even after the business collapsed, she had tried to remain committed to him, for the sake of her love for him, her morals and her kids, but he couldn't help but be an arsehole.

She began dating Daniel after rejecting his advances continuously for 3 years, purely because due to loneliness, ironically not loneliness stemming from the need to be with someone, but loneliness as a side effect of having to both handle the kids as they took steps towards adulthood and keep her ex from being a detriment to himself, exhaustive loneliness was the easiest way to describe it.

Frustration drove her towards Daniel and away from Terry. She wanted a reaction out of Terry, she wanted him to shape up, wake up and come to get her, but alas, he didn't react for a while and when he finally did, he made a complete fool of himself, he seemed prone to that these days. A broken nose and trip to the hospital only served to further damage any remaining dignity and pride she had left, not because he lost, but because the fight - if you could even call it that - was entirely unnecessary.

Honestly, the whole debacle and the events to follow were like watching an animal suffer and wanting to put it out of its misery as a kindness.

Daniel was a sweet man and before a lover, a good friend, a friend she could confide in, a friend who actually listened to her rather than burden her with more problems than she needed. He did his best by the kids despite having no relation to them and always seemed to be on her wavelength.

There was a certain charm to him that she couldn't explain, maybe it was ability to take charge of a situation, his manliness, his authority, his dependability or perhaps his kind spirit. She wasn't sure what it was, but she was glad he was nothing like Terry.

Would she ever consider taking Terry back if he changed for the better? Whilst given what she had already undergone warranted a *hell fucking no* to that question, she'd be lying to herself if she said that there wasn't still a part of her still clinging onto the probably fruitless hope that he would one day wake the fuck up and sweep her off her feet, but the real question was by the time he finally mustered up the balls to do so, would she still have the patience to accept him back into her life, he was already teetering on the precipice of her tolerance levels. 17 years of marriage was no easy thing to dismiss if it were even possible and to top that, they were practically inseparable before that, the very epitome of secondary school sweethearts.

Though there was no question surrounding Daniel's successes, she didn't want to marry him for his money, nor did she need any of it and no one could accuse her of that. She had always made and used her own money, his company however, was appreciated.

This morning for an example, Terry made her late, Daniel got her to work on time, polar opposites, one unreliable, the other reliable, they balanced each other out.

Working in St Pancras, of course congestion charges were a must, but fortunately that wasn't something Daniel worried about. With Daniel, everything felt so seamless, so simple, they worked in tangent, never argued and saw each other on equal terms, what could be better?

So why now was she still so irritable and thinking of her ex?

Think happy thoughts, she repeated in her head, at least the kids were out of the house now, though whether they would get to where they were planning to go on time or at all for that matter, was another question.

"Natasha?" The calling of her name brought her right back to reality.

"Yes?"

"You probably missed my question. Do you have a copy of the reports you sent me last week? I thought I had CC'd everyone into the copy I sent over to James, apparently not", her colleague replied.

"Give me a second..." Natasha replied, shuffling through the files she had on table and eventually finding something pertaining to the records requested.

"I do", she replied, pulling out the documentation.

She returned to her cubicle an entire hour later and glanced over towards her mobile to find a missed call from Terry. For heaven's sake, what now?

She attempted to call him back, only to be rewarded with a ringing line, concluded with his answering machine.

"Hm... that's odd", she muttered to herself. Sharing the cubicle, her colleague, Elmira Dowling, returned and placed in front of her a piping cup of tea.

"One sugar and a pinch of milk, just how you like it. That should perk you up, you look as sour as a lemon this morning, babe, something the matter?" Elmira enquired, taking a seat beside her.

"Terry", she replied simply.

"For fuck sake, what's he done now?"

"Who knows with that man".

"That man is a thorn in your side, babe. You need to get him out of your life before he sucks you dry, only so much you can take". Natasha laughed.

"He's the father of my kids, I couldn't and wouldn't do that to him".

"Too soft, babe. You need to teach him a lesson or two, kick him up the ass, make him realise what he'll lose. Did I ever tell you about my friend Jemimah? She was having man troubles and one day he took liberties, needless to say, she whipped his ass, made him her bitch and now he's on curfew. Maybe you need to simply crack the whip, babe".

"In his head he already believes he's lost everything except his kids. I couldn't take them away from him too. He might look tough but he's pretty fragile, I wouldn't want to be responsible for anything crazy he'd do to himself if I did that, I don't need that on my conscience, besides, my mother-in-law already gives me enough grief for not staying with him".

"Dragon bitch?" Natasha laughed. That was Elmira's nickname for her.

"Yes, her. Hold on honey, I'm going to give Ria a call". Natasha left Elmira ranting to herself and called Ria, but a repeated message that the number was unavailable was the only response. This mystery was getting more and more disconcerting by the second, they couldn't possibly still be on the underground, surely.

"She's not answering..."

"I wouldn't worry too much, she's probably distracted with something or on the underground", Elmira replied.

"They can't still be on the underground and that girl never peels her face away from that phone screen. Besides, it's not just ringing and then going to the answering machine like Terry's, it's just saying it's unavailable".

"Don't worry, it's probably nothing".

"Yeah... maybe you're right, I just have an irksome feeling and it won't go away".

"Try calling again in a few", Elmira suggested, stuffing her face with Yumease Biscuits.

"Yeah, that's my best bet".

A little past 1:08 and Natasha's phone began ringing. It was Ria.

"Ria? Are you okay, darling?" Natasha asked, picking up the phone.

"Mum! You won't believe what happened to me! I was on the train and then it just suddenly stopped, like literally. We were sat there for ages and then they finally made us evacuate the train and walk back to Sloane Square. There was this massive crowd and everyone started screaming and running from something and I managed to get upstairs and run away! Then I heard gunshots! But I didn't stop, I just kept running and took a train to Clapham Junction and got a new battery. Then dad called and..."

"Hold on, hold on, hold on, you are saying everything in a single go, honey, I barely heard a word you said. You were on the train and you had or evacuate?"

"Yes!"

"How?"

"We got off at the back and walked back to Sloane Square station on the tracks".

"Why? What did they say?"

"They didn't know at the time, but I know now it was terrorists".

"What? Terrorists?" Natasha's outburst drew the attention of her colleagues.

"Yes mum, it was definitely a NOMA attack, I'm sure of it!" Natasha immediately switched to investigation mode, opening up a new tab on her browser in search of breaking news and it didn't take her very long to find it, for there at the top of search listings was *Anarchy Hits the Streets of London*, accompanied with endless listings, articles and live streams pertaining to the events.

"Where are you now, honey?" Natasha asked, as she scoured the internet looking for more information. There was a horrendous noise on the line and when it ceased Ria spoke again.

"Sorry Mum, those were helicopters. I've never seen so many, the sky was filled with them!"

"Where are you, Ria?"

"Clapham Junction".

"How did you get there? I thought you were at Sloane Square?"

"No mum, I told you I had to run from there because I heard gunshots".

"Gunshots? Jesus Ria! Where is your father? Let me speak to him now!"

"He's not with me, we got separated before we got on the train because of the crowds, he was on one of the ones behind me. He's okay though, I called him a few minutes ago, he's on his way here".

"How the hell did you get separated? I knew something like this would happen! What if something had happened to you? What if someone had..."

"Mum! Mum! I'm okay, I'll be fine. George is with him. I'll just wait here for him to get here, okay?"

"Unbelievable. Ria, I'm going to try your father again, I'll call you back in a minute, okay?"

"Okay, mum".

"Good girl, stay where you are, don't move".

"Yes, mum", Ria moaned. Natasha put down the phone and immediately began furiously tapping in Terry's phone number, as Elmira tuned into a live video feed from an INBC helicopter.

"Shit, this is pretty serious. They've barricaded the roads. I can't believe this". She turned up the volume and had already begun to attract the attention of neighbouring cubicles.

Terry's phone just rang endlessly, but no one answered yet again.

"Dammit Terry! Answer the fucking phone!"

But Terry had valid reason for not answering, for just then, he was coming around from a crash that could have just as well killed he and his son.

CHAPTER 8 - TERRY

1:10pm - 1 Hour, 25 Minutes since outbreak

. . .

"Morning Cindy!"

Hello!
How can I assist you?

How is the weather today?

Send a message for me

Book an event for me

Give me directions

Book me a hotel room

Just speak.

C.I.N.dy has you covered.

Say hello to the most fantastic phone to date!

tPhone Z

Go ahead.
I'm listening...

. . .

The sound of his cheesy Anna Swenton ringtone filled the overturned bus and continued on for some time before eventually stopping.

Terry himself roused from his dazed state, unsure of where he was for a moment. His head was throbbed and his vision could barely focus. Disoriented, he groaned as he rolled onto his side, every bit of his body ached.

His phone resumed ringing, snapping him out of his daze, before once again falling silent. Something trickled down his face and upon raising his hand to inspect it he discovered blood.

"Shit..." He groaned, but it seemed superficial. He was covered in glass. He glanced around, inspecting the wreck and was suddenly hit with the reminder of his son.

His eyes darted to and fro looking for George, but for a moment he couldn't find his boy. It became clear why, for he spotted his boy covered, almost hidden away by glass and damaged chairs.

Terry scrambled to his feet and ran over to push the broken chairs off of his son. He then brushed off the glass and held his unconscious son in his arms, or at least he really hoped he was unconscious.

"George, speak to me". He gently shook George, hoping his boy would stir, before running his fingers through his hair and bringing his mouth closer to his ear to check he was still breathing. He was, thank goodness.

"George, wake up, son".

George did finally stir and groan, much to Terry's profound relief. His eyes gradually opened.

"I'm thirsty..." He groaned with a cough.

Terry chuckled.

"Let's worry about getting you out of here first, okay?"

"Where are we...?"

"The bus, it crashed. Does it hurt anywhere?" Terry asked, checking his son over. George attempted to move all limbs.

"I don't think so, my body just aches".

"Okay, that's good. You have a few scrapes and bruises, but you should be fine".

"You're bleeding, dad".

"I know, I'll be okay, don't worry about me. Can you get up?"

"I think so".

"I'll help you up, hold on to me". Terry assisted his son to his feet. "Holding up well there, son. That's a good lad".

"Help me..."Came the weak voice of someone towards the back of the mangled bus.

"Hold on! I'm coming back!" Terry shouted. With everything on its side, it would be no easy exit. Terry looked around, there were some shattered windows above, formerly the side windows, but they looked particularly perilous with all those shards of glass still protruding out. The alternatives were the front and back windscreens, the back doubled up as an emergency exit, but it didn't look accessible at the current moment in time, what with chairs, handlebars and people piled up on top of one another. It looked as though the front windscreen was going to have to be their way out.

"Wait here", Terry instructed, leaving George aside for a second to check the front windscreen. As he approached the windscreen, he spotted the driver's arm hanging through a shattered hole in the driver's booth doorway glass. Blood seeped down, dripping onto the bus doorway, proclaiming without words the grisly demise of the driver. The entire front of the bus was a mangled mess, but a small, albeit dangerous, gap in the windscreen would allow for them to squeeze through with some tact.

He returned to George.

"Okay little man, I'm going to hoist you up through that gap in the windscreen, when you get out, get as far away from the bus as you can and wait for me. Don't go off with anyone".

"Okay, daddy", George replied, a tremble in his voice.

"Mind your head, lad, don't look up into the driver booth". Terry helped him across, kicking out protruding glass from the windscreen.

"Be careful, don't touch the remaining shards of glass or stand on them if you can, climb out slowly and carefully, there's no need to rush, don't take any unnecessary risks".

"I'll be okay, dad", George replied, grabbing the side panels for balance.

Terry watched over his son, as he squeezed his way through and scrambled to his feet.

"You okay out there?"

"I'm fine".

"Okay, now get out of harm's way, I'll come find you after I'm done helping these folks".

"There's people all around. There's smoke coming from the bus, dad!"

"Don't panic, I'll be with you momentarily, lad".

"I don't want to go without you, dad".

"You'll be okay, I'm just behind you". Terry watched after his son, glad that he had thrown himself on top of the boy and in doing so managed to prevent what could have potentially been fatal.

There were more weak moans and groans from people trapped in the bus now. Terry pushed aside seats and shifted any other debris blocking his way in an attempt to reach people. His first port of call, a woman sat sobbing next to her unmoving husband.

Terry crouched down next to them and checked to see if the man was breathing, but no air escaped his lips.

"He... he won't move, why won't he move?" The woman croaked in her panic and anguish.

Terry attempted basic first aid, but to his dismay the man didn't respond.

"Hello! Is anyone in there?" Terry heard someone outside shout.

"There are people in here! They need immediate medical assistance! Call an ambulance!" Terry shouted back.

"This is the police, what is the situation?"

"The driver panicked and drove into your barricade with all of us on board, he's dead. My son is out there", Terry replied.

"Yes, we have your son and the driver opened us up to danger, we can't help you right now and there are no paramedics on scene. Is anyone in there dangerous".

"No, we are all just passengers, it was the driver that crashed into you. Can't you help?"

"No one can attend, you'll have to find a way out yourself".

"What? There are people fucking dying in here! What do you mean you can't attend? We need emergency assistance right now!"

"Hold tight! There are some people willing to help. Do you smell gasoline or is there anything besides injury that poses immediate danger?"

"No, but people are in critical condition here and I can't guarantee some of them will make it if help doesn't come quickly!"

"We have to secure this road, but help is on the way".

"Thanks... for nothing", Terry grumbled under his breath, but it wasn't long before he heard the ruckus of people surrounding the bus in an attempt to help.

"Can you open the emergency back window? We can get in and pull people out", someone asked. Leaving the woman and her husband - believing he was now a lost cause -, Terry made his way further towards the back of the bus. From what he could see, getting back there would be no easy feat without bypassing the injured people along the way and potentially harming them further.

A man's leg was trapped and from the looks of it, badly twisted.

Terry recognised this man, this was the son of a bitch who left that girl to die. Terry had half a mind to leave him there, but that would make him just as heartless as the bastard. Not wanting death on his hands, Terry tried to move the seat, only for the man to yelp in agony and immediately proceed to vent.

"What the flaming fuck do you think you are fucking doing you fucking asshole! Help me, don't fucking make things worse!" Terry could have punched him right then and there, but this wasn't the time or place. Instead he disregarded the remark and apologised.

Not without more pain, he managed to free the man. The douchebag didn't even say thank you. He simply crawled away, mumbling about how important he was and how he wasn't even supposed to be here. What was he doing on a bus then?

By the time Terry had freed the man, two people had managed to climb on top of the bus and lower themselves in through the shattered side panes.

"Oh, thank the lord. Careful, it's not steady", Terry warned, as they approached him and the ungrateful man. "Where are the paramedics? What the hell is going on?"

"I'm the wrong person to ask, mate. All I know is that they don't want to bring anyone to this place, nor are they letting any cars through towards South Kensington, both ways are blocked. I got caught in the blocked traffic, was trying to U-turn when I saw this bus come crashing through. From the way you guys were driving and the crash, I'm willing to bet you know more than we do", one of them replied.

"Believe me, I wish I could answer that question. The driver is dead, shit hit the fan back up towards South Kensington and I couldn't tell you if it was a terrorist attack or people having just lost their fucking minds. I just know that that entire region is ground zero at the moment".

Terry shifted a cluster of broken seats to reach a pile of people, either dead or unconscious, at this point it was hard to tell.

"There is a peep of space at the front to exit from, though I mean it when I say *peep*, my son only just managed to get through. If you could help me over here however, I could open up that back window".

Immediately they got to assisting him in clearing the way and opening up a route to the back, which meant in some cases stepping over those in less critical condition, at least momentarily.

The rescue operation proved something of a significant challenge, but only until he was able to clear a path to the back window, where upon he immediately proceeded to break the safety pin and pull the lever keeping their exit sealed. With a clicking sound, the locking mechanism released and the window opened. Almost immediately, random kind volunteers rushed in through the new entry point to help them carry the passengers out to safety.

As the last survivor was carried out of the bus, the remaining dead were then covered and also carried out of the bus. Eventually everyone was out, including the headless girl, whose friends and family, especially her parents, Terry couldn't help but feel emotional for, what a horrific and tragic way to go, not that dying in a bus crash was any better, but at least those bodies were intact. Terry couldn't even begin to imagine their anguish. As morbid as it may seem, what if she was one of his children, what if that was Natasha?

No, he couldn't think like that, he was his family's protector and he wasn't about to let anything like this happen to them, he wouldn't be able to live with himself.

He outside of the wreckage gulping in the fresh air, thankful he and his son had made it out alive. He was covered from head to toe in the blood of his own and of others, exhaustion had taken its toll and after all this drama, he wanted nothing more than a cold shower and a serious counselling session.

News helicopters hovered overhead and the wreckage had drawn quite the crowd of shocked and curious onlookers, some taking photos of the covered corpses on the ground with their phones.

Did no one have a shred of common decency anymore? Why would you take a photo of something like that? Terry shot them a scorning look, not that it mattered, people were going to do what they wanted and he would just have to accept that this was a generation of looking at everything through lenses and on small screens.

He spotted his boy being held back by an officer and approached them.

"Daddy!" George called out to him.

"Your son?" The officer asked.

"Yeah, he's mine", Terry replied, running to and embracing him. He glanced up at the officer. "Didn't you hear us calling for an ambulance?"

"Didn't you hear my colleague inform you that no one could attend? Priority is on containment and so it will remain until further notice".

"Who is giving out your orders? We could have died in there! People *did* die!"

"Your driver disregarded a clear barricade, which in turn sent you careening off the road. Given the potential threat this posed during a time such as this, you are only too fortunate we didn't shoot. We could have just as easily assumed you to be terrorists or co-conspirators, so consider yourself lucky penguins. If you have a problem with the way this was handled, I suggest you take it up with your driver first".

"He's dead".

"Well then, I guess that cuts down the number of people willing to listen to your complaints by a whopping one hundred percent, what are the odds of that?"

"There's no reason to be so rude. Since you couldn't help us in there, do you at least know what is happening or where we can get a lift?"

"First of all, if I knew that I wouldn't be standing here, secondly, did I give you the impression I was a taxi service?"

"I need to get to my daughter".

"Not my problem, now move along, I have a job to do".

"A little bit of authority and you guys turn into raging asshats!"

The remark was ignored as the police officer stepped past him.

Terry sighed and returned his attention to George.

"What are we going to do now, dad?"

"We are going to find some way to pick up your sister", Terry said, checking George for any missed injuries.

"What are we going to do when we get her?"

"I'll figure that out when we find her".

"Excuse me, I couldn't help but overhear the conversation you had with that rather unhelpful officer", came a female voice. Terry and George looked up to find a woman standing before them with a beaming smile on her face.

She wore a long yellow dress, silk scarf and knee high, heeled, brown leather boots. Her curly brown hair dropped to her shoulders. She reminded Terry of an ever so slightly older Nora Heymond, that American actress from a vampire hunting TV series he'd been watching quite a bit of recently.

Terry stood up to face her.

"I parked my car nearby, I could give you a lift to wherever it is you need to go".

"That's far too kind, thank you, are you sure? You don't need to go this far out of your way for us".

"Well I heard that you were trying to reach your daughter, so I wanted to help in any

59

way. Do you know where she is?"

"Clapham Junction, were you headed that way?"

"Err, no, not exactly".

"Well I couldn't ask you to deviate from your journey, it's okay, we'll figure something out".

"No, no, it's okay, I insist. Besides, I was heading to east London and stupidly decided to cross town to get there, but that doesn't look as though it's happening any time soon this way, so it looks as though I'll be heading south first anywho".

"Are you sure it's no hassle?"

"No, not at all", she laughed.

"Okay, well words alone couldn't begin to show my appreciation right now, Ms..."

"Charlotte Andrews and the pleasure is all mine".

"Thanks again, Charlotte. My name is Terry Burnham and this is my lad, George, we were trying to reach my daughter, Ria".

"It's really nice to meet you, George". She shook his hand and he smiled meekly. "What do you say we shoot?"

Terry turned to George.

"Want to climb on my back?"

"I can walk, I'm not a little kid, dad". Terry chuckled somewhat nervously. George was putting on a brave face in front of him, but Terry could tell he was shaken up, his son couldn't even look him in the eye. Nothing would remove the horrors of what was seen today from his poor little mind. Terry himself was just about clinging on to sanity after the death and destruction he had already witnessed, so one could only imagine what his boy was going through.

She led them back to her car, a small black hatchback Aradin.

"Hop in", she instructed, unlocking the doors.

Terry ensured George was all safely buckled up, before hopping in himself, but before he even had the time to get comfortable, there were a series of screams. Terry turned to see people scattering like sweets from a bag.

"What on Earth could be going on now?" The woman asked.

"Probably best we don't wait around to find out", Terry replied, to which she agreed wholeheartedly, revving the engine and swerving out of there.

Cars weaved in and out of intersections, ignoring traffic lights and very narrowly missing each other, it was only a matter of time before there was one or more accidents similar or worse than the one he experienced today, a memory that simply would not leave his mind, along with all the other horrific events that had taken place today. Hazard after hazard seemingly awaited them at every turn, all the while, helicopters, police cars, riot vans, fire trucks among others, raced past them directly towards the chaos and it wasn't until the road was a little safer was Charlotte able to cough up the words she had been choking on since she slammed her foot on the peddle.

"What the hell was that back there?" She asked, glancing in Terry's direction.

"No idea, but I can take a lucky guess that it wasn't in our best interests to find out", it was probably best to avoid trying to explain the horrors of what he had already witnessed to her, what with his son in the car. It was bad enough confronting the reality of it himself, far less putting his son through it.

"You both certainly look as though you've seen your fair share", Charlotte noted, interrupting Terry's trail of thought, referencing their wounds, blood and dust covered clothes and pale faced expressions.

"It's... .been an ordeal", Terry replied.

"I'm sorry to hear that. Anything else I can do to help?"

"No, you've done more than enough and besides, I don't think anything will help undo what has already been done".

Charlotte silently glanced at him.

"I can tell it's eating at you, I won't probe, but can you at least let me drive you to a hospital after we collect your daughter. No arguments now, I couldn't live myself knowing something happened to you because I didn't want to do that little bit extra".

Terry didn't argue back, instead he accepted her offer with a smile. He couldn't help but feel guilty having exposed his son to that massacre and mayhem. He knew he had done all he could to protect his boy, but what his son was going through mentally after seeing all that was beyond all that Terry could imagine.

"How are you holding up back there, kiddo?" Terry asked, looking around at his son.

"I'm okay".

"Glad to hear it".

"If you don't mind me asking, how'd you end up in that accident?"

"Erm, well, we were on the train to South Kensington, had to get off because something was happening, took a bus, had to flee that bus when people started running and behaving erratically, jumped onto that bus you saw, the driver panicked, drove into that road block and here we are".

"Behaving erratically, you say?"

"Yeah, like... they were afflicted with something, madness maybe".

"Probably hysteria".

"Probably". He doubted that, but it sounded more digestible than the truth.

"Do you have anyone you need to call, like your daughter for example?"

"I did earlier, before the bus crashed, that was a while ago though. I'm sure I heard my mobile ringing in the bus wreckage, but I had no success finding it".

"Here, take mine", she insisted, rummaging through her purse as she drove and handing him her mobile, after tapping in her password.

"Do you remember her phone number?"

"Dammit, I don't".

"I do!" George declared and recited it for Terry to dial.

The phone rang for a while before Ria picked up.

"Hello? Who is this?" She asked.

"It's me, dad. I'm borrowing a phone".

"Terry? Where are you? I've been waiting here for ages!"

"Sorry, Ria, something came up".

"What could be so important that you aren't here on time... again?"

"I'm on my way, Ria. We ran into a little trouble".

"It's always the same thing with you isn't it".

"Never mind that, have you spoken to your mother at all?"

"Yes, and she isn't happy, just so you know".

"That's expected, we'll be there shortly".

"How short is *shortly*?"

"Don't be cheeky, we will be there shortly, that's all that matters". She sighed.

"Fine... I'm waiting".

CHAPTER 9 - RIA

1:32pm - 1 Hour, 47 Minutes since outbreak

. . .

FACT FILE #3:

Aradin Motors (AM), is a German multinational corporation headquartered in Stuttgart, Baden-Württemberg, that designs, manufactures, markets, and distributes vehicles and vehicle parts, and sells insurance services. AM also manufactures cars and trucks in 52 countries. The company was founded by Whistler J Aradin in 1906 as a holding company. The company was the largest automobile manufacturer from 1920 through to early 2000s, where recent competition has eaten into market share and forced the company to reconsider its options.

AM in 20▮ sold over 9.4 million vehicles, much of which was to service industries, including the police and firefighters.

. . .

Ria hung up the phone on Terry.

He always did this and here he was doing it again, late as usual. He wasn't even dependable during a crisis like this!

Containing her irritation was going to be a trial, but at least she was in the town and towns meant shopping.

Despite the belief that it would take a while to calm down, one look at a dress in a shop window and she was back to her usual self. It was a very pretty dress and she was almost certain it would go well with that summery hat she had back at home and the necklace her mother bought her for her birthday.

Maybe this wasn't the right time to be thinking of clothes, not after the ordeal she had been through.

She checked her mobile and spotted quite a few topics trending on Chirper, all of which related to London. So, it was that the world had already heard about the terrorist attacks it would seem. None of these tags were related to terrorism however, in fact, they were all quite alarmingly different to anything she would have ever thought up.

The top five trends were purely dedicated to the events occurring in London and looking at the pictures, mostly overhead views, it was clear to see that what was happening here was probably even more than just a terrorist attack. It looked like a riot, a violent one at that.

A thought suddenly popped to mind, what if she shared her ordeal, it would surely be a tale to tell amongst her friends later, right?

With that, she video recorded herself talking about what she had seen and experienced thus far and uploaded it to her Vyou, for fun, tagging it #riasinlondon.

Within moments, a few of her friends had liked the video as well as her previous chirps and were re-chirping them. It wasn't much, but it was a start.

She stopped before a crowd of people amassed outside of a tech store. It didn't take long to work out what they were all gawping at, there in the windows were those new super sharp televisions showcasing in pristine quality the horrors of the events occurring in London.

An INBC helicopter hovered over the scene of chaos in South Kensington and Ellie Branning, the designated reporter as shown at the bottom of the screen, tried to explain what was being seen at the scene taking place on the ground, whilst the cameraman zoomed in for a better view. On the ground were panicked people fleeing for their lives and chased by... other people.

There was a series of gasps from the crowd, as a man was slammed up against a car and mauled. Men, women, children, pets and even the elderly, no one was excluded from the violence.

The cameraperson remained focused on that one man and his assailants until they could do so no more, the man had been ripped to shreds and the scene too grisly even for the news.

The camera panned away to other fleeing people being chased and doing the chasing.

"I can't believe this is happening", Ellie said and her words were echoed by the crowd gathered around the TV screens.

The reality of the situation had finally hit Ria and with all the impact of a meteor. After seeing those scenes, she was genuinely terrified. What if she had been caught in that? Ripped apart like that man? She sure hoped this anarchy was contained before it reached her or anyone else.

She moved away from the screen, away from the crowds, away from the morbid scenes unfolding before her and tried to calm herself down again.

Where was her father already? This was ridiculous, already six minutes had passed since he last called and he remained nowhere in sight. She pulled out her phone and checked the battery, it was already down to 98% and a full hour hadn't even passed yet.

Lacey messaged her and it was evident that she too had seen the news, for her message read of hysteria and complete irrationality.

Ria suggested she calm down, that the police would handle it and reminded her that the media had a habit of blowing things out of proportion, though it was difficult to determine who she was trying to convince here, Lacey... or herself.

Still, Lacey was at least home safe, watching this all on TV a few roads away from where Ria used to live in West London, she was far out of the danger radius, which was more than could be said for herself.

She sat down on a bus stop seat and waited there for Terry, hoping he wouldn't be much longer.

She didn't have to wait very long, for eight minutes later her father's edited clown face appeared on her vibrating phone.

Giving him directions to where she stood, it took him a further two minutes to reach her and when he finally did, he pulled up in a car she did not recognise.

Had he not stepped out of the car, she wouldn't have known it him at all.

"Ria, get in the car", he ordered and proceeded to open the back door of the little hatchback. Ria stared blankly at it for a moment.

"Whose car is this?" She asked.

"A woman offered us a lift, I'll explain when you get in". Ria reluctantly obliged.

"What the hell happened to you, Terry? You totally look like shit". He did look like shit, he was covered in grime and blood, it looked as though he had been through a death-defying obstacle course.

"Mind your mouth and like I said, I'll explain in the car", he replied. She climbed into the car to find her little brother George who also looked like shit.

"George!" She cried, refusing to hug him if only because of the state he was in. She couldn't deny her delight to see him after the morning she had had, but he too looked as though he had experienced some serious shit and with all those cuts and bruises covering his body, she was willing to bet it was worse.

"Ria!'" He yelped with glee and embraced her as though it were the last time he would ever see her again.

That was when an unfamiliar woman at the wheel turned to her and waved.

"You must be Ria, hello, I'm Charlotte".

After awkward introductions, they were well on their way to God only knows where.

"Where are we going and what happened to you two?" Ria asked.

"Hospital to make sure we didn't sustain any internal injuries we don't know about, but where do I even begin?" Terry replied with a sigh.

With that, Ria knew she was in for a rollercoaster of a story and boy was it indeed. By the time Terry had ended, Ria was well and truly exhausted, but had a newfound respect for him, less confidence in her theory that this was NOMA or even terrorism related for that matter, apparently an altogether new concern she never once thought she would ever have and a story she wanted to share with the world, which of course she immediately proceeded to do.

Her last video had picked up steam with her peers, it was already among her most favourited and shared chirps. This would surely make her talk of the classroom when this whole thing settled down before end of term, it had to settle down after all, right? With that many police and helicopters, they'd control this, surely.

"Where were you going before all of this?" The woman, Charlotte asked.

She was very pretty and Ria instantly disliked her, or at least something about her, though she couldn't quite put her finger on what that was. Maybe it was the way her father was so casual with her as though he and she were already on a friendly basis, the last thing he needed was more distractions.

Ria kept a sharp unmoving eye on her whilst she documented her father and brother's ordeal on social media.

"We were spending some quality time together, we were on our way to the museums in South Kensington, the science and natural history museum, we haven't been there since Ria was six and she loved it, so I thought it would be nice to go again, nostalgia I guess, though it was a surprise", Terry replied.

"That sounds nice", Charlotte replied with a smile. Ria couldn't have been more aghast with that revelation if she tried, a great big wave of disappointment washed over her face and showed in her expression.

"Seriously, dad? That's as lame as it gets. I'm sixteen, not six, that was ten years ago. What made you think I'd enjoy something I enjoyed when I was six? See, this is how out of touch you are. We should've just stayed home, at least then we wouldn't be in this mess and George wouldn't have been hurt", Ria grumbled.

"I just wanted to do something special with you guys".

"Then take us to a concert or heck, a day trip into Camden or anything that doesn't feature on the *lame-o-meter*, especially not on the critical, avoid at all cost, side".

"What do you know about Camden and George is far too young to go to concerts".

"Everything, my friends are always in Camden, it's like totally the coolest place to hang out".

"Do your friends' parents know they are loitering in Camden?"

"One, it's not loitering, two, of course they do, they let their kids have fun, remember what that word means, dad? Fun? It's the opposite of what we are having now".

"No need to be rude, Ria", Terry replied without looking at her. Ria slumped back into her seat.

"Have you even spoken to mum?"

"Good point, do you mind if I…" He shamelessly begun to ask Charlotte.

"Oh yes, no problem, go ahead", she interjected before he could finish asking.

"Don't be a twat, dad, don't you think you've asked for enough as it is? Here, take mine!" Ria snapped, leaning forward and thrusting her mobile in front of his face. "Besides, you'll only have to ask me for her number anyway".

"That was uncalled for, but thank you", he replied, taking her phone, "which reminds me, here". He dug into his pocket and pulled out her battery. It was scuffed but surprisingly in good state given the condition he himself was in. She now had two and she'd need two to keep up her social documentation throughout the day.

He searched for her mother on her phone and rang.

CHAPTER 10 - NATASHA & DANIEL

1:54pm - 2 Hours, 9 Minutes since outbreak

. . .

FACT FILE #4:

CYPHER, sometimes referring to itself as **noX**, **N**ew **O**rder E**x**iles, is a group of anonymous hackers, activists and in some circles referred to as political terrorists. They pride themselves on bringing down the establishment, exposing corruption and restoring power to the people.

The group gained infamy with the website **LeakPod**, which saw the private correspondence, tax evasion proof and other damaging information of thousands of important figures in the limelight.

Supposed leader of Cypher, an anonymous individual going by the name, **The Jackel**, is a wanted fugitive, but Cypher has done well to conceal their identities, with only a few members arrested over the course of the last few years and new members replacing them quicker than they can be caught.

. . .

Natasha had attempted on several occasions in the past half an hour to reach Terry's phone to no avail and was beginning to grow both concerned and impatient. On the last attempt, the line cut off unexpectedly and wouldn't allow her to connect at all. What the hell was going on?

Matters on the news were making things no less disconcerting. A crowd of her colleagues had seemingly accumulated around her cubicle since Elmira had turned it into a fucking bookie with all the accompanying fun, speculation, opinion and of course aggressive support for those fleeing for their lives verbally expressed.

Elmira lived alone and her parents lived way down in Kent somewhere, so there wasn't anyone, related anyway, for her to concern herself with. Their fret levels weren't anywhere near comparable, it felt as though her woes were stockpiling and panic as a result of lack of information had set in, but before she could even consider grabbing her coat and leaving this damned office, Ria called.

"Ria, has your father arrived there yet? He's not picking up his phone and I'm getting really worried!" Natasha begun.

"Natasha, it's me", Came a voice she recognised.

"Terry! Jesus, where the heck have you been? I've been worried sick here! I have a daughter way off of where she was supposed to be, you and my son went AWOL and a city fucking falling apart! Why the hell weren't you answering your phone and where is Ria? Is George okay? If anything happened to him Terry, I swear..."

"He's fine, Natasha, calm down for a second, we are all fine", Terry interjected, "A little shaken up, but otherwise fine".

"Don't tell me to fucking calm down after the panic induced stroke you almost gave me! Are you going to explain not answering your phone? Or for once do you not have a crap excuse?"

"We were in a crash..." Natasha was speechless, what was she supposed to reply to that? For once he had completely silenced her.

"W... what?"

"The short of it is that we got separated from Ria in a crowd, but I figured we'd just meet her on the platform at South Kensington, all trains were suspended, George and I tried to reach her by a bus and ended up slap bang in the epicentre of what I can only describe as hell. We managed to flee and board another bus, the driver however, panicked, started driving like a complete lunatic and crashed into a police roadblock. Needless to say, we were among the lucky few to be alive and well, but I lost my phone in the process".

"Terry... I... are you guys okay?" Natasha asked. Elmira glanced over concerningly.

"Terry and George were involved in a crash", Natasha whispered, covering the mouthpiece with her hand.

"Seriously? Fuck, are they okay?" Elmira asked.

"We're shaken up, but we're alive, that's the most important thing. Natasha, what

69

I've seen today... there are no words. I need to talk to you... in private", Terry continued.

"Yeah... okay. Where are you now?" Natasha replied.

"A kind woman has given us a lift, we've just picked up Ria and we are heading to the hospital".

"Which one?"

"St Thomas most likely".

"Should I come down there? I'll leave right away".

"No, it's okay, I've got this, we'll be okay at the hospital. Stay put, it's probably safer inside at the moment. I'll call you back when we get there and if you see or hear anything suspicious, call me".

"Like what?"

"Just call me".

"Okay, I trust you, give the kids my love and get there safe".

"Will do", he replied and the phone line cut. Natasha put her face into her hands and sighed. Today was a disaster and it only looked to get worse before it got any better.

"Natasha? What's happening?" Elmira asked.

"They're okay... but Terry sounded...”

"Sounded?"

"Off...”

"Off?"

"Yeah, different somehow, uncertain".

"Typical Terry then?"

"No, I know Terry, this wasn't him. He sounded more... assertive than normal, as though something knocked the senses into him. He wanted to talk to me about something in private”.

“Shit...”

“He was at the thick of it when everything started happening, I feel as though whatever they had seen is weighing heavily on his mind".

"You almost sound as though you care about him, isn't this more about your kids?"

"He's the father of my children, Elmira, of course I care. Also, the kids are relying on him, if he's not in the right frame of mind...”

"They'll be okay, Natasha, I'm sure Terry will keep it together, this is make or break".

"You don't know Terry, he's as emotionally brittle as a Ghoriba cookie".

“A what?”

“Oh, it's a Moroccan... never mind".

"You should just go down there, or call your man, ask him to go and check on them or pick them up".

"Undermine and damage Terry's pride any further? No, I can't do that, besides he said he could handle it".

"Like he handled all those other situations? Call Daniel, at least just let him know what's going on, he deserves to know!" Elmira threatened. Natasha wrestled with the idea for a while before picking up his phone and calling him.

2pm hit and Daniel knew nothing of the events unfolding outside, he had been in meetings with his top clients all morning and these bigwig corporate directors weren't the dallying type, terrorist attack in London or not, business had to go on. Natasha would text or ring him if she needed something.

This morning hadn't been kind to him and it was much in part due to that worthless fool, Terry. He didn't mind holding up clients for Natasha or the kids, but holding them up for Terry's fucking incompetence ticked him off, that guy needed a wake-up punch or two, evidently the first one a while back wasn't enough.

His morals were in question, his priorities were in question, his whole fucking life style was one big question and as someone who had worked his fucking arse off from day one, Daniel hated to even be in that man's presence, Terry was a disgrace and an insult to his intelligence.

It was only a matter of time before Daniel took everything from him, his wife, his life, his kids and anything else he had. It wasn't a cruel way of thinking in the slightest. Strength, success, confidence, tenacity, charm, appearance, natural good looks and a winning fucking smile got you by in this battle of a world, nothing else. The weak will be slaughtered like lambs, for there was no place for a person not willing to raise their sword against the challenges life put before you.

That loser wasn't a concern to Daniel in the slightest, he was however a nuisance and the sooner he was removed from Natasha's life, the better. It was just a shame he was the father of her kids, otherwise he would have been long since gone.

Daniel's thoughts were predominantly on the kids, he suspected they didn't quite like him and that was okay, eventually they would both come around, Rome wasn't built in a day.

Daniel was never great with children, his own father had been a waste of space, forcing Daniel to mature beyond his years in order to do what his father could not and his mother, bless her soul, did right by him, but was diagnosed with Osteogenesis imperfecta otherwise known as brittle bone syndrome, which often left her unable to do most things everyday people took for granted.

He had never had children of his own or been married before, just an endless stream of pointless relationships with clueless women, then along came Natasha, a woman with the tenacity of a bull, the ambitious acumen of a businesswoman, the confidence of a soaring eagle, the beauty of a maiden and the heart of a goddess. This woman had stolen his heart, except the only thing holding her back was that fucking tool, Terry, a man who reminded him of the father he loathed.

Daniel eventually found sleeping with other women meaningless and instead focused his entire existence on trying to make Natasha his woman, even if it meant taking a decree of celibacy until she accepted him. As fate would have it - luck was for losers - Terry broke her heart and who should she eventually turn to? None other than himself. So, it all

71

worked out in the end.

It was during his meeting with a said client that his phone rang. Now in most settings he would have disregarded it, but in this instance, he recognised the unique vibration sequence and pulled it from his inside jacket pocket, it was Natasha and she knew all too well not to ring him during work hours unless it was an emergency, given that she had never done this before, it was most likely just that.

"Hold on just a second, sorry to interrupt, I just need to take this, I won't be a minute", he assured his client and stepped out of the room.

He answered his phone.

"Natasha?"

"Daniel".

"What's wrong, sugarcake?"

"I wouldn't ask you this under normal circumstances, you know I wouldn't, but I'm seriously worried and..."

"Hold up, hold up. Now calm down and explain to me what happened from the beginning". So, she did, or at least as best she could and kindly requested he go and check on the kids at the hospital, to which he obliged and once again found himself cleaning up Terry's mess.

The whole debacle thing in central London was a little fuzzy to him, Natasha had been rather vague with the details, possibly because she didn't quite understand what was happening herself, but it concerned him all the same.

After their phone call, he popped back into room to postpone the meeting due to an emergency that required his immediate attention, before departing shortly after the clients left, grabbing his car from the building carpark.

As he sat in the car making his way to St Thomas Hospital, he switched on the radio and was presented with station after station of the broadcasted events in London, but it was the breaking news that caught his attention.

"Oh my God! Oh my God! People, a helicopter has just gone down, I repeat a helicopter had just gone down. It's too early to tell but it is believed to be INBC's helicopter. Check your televisions, tune into their stations, you'll likely hear or see the live feed has cut..." Daniel switched to INBC radio. "... not getting any coverage as of present, sorry about that ladies and gentlemen, it appears that the helicopter providing us with up to date news live on the scene has gone down. We are not sure of the cause, but we hope that the crew of the helicopter are okay. On board were reporter Ellie Branning, cameraman Zachary Lincoln and pilot Steve Phillips. We will keep you updated on what happened. In the meantime, we are reverting casting to our other helicopter..."

What the hell was going on? He thought to himself and the situation over the radio continued to deteriorate. People were dead, others were fleeing for their lives and not a single station failed to cover the news, albeit to a lesser degree than the established news stations. The traffic ahead too eventually came to a complete standstill and for 10 minutes he remained in exactly the same spot.

Impatience eventually got the better of him and he stepped outside of the car to investigate, possibly the worst decision he had made all day.

People were stepping outside of their cars and standing around looking to see what the holdup was. They suspected all too well what the holdup was, but as human psyche would go, none would want to admit it, for accepting it as real meant that it was real and far more serious than either of them could ever imagine.

Up ahead the roads were blocked, someone would inform them and above their heads flew several army helicopters. Even from this distance Daniel could see the soldiers leaning out of open helicopter doors and equipped with L85A2 carbine assault rifles with fitted scopes, standard British warfare equipment, but were they really required in this instance? Was it *that* bad?

Daniel knew his guns well, he had fired several during his trips to the US and at one point he had even wanted to be a soldier, proudly fighting for his country putting those fucking terrorists and commies in their place.

Instead he found another less blood-soaked alternative to be a part of his country's great justice system in the form of law. Still, just seeing the boys out on the field right now brought out his inner soldier and were it not for Terry's incompetence he wouldn't have been able to witness this crucial moment.

Something told Daniel that today would be history defining. People would ask what he was doing on this day in future and what would his reply be? Checking up on Terry's kids at the hospital?

Daniel was distracted by the frantic screams and shouts of people ahead. People climbed on top of their cars to get a better look, but towering at 6 foot meant he had no need to.

At the junction ahead, people were fleeing in his direction from something, possibly multiple somethings

Daniel backed off, backed off towards his car as the fleeing people and their pursuers drew closer. Just behind them, army helicopters took position, hovering overhead and soldiers on board fired down into the traffic, supposedly taking shots at the pursuers, but the gunfire was enough to scare the shit out of any and all at ground level. For what purpose would there need to be army helicopters carrying gun wielding soldiers and for what purpose would said gun wielding soldiers need to be firing down on the masses. The answer was not worth finding out and people either retreated to their vehicles or fled.

Running probably wasn't going to save him, he'd eventually get caught in this crowd, even if he car-jumped from bonnet to hood.

Would taking shelter in the car help? Not from bullets, but he'd be a whole lot less exposed, especially if he kept his head down.

He dived back into his car, locking it behind him and hunkered down, as people ran past either side of his vehicle and even over the top of it.

Had the circumstances been different, he'd have kicked their asses for using the top of his car as a stepping stone.

Stuck in the midst of this traffic, he was going nowhere quickly. He delved into his pocket in search of his phone, but fumbled pulling it out and dropped it down between the seat and door. As he dug down in search of it, he was startled by a loud bang at his windscreen. Pressed up against the windscreen was a heavily bleeding man's face, his eyes silently pleading with Daniel to save him.

Behind him and atop the hood of Daniel's car stood the woman seemingly responsible for his injuries and she certainly looked the furthest thing from mentally sound. Foaming at the mouth, covered in horrific bites and lacerations and her eyes rabid and crazy, this erratically twitching woman wore a very formal but ripped business pencil skirt, not exactly his choice attire for someone outright slam dunked into the looney bin.

She grabbed the man by his hair and sank her teeth into him like a rabid animal or fucking vampire, ripping chunks out of him as he screamed. Try as he might to escape her grip, this crazed woman held him down with a strength no human with her physique could possibly possess. Her fingers dug into his skin as he flailed, trying to hit her and soon she was accompanied by another and the two, using their combined strength, pulled the man to the ground like a pack of ferocious animals.

Daniel didn't need to look, the man's screams were more than enough insight into what was likely happening, but what the fuck was that? What the hell was happening right now? This had to be some cover-up exposed to the public or some shit. It was unreal, was he dreaming?

He quickly ensured all doors to the car were well and truly locked and windows wound right up, before delving into the glove box to find something to defend himself with, but there he found nothing. He could only think of the tools he had in the boot, but how the hell was he going to get those? Dammit, he should have grabbed them before diving back into the car.

Without warning there was a loud smash and Daniel was forced to shield his face from a rain of shattered glass from the windscreen that fucking crazy woman had put her head through. It must had taken something substantial to be able to do that, in one go to boot. With everything happening right now, maybe it was best to abandon all logic and simply focus on survival.

He grabbed an umbrella from the opposite side door compartment and began a barrage of attacks on the crazy woman, but anyone who could smash their head through a windscreen and behave as though nothing had happened, despite several lacerations to her face and who knows what sort of cranium damage, was probably not going to be deterred by a few pathetic blows to the head with an umbrella.

Just when he thought his woes couldn't compact any further, through his side window another one of the crazies lunged head first, scattering more glass everywhere, but both he and the woman who had smashed her head through the windscreen found themselves pulled aside to allow for more crazies to claw at the windows in attempt to widen the gaps, this irrespective of the razor sharp glass slicing through and digging into their fingers. They were frantic and unrelenting, foaming at the mouth and twitching even more violently than before.

Daniel knew then that he had seconds to decide what to do, seconds that determined life or death. He didn't want to die this way, not to these crazies, he would escape, he would get away from these fuckers. He wouldn't allow the world to go on without him, he wouldn't allow Natasha to be with anyone else in his stead, especially not Terry. He would never let that fucking happen.

Just as that thought passed through his mind, another head smashed through the side window closest to his head.

CHAPTER 11 - GEORGE

2:24pm - 2 Hours, 39 Minutes since outbreak

. . .

. . .

George, his father, his sister and the kind lady who had offered them a lift, Charlotte, sat in the hospital waiting room awaiting their check-up. Their injuries weren't heavy, although his father appeared to have quite a nasty cut to the head that would probably need stitching.

There was no mistaking the air of tension in the hospital, things were definitely awry and George was willing to bet it was to do with what he had seen.

He still didn't know what to make of what he had seen. Sure, it terrified him, but how could he properly convey how fearful he felt? What was the right reaction? Cry? What good would that do, his dad was clearly trying his best and he wanted to be as brave as his father, despite being confronted with images and sounds that would remain with him forever, this was the greatest test of his courage. This was a dog eat dog world as Daniel would always say, only the strongest would survive. Based on his words, George knew he had to remain strong, but if strong meant pretending nothing had ever happened, he was as weak as it could get. Outside he was only *just* able to maintain a calm persona, but inside he was falling apart, cracking at every point and those cracks would eventually appear on the outside, there was no stopping them, he was losing his cool and the memories of what he has seen and experienced were plaguing him.

"Are you okay, kiddo?" His father asked, sitting opposite from him and snapping George out of his thoughts. His face was wrought with concern.

"I'm okay".

"You don't look so great. You don't have to hide it, if what you saw is still bothering you, I'm here, tell me. Come, we'll talk".

"He said he's okay, Terry", George's sister grumbled. She sat with her arms crossed looking up at the news bulletin on the waiting room TV screen.

"I'm okay dad", George assured his father.

"Okay, but I saw what you saw too, I experienced what you experienced, so I understand, I'm here for you".

Ria glanced over, but said nothing. It looked as though what George's father had said might have struck a chord with her.

"Yes dad", George replied coyly. His father turned to Charlotte.

"So, what were your plans today... actually that's invasive, you don't need to answer that. Ignore me, I'm just a bucket of nerves now and anything is better than silence"

"That's okay, I don't mind answering the question. I was on my way to see my boyfriend, he lives in East London. He's been in Boston for two weeks, so we hadn't had the chance to see each other until today".

"Sorry to hear that. Have you called him?"

"He called me whilst we were driving, I called him back after parking the car. He's okay, but he's just worried sick about me and a little shaken up about everything going on, he's watching it all on television".

"I can only imagine".

"I guess some sort of force of nature is trying to keep us apart".

"Yeah, if you believe in all that spiritual pixie dust, smoke and mirrors crap". He laughed.

"There's nothing you believe might be true? Like fate? Destiny? That sort of thing?"

"Nope, I don't believe anything is predetermined. Take our meeting for example, I believe it was sheer coincidence, a convenient and pleasant coincidence, but a coincidence all the same. All you two need is love, love is far reaching, doesn't matter what's in between". Charlotte smiled.

"Look at you", she teased, "you must have the most perfect relationship".

"Actually..."

"My mum and Terry split up. She's off with her new guy and dad is all alone", Ria interjected.

"Ria!" George's father snapped.

"If you didn't want your business spread out, you shouldn't go meddling in other people's business".

Charlotte waved her hands trying to fan the flames.

"It's okay, I really don't mind and I'm sorry to hear that, Terry".

"It's okay, it just didn't work out".

"Such is life".

No more than five minutes later their names were called. Standing up, they followed a female doctor towards a small room where Ria and Charlotte were politely asked to remain outside.

George and his father stepped into the room and the doctor immediately approached his father's wound.

"Check my son first, I'll be okay", he insisted and so she did, finding nothing out of the ordinary that was of immediate concern, but to be on the safe side, she had him checked over by another assistant doctor in a separate room whilst she addressed his father's wound.

"Most, if not all you have is superficial, nothing a few plasters won't fix".

"That's good", George replied, knowing that just surviving that crash with mere scrapes and bruises was something of a miracle.

She began tending to him and making small talk as he lay on his back facing the ceiling.

"So, what happened to you, little mister?"

"We were in a crash", George replied.

"That much I know, it must have been terrifying".

"It was, but..."

"But?"

"There was more scary stuff".

"Oh? Like what?"

"A woman's head was pulled off on the bus and the blood was everywhere". The doctor stopped checking him over and stared at him in disbelief. Did she not believe him?

"Pulled off?"

"Yes, those people tried to pull her through the window, but they couldn't, they could only pull her head off".

"Is this some kind of joke, it's not funny". Clearly this woman hadn't seen what was going on outside.

"I'm not joking, it really was. The people also attacked other people as well".

"Which people?"

"The bad people, they chased my dad and I down the road onto the bus, then the bus driver was scared and he started driving really fast and he crashed".

"How did you get here?"

"We came here, Charlotte gave us a lift in her car. We had to pick up Ria first".

"Girls names, are the two girls you speak of outside?'"

"Yes", I replied.

"Your sister and mother?"

"Charlotte isn't my mum, my mum is at work, Charlotte just gave us a lift in her car".

"Okay. So, these people you say chased you, what did they say, or do, or look like?"

"They were swearing and..."

"And?"

"Attacking people. They looked normal, but they were being very strange".

"And they chased you and your dad? What about your sister and the woman you call Charlotte?"

"No, they weren't with us".

"That's good news. Did these people chase others?"

"Yes, there was lots of blood". She stared at him in silence. It was made abundantly clear that she didn't quite know what to believe. She stood up.

"Wait here for me, okay dear", she instructed.

"Okay", George replied. She stepped out of the room for a few minutes, leaving George glancing around the room. Basic check-up utilities sat on drawers and posters pertaining to health were pasted across the walls. At 8, George was already not fond of hospitals, there was always something creepy about them.

The doctor returned with a disconcerting expression upon her face.

"Did any of those people touch you?" She asked straight away. George shook his head, he would probably be dead if they had.

"No". George shook his head.

"Are you sure? You can let us know if they did, don't worry, you'll be okay". George shook his head again.

"Nuh uh".

"Okay, to be on the safe side, we need to monitor you and your father ", she insisted. With that, they were escorted to another room, secluded from the rest of the patients and there, told to stay put. George's father was most unhappy with these circumstances.

"You think we are infected with something?" He demanded.

"That's not what we are saying, we are just taking precautions".

"Precautions from what? Just come out and say it, you think we are one of them?"

"That's not the case".

"The least you could do is tell us what we are dealing with, before sticking us in a room and locking the door".

"It's an infection and it's highly contagious".

"What... like Ebola or swine flu?"

"Worse than that if what I saw on television is anything to go by, bear with me, I've only just gotten details on this, we've had no patients from central London, you two are the first, so naturally everyone here is a little on edge, we have sick vulnerable patients, so it's the perfect cesspool and breeding ground for infection. On top of that, they don't even know how exactly it is spreading or who brought it here first, so please try to understand our dilemma".

George's father slumped into a chair whilst George sat at the edge of one of the two beds in the room. But they weren't alone, for having been in contact with us long enough, Charlotte and Ria were told to stay in the same room and there they remained for all of twenty minutes without word. George's father grew impatient and went to demand an explanation. Banging at the door, he demanded attention and soon enough he was answered from behind the door.

"Sorry sir, we have the CEU response team coming to check you and the doctors who tended to you".

"CE... what?"

"CEU, containment and evacuation unit".

"Come off it, wouldn't we have shown symptoms by now? How many times do I have to say that we had no contact with them whatsoever!"

"Please try to understand, sir, we have to take every necessary precaution to ensure this infection does not spread further. As it stands, we don't know yet how it is spreading and as such, there is very much the possibility that you have been infected, but the symptoms are delayed due to your immunity system, or you could be host to the infection, but it doesn't affect you due to genetics. There could be any number of possibilities, so please be patient a little longer and we'll try to have you out of there soon enough".

"How much longer?"

"I can't say exactly".

Exasperated, George's father sighed and conceded.

They could be here forever for all they knew.

"Is a state of emergency being planned? This all kind of came out of nowhere, what happens now?"

"I... I honestly can't say, that's not my jurisdiction nor to my knowledge. What I know is limited".

"My wife... The mother of my children is still in the centre of London, what happens to her?"

"From what I know, the police, CEU and British army are handling the situation".

"The frigging army? How bad is this thing? Was this some sort of terrorist attack?"

"It's all up in the air at the moment, all there is, is speculation and as you know, speculation alone is no grounds for legitimacy, regardless of how convincing it may seem. I do however understand your dilemma; do you need a phone? You are more than welcome to contact her".

"We have mobiles".

"Then I suggest calling her and telling her to leave central London for her own safety. It may not be required and the situation may be resolved before we know it, but as these things go, I'd be on the safe side".

"I'll do that, but what about us, are we safe here? All of that is happening just across the bridge, right?"

"The bridge has been blocked and barricaded by the CEU, nothing is forcefully breaking through that blockade".

George's father sighed again.

"Fine, could you at least give us food and drink, we're hungry and thirsty".

"I can't risk opening the door, sir".

"So, we are to starve here?"

"No, just be patient, the CEU will inform us of what we can and can't do, we can make a risky decision like that ourselves".

"So, you're going to keep us locked in here like animals? Dammit, who the hell are you?" George's father snapped, banging on the door.

"Dad!" George cried. His father turned to look at him and immediately calmed down. Composing himself, he turned towards the door.

"We're waiting", was all he said, "Don't keep us waiting too long".

"Yes sir", she replied and he came back to sit down.

"I'm calling your mother".

CHAPTER 12 - NATASHA

3:28pm - 3 Hours, 43 Minutes since outbreak

. . .

. . .

Natasha considered leaving the office, in fact, everyone was and who could blame them? Nobody felt safe, nobody felt secure and with family caught in the midst of the anarchy, it was torture just being here.

Natasha for one had everything to worry about, her kids and their father in hospital, not exactly too far away enough from the chaos, she had a fiancé who was now no longer answering his phone and her blood pressure wasn't benefitting from any of this.

Stress had her stomach in a knot and her heart thumping harder than ever before.

Why wasn't Daniel answering his bloody phone, why? Did something happen to him? She dreaded to think it, but had to face the dire possibility that that could very much be the case, since this was unusual for him. Try as she might, she was only able to reach his voicemail.

"Fuck, maybe this is a hint to get out of here", a colleague behind her suggested.

"They'll get control of it; the army is pushing in there. You know how the media is, it probably ain't as bad as it seems. Besides, if we start panicking, that ain't solving nothing", Elmira replied.

"Fuck that, there are people packing up and leaving already".

"They have family in there, Natasha too. Are you going Natasha?" Elmira asked, turning to her.

"I am, though they're at the hospital".

"Here's hoping they're okay". Just as Elmira said that, an email popped up from the office manager.

'To all employees, due to the events occurring in London, it has come to our attention that some of you will have family members within or close to the scene, we understand your concerns and let it be known that our thoughts are with you. In light of this situation, many of you will want to leave, as such we formally allow you to leave, not only that, should the situation not improve by tomorrow, it will be understood if you choose to remain at home, you will be paid for this day. Everything else beyond this will be left until further notice. I hope you get home safely and that you family members and friends are safe and well. Thank you, Bishop'.

It was a considerate message, even granting them leeway for tomorrow and Natasha couldn't have appreciated it more right about now.

"We can leave, just got an email from Bishop. You can also stay home tomorrow if the situation doesn't improve", Natasha alerted the others.

"And not get paid? No thanks, I'll be here 9 am sharp, this company is already stingy enough as it is, why would I voluntarily miss a day worth of pay?"

"It states that they are willing to pay us tomorrow as though we'll be here".

"In that case..." she got up and begun packing. Natasha joined her as others departed the two women's cubicle to return to their own and prepare to leave.

"You heading over to the hospital now?" Elmira asked.

"That's the plan".

"What about Daniel? Is he there yet?"

"He isn't answering".

"What the fuck is up with these men today?"

"To be honest, I'm worried that something happened to him, it's not like him to ignore me and his phone automatically connects to CINdyGo for vehicles the moment he gets near it, so he wouldn't have to even touch the phone".

"Well I hope he calls you back. In the meantime, let's get out of here".

Having packed their things, they made their way out of the cubicle section of the office towards the elevator and stairway. They weren't the only ones standing there, quite a few people on their floor were also using the opportunity to make a hasty exit, some conceding to impatience and taking the stairs.

As the door to the elevator opened and everyone poured in, Natasha's phone rang.

The elevator was quite a squeeze with Natasha and Elmira having stepped in first, unfortunately resorting to them being crammed into a tight space at the back like sardines; this made the attempt to reach her phone in her handbag quite the challenge. It was only as they had almost reached the bottom did she manage to slip her fingers around it, pull it out and answer it.

"Hello?"

"Natasha, it's Terry".

"Terry, what's happening? Are the kids okay?"

"They're fine, staff have quarantined us at the hospital, they're waiting for the CEU to make the next move".

"CEU?"

"Yeah, they deal with outbreaks. We were at the epicentre of this shit, so naturally they're not taking any chances".

"Okay, well I'm just making my way there now".

"Whatever you do, don't travel through London, take the long way around, it might take longer, but it's safer and it's the only way you'll make it across the river, they have all the bridges within the radius of South Kensington blocked and it wouldn't be farfetched to think raised. It would be suicide travelling that direction".

"Okay", Natasha replied, feeling even more concerned about Daniel now. The elevator arrived at the bottom floor to the sound of a chime.

"It's spreading pretty fast, so be careful".

"I know that, Terry! I'm not..." Her sentence was cut off midway, as the doors parted, allowing for the receptionist and a security guard waiting for its arrival to pour in, lunge at and drag the man standing closest to the front out. In the confusion, those watching could do nothing but gasp and stare in horror, as a man was brought to the ground and savagely mauled, fighting for his life. It wasn't until the security guard, leaving the receptionist to attack the man, lunged at the rest of them, did anyone start screaming.

Blood splattered across faces, the ceiling and all along the sides, as it turns out, the security guard had sunk his teeth deep into another man's neck spraying his blood everywhere.

Behind the commotion before them, the lobby glass doors shattered with the combined weight of several frankly suicidal people throwing themselves at it with complete disregard for their wellbeing. No sooner did they all fall through, collapsing on top of one another like a rugby pile-up, they were back on their feet again, not even stopping to give themselves the once over after what had to be a pretty nasty accident.

Caught up completely in the moment, Natasha entirely forgot that Terry was on the phone

"Close the fucking door! Close the fucking door!" A man besides them screamed, squeezing himself up against the back and using his legs to push those in front out to their assailants in order to protect himself, whilst they themselves grabbed onto the side panels to prevent themselves from spilling out of the elevator.

Others banged at the buttons relentlessly, with hopes the door would close, but the motion sensor installed for safety measures prevented it from closing, so instead they were trapped in a perilous cycle of it repeatedly beginning to close, only to sense an obstacle and open again, exposing them to the dangers once more.

Realising they were getting nowhere like this, panic set in and with panic, came its cousin, desperation and desperate people did despicable things in the name of self-preservation. Everyone at the back began to push forward, forcing the man being eaten alive, his assailant and other innocent terrified people out of the elevator.

Those who had poured through the shattered lobby windows pounced on the people at the front like a pack of rabid dogs. One man was dragged out of the elevator kicking and screaming, a woman scrambling to squeeze her way back onto the elevator, pushed to the ground by someone on the elevator and immediately set upon by the feral people.

Before the fucking painfully slow doors could close, more assailants stuck their hands and heads through, making it open again. Measures put in place to prevent accidents and death were ultimately having the adverse effect, the irony was alarming.

Those in front kicked and punched at the assailants to force them to retract, but the doors opened again.

Two more managed to make it in, one sank its teeth deep into the shoulder of a new female colleague, Georgina, ripping her flesh like tender meat from bone.

Fighting back, the two crazed assailants were pushed out by those within the elevator, whilst others hammered at the buttons until the doors finally closed and the elevator began to ascend.

A shudder passed up Natasha's spine and she slumped to the floor in shock and mental exhaustion. The level of panic certainly hadn't dissipated on account of the closed doors, if anything for some, the horrors of what they had just witnessed became all the more apparent when contrasted with the apparent normalisation of their situation now, no thanks to the elevator music and company jingle automatically coming on, as though mocking them.

"Welcome to Teddy and Briggs corporate accounts and auditing firm, it is our ethos to ensure that all our clients receive the level of quality in service that they would expect from one of the best accountancy firms in the country. Leave with a smile. Have a great day!"

Her hands trembling, Natasha raised the phone to her ear.

"Natasha? Natasha! Are you there, Natasha? Natasha!"

"I... I'm here", she murmured.

"Shit, Natasha! What the hell was that? Are you okay?" She looked down at herself.

"Blood... so much of it... Terry, they..." Why was constructing a sentence such a challenge? She could barely think straight and she wasn't the only one in an apparent state of shock, for those around her were either staring blankly into space or crying.

Natasha didn't even want to guess what the mixture of liquids on the elevator floor were, she knew that they were all from the human body and that was more than enough.

"Natasha? Natasha!"

"I'm... still here... but..."

"What's happening?"

"I... I don't know".

"Shit, you're in shock".

"No... no, I'm okay... I'm just... blood". She wiped the blood from her face with her sleeve and the elevator came to a stop on her floor, where she and the others clambered out of the elevator. Elmira who was in a little better frame of mind took the phone from her and begun explaining the situation.

"We are back up at the office floor... no, we didn't get bitten, just blood splatter from those who were... no, they're not with us".

Natasha found herself staring at the others as they wandered around aimlessly, panicking and deciding their next course of action.

Georgina, the young woman who had sustained that nasty bite injury, wouldn't stop crying and screaming. She also downright refused to let anyone help her, lashing out at anyone who tried to help.

Why had Terry specifically asked if anyone had been bitten? This question swirled around Natasha's head as she stared at the hysterical Georgina with suspicion.

"Quick, barricade the elevator doors and get back into the offices!" Her co-worker shouted. With that, they cooperated in order to prevent any of those crazy people following them up, before making their way back into the safe confines of the office, where the shocked and the injured would take a moment to rest their bodies and minds, whilst others kindly tended to their wounds and fetched them water.

Natasha took a seat at the edge of the chair, holding her head to reassure herself and steady her nerves, but that proved to be more difficult than she ever could have anticipated. Those screams, all that blood, that entire scene replaying in her head over and over like a scratched CD.

Elmira returned with a glass of water and crouched down in front of her.

"Here, Natasha babes, drink this", Elmira instructed, whilst simultaneously attempting to calm a panicked Terry over the phone.

Natasha couldn't prevent her hands from trembling, just holding the glass without spilling it was a challenge.

Elmira begun cleaning Natasha's face with damp tissues from the kitchen.

"No, Terry, she's still in shock, she's covered in blood... no, I told you, she's fine... she'll be okay with me, we'll get out of here and get to where you are or barricade ourselves in here... okay, I'll have a look". Elmira stood up. Natasha grabbed her wrist, she definitely didn't want to be left alone.

"I'll be back babe, I'm just going to look out of the window to see how bad it is down there", her friend and colleague reassured her and with that she took off, leaving Natasha alone momentarily with her thoughts, returning a few minutes later looking rather pale.

"We are in serious shit, it's all hell out there".

"What... what are we going to do?" Natasha asked, realizing the severity of the situation.

"I... honestly have no idea, Terry said he'll call back shortly".

"What the heck is going on?" Came a familiar voice. They turned to see Bishop, their office manager, who had only just stepped forth from his office at the back along with the assistant manager, Hannah.

"I don't even know where to begin", Elmira replied, "we were attacked by strangers downstairs".

"Wait... what? Strangers?"

"The ones killing people on the news".

"Seriously?"

"Yeah and they attacked us whilst we were in the elevator, pulled a few people out and started ripping them apart right there in front of us. We managed to close the door, but not without serious effort on our part and get back up here, but *she* got bitten". Elmira pointed towards Georgina.

Bishop and Hannah were speechless, so Elmira continued.

"Think that shit was something? Hear this, fucking *security* tried to eat us alive and just when we thought that that was enough to deal with, more of those crazed fuckers smashed right through the entrance glass, total disregard for their lives. Anyone crazy enough to throw themselves through a glass panel is one we'd be crazy ourselves to attempt to tackle".

"You seem calmer than the others", Hannah replied.

While that may have looked the case from the offset, Hannah didn't know Elmira the way Natasha did, she was definitely shitting bricks right now and masking it with courage to remain sane, she did the same thing when she received a call that her brother had been involved in a car crash all those years ago, which ultimately claimed his life, but Elmira remained so upbeat throughout the ordeal, that you'd be led to believe that she didn't particularly hold him in high regards, nobody except Hannah saw her mental breakdown following the funeral, it was so severe that Natasha had to take a few days off to spend with her *just* to make sure she didn't do anything reckless.

"Have a look outside", Elmira suggested, pointing towards where she had gazed down.

With raised brow, Bishop led the way and no sooner did he reach the window pane, he gasped, "My god". Elmira need explain no further, the scenes beyond that glass were more than enough explanation

He returned to the rest of the group as pale as Elmira before, maybe even more so.

"What the hell do we do now?" He asked as though having conceded already.

"Two choices, we plan a way out and try our hand at escape or we stay here and wait it out", Elmira replied.

"How can we wait it out? God only knows how long we'll be waiting here", Hannah replied.

"Maybe we can't go down, but we can still go up, so we could put an S.O.S on the roof or something, someone has to see it, right?" Bishop replied, but before Elmire could reply, they were distracted by the cries of the others close by.

"Georgina? Georgina! She's not responding! Her eyes are glazed over and she's just mumbling something to herself and twitching!"

Others rushed over to help, Natasha however pushed herself further back into her seat anxiously. What did Terry mean when he asked if they had been bitten? Georgina had been bitten, what did that mean?

Georgina was the new girl of the office, having only started a few months ago. She was young, full of life and extremely helpful, borderline abused for her kindness. Maybe as a result of naivety and wanting to show her best side or simply cultural differences, she went above and beyond for people in this office, only to be bickered and bitched about by the two-faced wolves. She had only just finished university and this was her first career job, a baby faced twenty-two-year-old freshie with the fire of passion and drive to compete with the volcanoes of Hawaii.

"What's wrong with her?" Someone asked.

"She's just muttering something under her breath and shaking as though she's cold", Lizzy, their colleague tending to her, replied.

"Give her something warm".

"I wrapped her up in a blanket when she started trembling and she threw it off, complaining that it was too hot, look over there", Lizzy replied, pointing towards the blanket on the floor, "she's shaking even more now".

Bishop approached the cluster of staff surrounding Georgina and peered over.

"We managed to stem the bleeding, but... I don't know, something's not right".

"She got bitten. Do you think...?" Their colleague, Todd, begun to put two and two together.

"Do you think what? She's infected with something?" Another colleague, Louis, answered.

"I mean think about it, the guard and receptionist downstairs, we all saw them this morning and they were fine, so unless they were part of some major fucking conspiracy to overthrow the company by attacking everyone like rabid animals, they weren't right in the head, something got to them and I'm willing to bet that they got bitten by someone else. Someone came in, security tried to restrain him or something, bitten. They both bite her, fucking epidemic".

"That receptionist has a name, it's Lorna", Lizzy retorted.

"That doesn't matter right now. If I'm right, we're all cosied up here with zombie over there and we have no idea how contagious this thing is", Todd replied.

As crazy as it sounded, Todd's words made an unsettling amount of sense and almost immediately some around Georgina began to back off.

"Don't be ridiculous! Are you listening to yourself? Bringing up some fantastical bullshit straight from a fictional TV Series or movie or something now of all times. How are you so sure it's a virus? You're talking like a fucking expert", Louis interjected.

"Internet, dipshit, they're speculating it is, I'm just a messenger".

"Looked a little more than that, people only start running around eating people in movies and those crazy psychos with cannibalistic habits".

"So, what the fuck was happening downstairs then?"

"Beats me, I was up here".

"How is she, Lizzy?" Bishop interjected, killing the little argument, now wasn't the time for bickering amongst themselves.

"Her temperature has spiked, but she's trembling as though she just returned from the Arctic", Lizzy replied.

"Did you give her water?"

Lizzy lifted a glass, "She's had three glasses already, she gulped them down like nothing I've ever seen".

"We need to get her to a hospital, this looks similar to the symptoms of rabies".

"She was bitten by a person, not an animal".

"And said people were behaving like animals themselves, no? What are the chances they were bitten and it's spreading like Todd suggested?"

"Yeah, but... shit, she's foaming at the mouth, someone get me a tissue", Lizzy requested, to which a colleague fetched one to hand to her, but before Lizzy could clean Georgina's mouth, Georgina coughed up a spray of blood all over Lizzy's face, who abruptly stood up with her hands out and gasped.

"Fuck!" Everyone gasped and some immediately sprung to action in escorting Lizzy to the ladies and proceeding to clean up Georgina, whilst others saw more than they needed in order to confirm Todd's suspicions.

"What the fuck?" Todd cried, "I told you! I fucking told you!"

"Take her to the toilets, keep her there", Bishop instructed, "I'm going to try to call someone, anyone". He left and made his way back to his office.

Hannah, evidently one of the few unfazed by Todd's mere speculations and scaremongering, took over and helped escort Georgina to the toilets.

Natasha stood up, feeling a little disorientated, she needed some cold water on her face.

As she followed behind Hannah and another two women escorting Georgina to the toilets, Georgina began to twitch more violently and her muttering got louder.

The girls stared at her and then at each other, as Georgina's mutters became a full-blown unsettling conversation with herself.

"Coffees, teas, that's all they ever ask for, never anything for me? Treat the new girl like a fucking incompetent retard, it's not my fault my mother slept with another man, it's not my fault my fucking lecturer was a fucking lecherous sexist asshole, it's not my fault James fucking left me, stop blaming me dammit! Nothing but users, all of them! Nothing but fucking users!"

The language and tone were unlike her. Had she lost it? This usually timid, polite girl, had now suddenly begun expressing herself in a way that seemed completely out of character.

"Hannah", she said, turning towards her bewildered assistant manager, with a somewhat drunk or drugged expression.

"Yes, Georgina".

"I have a secret".

"Well let's keep that to yourself for now, we need to get you to the toilets".

"Oh, but I want to tell you so badly, so I'm going to tell you anyway. I didn't want to say anything because you're like my fucking manager, it wouldn't have been *professional*, but I feel great right now, so fuck that".

"Georgina, don't say anymore, you're not in the right frame of mind right now".

"Don't tell me what to fucking do, you're not my fucking mother. The truth is, when I first met you, I thought you were a right stuck up bitch, you looked like one of those fucking frigid bitches with a rod stuck so far up their fucking ass that it's jabbing into the part of your brain that would make you a nice fucking person. I was telling my friends that you just needed a good fuck, *that* would loosen you up and you'd stop being such a fucking dictator".

"Georgina, stop talking", one of the other women escorting her replied in Hannah's defence, who was now visibly offended by the remarks.

Natasha gasped, for all the thoughts she may have had about Hannah as a manager, she would never be brave or stupid enough to say them out loud, far less directly to Hannah's face. Where had this sense of recklessness come from? Had the situation given Georgina a false sense of courage or was this just pain and anguish speaking on her behalf?

"Aww, why should I? I was under the impression Hannah liked talking and she's suddenly being a quiet bitch now. Truth is, I genuinely started liking you these last couple of weeks, you're not the fucking tool I thought you were".

"She said to stop talking!" Hannah snarled.

"Either that or you got laid good and proper, who was it? Ooh, was it an office affair? Bishop maybe? Those *meetings* with him, were you really just sucking him off beneath the desk?"

Hannah had heard enough. Without even a second thought, she dropped Georgina, leaving her to the other women.

"You've stepped across the line! Who do you think you are? You are new here; don't you dare speak to me or about me like that!" Hannah snapped and as she turned to walk away, Georgina grabbed her wrist.

"Don't be like that, you're being a stuck-up little bitch again. Look, I didn't mean to be offensive, I was just being honest, let's make up". She raised her head and rolling down her cheeks were bloodied tears; her eyes were bloodshot and darting all over the place. The sight was enough to send Natasha's heart leaping from her chest.

Without warning, Georgina pounced on top of Hannah, bringing her down to the floor.

"Get off me, you freak! I'll fucking sue you!" Hannah shouted in fury.

"Let's kiss and make up", Georgina insisted and grabbed Hannah's head in an attempt to kiss her lips. Hannah screamed and attempted to fight her off, whilst the two other women leapt onto Georgina's back to help. Natasha too scrambled over to help in any way, but with a frightening strength, Georgina shoved them off and into nearby walls and objects, all without much effort whatsoever.

Natasha sat up and rubbed the back of her throbbing head, she had had an unpleasant collision with the edge of a table upon her fall. As she pathetically sat there watching, the scenes before her continued to unfold for the worst.

Georgina a petite girl with barely any weight to her, needed only a single hand to subdue both of Hannah's without a struggle, what kind of voodoo magic was this? The other hand-held Hannah's chin locked in place in order to kiss her... or at least that was the way it initially appeared, but as Hannah's eyes widened, her legs thrashed as though experiencing unbearable pain and blood trickled down the side of her face, Natasha knew that this was more than met the eye.

Georgina retracted with a blood covered mouth and Hannah's tongue in tow. A quick jerk backwards of her head and she ripped Hannah's tongue right out of her mouth with her teeth.

Hannah's scream was piercing. Blood sprayed from her mouth and tears rolled down the sides of her face. She thrashed in agony, but with Georgina sitting on top of her, she was going nowhere soon.

Georgina chewed before swallowing the tongue, as though everything Natasha had just seen wasn't already enough to churn her stomach. Natasha spun around and grabbed a nearby bin to puke into.

"Dirty girl, Hannah. You like tongue action, huh?" Georgina said and burst into hysterical laughter, as more people arrived, including Lizzy and the others in the toilet, who had stepped out to investigate.

Georgina's eyes looked manic, filled with anger and hatred and her laugh was sadistic, almost demonic.

"You have luscious lips, how about we give our audience a show". Hannah, tears streaming down her face, tried to shake her head, but Georgina ignored her and leaned in.

Despite the pain, Hannah attempted to pull her lips in, but that didn't seem to faze Georgina who instead just sank her teeth into the surrounding skin of Hannah's mouth, drawing blood, until Hannah had no other choice but to release, but in doing so, Georgina ripped both her top and bottom lips off like a savage dog.

"Stop it!" Lizzy screamed, as Hannah kicked and thrashed and several people including her, once again attempted to pull her off of Hannah.

Georgina threw them back with ease and continued feasting on Hannah's face. If they stood any chance whatsoever of rescuing Hannah, they would *have* to resort to extreme measures, *that* was absolute. They had to face facts, this woman was Georgina no longer, it was a monster and a monster not unlike the ones downstairs and on broadcast.

Lizzy returned with a fire extinguisher and hit Georgina around the head with it, knocking the girl to the floor and off of Hannah.

"I'll fucking kill you for that, you bitch!" Georgina roared, twitching uncontrollably.

"Fucking come at me then, psychotic bitch! I'm from fucking Islington!"

As Georgina got to her feet and lunged over at Lizzy, Natasha wasted no time in grabbing a keyboard, pulling it free of its socket and hitting Georgina over the head with it.

She retracted just enough for Lizzy to hit her again with the extinguisher, leaving a blood covered dent in its side, but still, this woman remained resilient. With the number of blows she had taken to the head with large objects, it was any wonder how the hell she was still able to stand. What the fuck had she become?

"Spray her!" Natasha shouted. Lizzy immediately began removing the safety pin from the top of the extinguisher and before Georgina could launch another attack, she blasted the extinguisher in her face.

Others who had heard the commotion and rushed over to find a macabre scene unfolding before them, a demented Georgina and Hannah's half eaten face.

"Get her out of here!" Lizzy ordered, "And someone help me with this freak before she does to us what she did to her!"

As the useless male audience just stood there gawping, too cowardice or selfish to help, Natasha sprung to action, grabbing Hannah and helping the weak and groaning woman up to her feet.

"Don't just stand there, fucking help me out here!" She snapped.

"Fuck that!" Todd replied. "I was right on the fucking ball! I warned you! You saw what happened to Georgina, that woman will turn into one of them too, fucking zombie!"

"Georgina isn't dead, you fucking twat! Help me!"

Though the crowd, Elmira rushed to Natasha's aid, the only person Natasha could ever truly rely on. The others remained behind, arming themselves with anything they could use to take down the rampant Georgina.

CHAPTER 13 - RIA

3:45pm - 4 Hours, 0 Minutes since outbreak

. . .

FACT FILE #5:

The **C.E.U (C**ontainment & **E**vacuation **U**nit), is a relatively new European initiative, publically launched in 20▮▮ with the intent of tackling and minimising the potential collateral inflicted by increased terrorism and looming world war conflicts.

The initiative is brought about by the conglomerate of the national military, private military units, **Sector6 Dynamics** representatives, government representatives and the Directorate of Military Intelligence (DMI), consisting of MI1 (Interception and cryptanalysis), MI5 (Counter-espionage and military policy), MI6 (Covert overseas collection and analysis of human intelligence) and MI16 (Scientific Intelligence), commonly referred to as **Peza Research**, the only privately funded arm of the DMI.

The objective of the C.E.U, made up of two arms, is 1) to quell and contain violence and 2) secure and safely evacuate all non-hostile civilians.

. . .

Ria watched Terry pace back and forth waiting for someone to pick up the phone. The longer it took for her mother to pick up the phone was the more impatient and irater he became.

"Why won't she pick up?" This was his third attempt to reach her.

He tried once more and after a while someone answered.

"Natasha? Natasha! What the hell is going on?" He was silent for a few seconds, before his expression changed.

"What do you mean switched personalities? What happened?" He began pacing again as he continued. "Okay, has anything got into your bloodstream, because I'm pretty sure that that's how it is spreading, not unlike any other virus... but none in your mouth or eyes right?" He sighed. "Good, but you need to get the hell out of there... yes I know, but you need to find a way down, there couldn't possibly be a worst place to be right now, if they swarm that building, you and everyone surviving in it are fucked... just focus on getting out... is Georgina still alive?"

Ria stood up and went over to the window to peer out. She couldn't see much, but knew that somewhere not too far, a battle was ensuing.

"Natasha, leave Hannah, she'll turn into one of them, she will kill you, Todd was right and if the situation in London and what I saw is enough to go by, she'll be attempting to bite a chunk out of your neck any time soon. Heck, go one step further, lock her somewhere she can't reach you, she probably won't reach a hospital any time soon, especially considering that we've been in quarantine this long already, that and even if you managed to get her out of the building and away from the chaos, those army soldiers and CEU operatives out there will probably shoot her and you on sight".

There came a knock at the door and several people in CEU branded white hazmat outfits stepped in. The real deal, a full biohazard suit, all in white, covered from head to toe with gas masks and all, just like in the movies. Accompanying them were armed police officers, maybe a tad excessive.

"Natasha, please just do as I say, your life is at stake here, don't do anything stupid, you've always been the voice of reason, I'm supposed to be the impulsive and irrational one. I have to go now, I'll be in touch again soon, keep your phone to hand", Terry hung up.

"What's happening to mum?" Ria asked.

"I'll explain later".

"What is happening to her?" She snapped.

"I said I'll explain later".

"Dad!"

"We have other concerns right now".

Exasperated with her father, Ria turned to face the strangers.

"I'm going to need you all to follow me", the one towards the front ordered.

"Finally leaving this jail cell, huh?" Terry replied.

"Indeed, you are, the sooner we get the process started, the sooner we can get you all to safety, though hopefully that shouldn't take long, this virus spreads quickly and you haven't turned yet, so that at least bodes well", one of the hazmat outfitted people replied, a female.

"I see you are referring to it as a virus, does that mean that you've at least established what this thing is?"

"We know what to look for, yes, it's appears to be either an unfamiliar voracious mutagen or an aggressive parasite, we've temporarily nicknamed it the Vora Virus or Parasite".

"Do you have a cure?"

"It's way too early to be talking cures, we still have the process of identification and establishing its source, because right now prevention supersedes purge".

"Do you know what the symptoms are at least?"

"Not to sound snide, but you probably have a better idea of that than we do right now, we've received so many mixed reports that it's difficult to pinpoint exactly what we should be looking out for and that's the problem. Here we have what could be the single greatest national disaster of the century and we don't even know what we are supposed to be looking out for".

"You don't even know what you're looking for?"

"If we did, you wouldn't have been detained here for so long".

"Well we saw people swearing and attacking people".

"This is London, if we were to quarantine everyone who swears, we'd have a major task on our hands".

"No... I mean *really* angry swearing, unnecessary so. I know that doesn't mean anything, but they were like mad people".

"Did you see anything more... visible, tangible even. Something we could recognise from a distance".

Terry thought long and hard.

"They were twitching, like they had a tick or something".

Ria passed her father and approached the people in hazmat.

"Let's get this over and done with, we can talk about this after we find some way to save mum".

She was led out into the corridor along with the others to an elevator. One by one they descended the elevator and were led outside to a series of temporary quarantine stations.

"You will need to go in one at a time, where you will be checked for contamination", one of the CEU operatives instructed.

"And should we fail? I mean, you don't even know what you're looking for, right?" Terry asked. They didn't reply and that was enough to unnerve him. "I'm going with my kids". Ria turned towards him, was he serious?

"Sir, please comply with directives".

"Not unless you can guarantee my children's' safety, answer my question".

"I have no obligation to, sir".

"Then I have no obligation to step into there without my kids!"

"Terry!" Ria snapped, "Don't do this now, we'll be fine!"

Terry ignored her and continued to embarrass her in front of several onlookers and in the process creating debacle where there need be none.

Spotting people calmly approaching them with batons and tasers, Ria could overlook her irritation for a moment in the interests of protecting her father. Today was not the day for games and patience was at teetering point, they would certainly not go lightly on him if he continued this ruckus.

"Dad, I'm going in, so you can stop this nonsense before we all get tazed".

She plucked up the courage and walked in, how bad could it be? As she stepped in, her father called after her, but this time she ignored him.

Inside the plastic station was another person in a hazmat suit surrounded by armed guards.

"Hello dear, are you next?" The female voice asked.

"I guess so", Ria replied.

"Can you put anything you have in your pockets in this plastic bag, as well as any metallic objects on your person", she instructed, approaching Ria with an open bag.

The guards behind looked more than prepared for things to get hairy.

Ria searched her pockets and found nothing of particular value, but she gave them her purse and jewellery. Once they were sealed, she was escorted to a warded off sector of the station where she found another lady in a hazmat suit.

"Hello".

"Hi", Ria replied, "So what's happening now?"

"Well, we are going to need you to take off your clothes, then we'll wash you down with decontamination…" She stopped mid-sentence, distracted by the unmistakable sound of gunfire. Though the sound of unexpected gunfire was rarely ever a welcome one, it couldn't have come at a better time, for the idea of stripping off in front of strangers didn't appeal.

Guards and CEU operatives scrambled out of the station and to the source of the gunfire, leaving her alone with one other operative, who from the looks of things, had completely no idea how to handle this extreme change of circumstances. Ria could only begin to imagine her panicked expression beneath that mask.

"Wait here!" The female operative instructed and took off. Ria had a feeling she wouldn't see that woman again.

Doing as she always did, she ignored the command, grabbed her belongings and made her way back out of the quarantine station. Outside was utter travesty, people running around like headless chickens, lack of direction and purpose. The gunfire resounded in the background, as medics desperately attempted to transport the sick and injured away from the hospital, manoeuvring several ambulances into a position to make that possible, but wasn't it all a little too late now?

Spotting Terry, Charlotte and her brother, Ria ran over to them.

"Ria!" Terry cried, evidently glad to see her. "What did they do to you?"

"Nothing, just took my stuff, but I got it back, they didn't get to do anything else because this all started".

"Good, glad. Let's get out of here, we're heading east. We need to find a route across the bridge and the further east we go, the more likely we are to find one".

"Won't we need the car?" Charlotte asked.

"We will indeed", Terry replied.

"Let me have my phone back", Ria demanded. Terry didn't protest this time, instead he handed it over to her without hesitation, much to her surprise.

"Thanks..." She replied.

"Let me know if your mother calls", he insisted, to which she nodded simply. She checked her phone to discover a torrent of notifications and a battery life of only 76%.

On her babbadoo messenger was a message from Lacey.

'OMG Ria!!!!! Have u seen ur Chirper!? Ur famous!!'

Positive Lacey was either pulling her leg, or exaggerating, Ria opened up the Chirper app whilst maintaining an air of scepticism, but much to her surprise, Lacey wasn't exaggerating in the slightest, if anything, her proclamation failed to serve as fair enough warning.

Ria stood there staring at the ridiculous numbers before her, in disbelief. This couldn't be her account, there was no way this was her account. She had gained 5000+ new followers in the short space of time her phone had been out of her possession and her chirps had been rechirped and favourited well over 8000 times, but how...?

She checked over and over, logging out and back in, just to ensure it wasn't a Chirper related glitch, but nothing she did changed the numbers she was faced with and they only continued to increase with each refresh and the notifications kept pouring in.

As a result of not having added anything since last having her phone, there was already speculation as to whether or not she was a goner, another victim of the chaos.

Excitedly, she took a few photos of the scenes around her, attached them to a new chirp and began typing away.

"At St Thomas, got quarantined, omg! Dad and brother almost got killed! Hearing shooting, so gotta go!" She posted it feeling a little chuffed at the new-found value of every chirp she published. There was nothing quite compared to the elation gained knowing your posts and chirps were appreciated, even if they were at the profit of devastation.

She switched over to Myface and typed the same thing, before recording a small clip and uploading it to Vyou.

"Ria! I hate to interrupt your social session, but we need to make a move now!" Terry snapped over at her.

"Coming!" She replied and caught up to the others.

"We won't be able to get to my car and drive it out of here under these conditions",

Charlotte pointed out.

"What do you suggest?" Terry replied, holding on to George's hand.

"Under the circumstances? Steal one".

"What? No! Even if we were to do that, how would we even get it running?"

"I've hotwired cars before".

"Who even are you?"

"I was a rebellious teenager once, what can I say. Don't tell me you were mummy's perfect little angel".

"I might have smoked a spliff or two, but I can't say I've ever had the urge to commit grand theft auto. Anyway, no, no carjacking, things have gone shit, yes, but not so much so we need to start adding criminal records to the list of shit we have to look forward to after the dust settles".

"*If* the dust settles. So, what do you suggest?"

"Given the situation, I actually agree with Charlotte", Ria added, "What else is there, Terry?" She asked her father.

Terry glanced around.

"Maybe... we ask someone for a lift?"

"Really, Terry? That's the best idea you could come up with? Have you forgotten how we even got here?"

"Okay fine! We'll take a car, but if anyone asks, we were your hostages. Hurry it up, get it over and done with before anyone sees us!" Terry replied, visibly agitated.

They all took off in search of a suitable car, old enough that security alarms and such wouldn't be so much of an issue and Charlotte proceeded to work her magic, using only things she had in her handbag. When she said she had done this before, her dad didn't expect her to get a car up and running in such quick succession, she made it look criminally easy.

He attempted to take over.

"Thank you, Charlotte, you've been a star. I can take it from here, you don't have to stay with us if you don't want to, you've done more than enough and I'm sure you are concerned about your boyfriend, I don't want to drag you into any danger, where can I safely drop you off?"

"Err, hell no, I'm tagging along, we've come this far and I really want to see the conclusion to this epic drama", she replied, to which they all three stared at her blankly. "The drama starring one father's unyielding determination to save his family in a situation stacked against him. I want to help until the end, besides, my family all live up north, only my boyfriend lives in London and he's on the outskirts. I wouldn't be able to live with myself knowing I left you and your children to go into the dragon's den, let me see this through to the end".

"Are you sure? You owe us nothing".

"Like I said, anything to help, that's the type of person my parents would be proud of. All or nothing, so what do you say?"

"Okay, let's make a move then", he replied, returning to the passenger seat.

"Righto!" Charlotte replied and wasting no time, she put the pedal to the metal, jerking them all backwards and having Ria clinging to her seat.

They were blasting down the roads eastwards, cutting in and out of traffic as they made their way to the nearest open bridge.

"How about we head for the Rotherhithe Tunnel? Do you think that that is far enough east to still be open?" Charlotte asked.

"Couldn't hurt to try", Terry replied, "Doesn't look as though our options are overflowing.

Ria feared for the wellbeing of her mother, her father had explained little to them in the way of informing them what exactly was happening to her, it was all left up to interpretation, but from the sounds of the conversation they had had, her mother was in something of a worrisome predicament.

Just as her thoughts had returned to her mother, Terry suddenly turned to her.

"Ria, call your mother, check to see she is still alright, tell her we are coming through Rotherhithe Tunnel".

"Okay", Ria replied and attempted to call her mother.

The first few attempts to reach her resulted in the frustrating sound of her mother's voice recorded for voicemail and Ria's heart sank a little further with each failure, as the possibility of her mother in peril and worst-case dead, only sent her mind aflutter with panic.

"Can't you get through to her?" Terry asked.

"I'm trying", Ria replied.

"God, I hope she's okay. Keep trying".

"That's what I'm doing".

She tried repeatedly until finally a reassuring click of her call being received.

"Mum?"

"Ria? Ria is that you?"

"Mum, thank god you're alright, what's happening? Are you okay?"

"It's bad, really bad. Hannah is... Hannah attacked us, she's not thinking straight and Lizzy... Lizzy is dead... I..." Her mother replied, sounding panicked and flustered over the phone.

"Mum, calm down, we are coming, we are almost at Rotherhithe Tunnel and we'll be over on the north side soon".

"What's happening? Is she okay?" Terry nagged from the front.

"Hold on, I can't speak to both of you at the same time, I'm finding out", Ria snapped back, "Mum, where are you now?"

"We locked ourselves in the meeting room, there's six of us, there is five of them".

"Them?"

"Our colleagues... no... not anymore, they've become what Hannah became now".

"Just stay there, mum, don't move and don't let them in".

"We are doing our best, but I don't know how long we can keep them out for".

"Okay, we will be there soon".

"Don't come here! Those infected people are surrounding the building, you'll never get in!"

"We are not just going to leave you there, mum".

"Get out of the city!"

"No mum, we are coming".

"Shit! They've shut down the tunnel, the barriers are down", Charlotte interjected, "What now?"

"Go straight through", Terry ordered. So much for not wanting to break the law earlier.

"Now you're speaking my language", Charlotte replied, "Hold on guys, we are going through".

Ria didn't have the chance to hear her mother's pleas for them to leave the city, for the car tore down the centre of the road, bypassing traffic and sending people on the road leaping to safety as Charlotte hammered at the horn.

Ria closed her eyes as they smashed through the barriers and the security guards jumped out of the way.

When she reopened them again, the windscreen was cracked, but everyone was okay. They raced through the empty Rotherhithe Tunnel as the reception to the phone call cut, putting an abrupt end to the line.

Ria hung on for dear life as the car skidded around bends a hairpin away from crashing. Upon reaching the other end of the tunnel, they smashed through yet another barrier and swerved onto Commercial Road, making their way up to Algate East Station.

Ria explained the situation as best she could to her father, which only served to make him all the more anxious to get there.

The streets were anarchy ridden as looters and opportunists broke into shops, car jacked and fought with innocent people to steal from them the little they had to hand. Even without the state London was currently in, it didn't take much to send the general populace into hysteria induced depravity.

"Drop me off at Old Street, I'll take it from there", Terry insisted.

"And the kids?" Charlotte asked.

"Get them out of London".

"What about you? If you manage to escape, do you not want me to meet you somewhere?"

"No, I don't want to take that chance. Even without the infected crazed to contend with, there are the everyday crazy folk, London just isn't safe. Don't worry about us, we'll find a way out. So long as the kids are safe, I can think straight".

Ria was pleasantly surprised, that was probably the fatherliest thing he had said in a long while. George wasn't happy with the arrangement however, suddenly bursting into tears.

"Daddy, don't leave us! Please stay with us, we'll come with you".

Terry turned to him.

"Little man, I'm not going to put your life at risk. You'll be safer with Charlotte outside of the city. You've seen enough danger for one day and I've been terribly irresponsible. You can't come where I'm going, it'll be incredibly dangerous and I'd be a bad father if I took you with me". Seems as though this chaos had awoken something in Terry, these fatherly words were flowing from his mouth like water.

"No! I don't wanna go without you!"

"Then who will look after the ladies? You're the next big man after me, it's our responsibility to take care of the girls. You're a man, right?" Ria almost felt inclined to laugh at the prospect of the shrimp protecting her, but she could understand what Terry was trying to do.

George sobbed and eventually nodded.

"You two need to be brave and stay with Charlotte".

"How are we meant to contact you?" Ria asked.

"No biggie", Charlotte replied, handing him her own, "seems we are having a little phone issue today. I don't have much battery power left, I think it's at twenty-five percent, so you'll want to preserve it as much as you can. I switched it to power saving mode nonetheless".

"Thank you, Charlotte", Terry replied, taking it from her, "Are you sure you're going to be okay, kiddo?" He asked George.

George nodded reluctantly, but said no more.

"Ria, call me the moment something happens, don't take any unnecessary risks".

"Will do", Ria replied as they made their way onto the last traffic crammed road.

"Shit, we are not going to get any further than this", Charlotte informed.

"That's fine, any closer to the place and I'll be putting your lives at risk, I'll take it from here", Terry replied. He undid his seatbelt and opened the door.

Watching him leave made Ria feel uneasy. He had his ways and he was far from the picture-perfect father, but... he was still her dad and she only ever had one dad. This was probably the last time she would ever see the big loser and the thought hurt her.

"Okay, I'm gone. Get to safety and stay away from the city. Bye kids, I love you both", he proclaimed. He opened the back door and George wasted no time in clambering over her to cuddle him.

"I'll miss you", he wept.

"Me too, kiddo, me too. Take care of yourself and be brave okay? I'm putting my faith in you". Soon enough they parted and he turned to Ria. The hug despite the situation was short and awkward, but before he could close the door on them, Ria stopped him short.

"Dad..." She said, looking down at her lap, it had been a while since she called him that.

"Ria?"

"Bring mum back safely, I'll never forgive you if you let her die".

"I'll do my best".

"And dad..."

"Yes?"

"Don't die either, come back to us". She glanced up at him after a moment of silence to see an annoying smile on his face.

"I'll do what I can", he replied and shut the door. Ria's heart suddenly sank faster than a brick in an ocean, her idiot father, the man who could piss her off beyond all measure, but would always have a place in her heart, was about to embark on a journey that could potentially claim his life, as well as her mother's.

The three watched Terry disappear amongst the cars and people, before Charlotte reversed the car and turned around.

"We better get out of here. I guess we'll head over to my boyfriend's house first and make our way out of London from there. Ria, could you do me a favour and text him, tell him what happened and that I'll talk to him via you", she instructed and begun to recite the number.

Ria sent him a text and left it at that. Her phone was still buzzing endlessly with notifications. She replied to Lacey, sending her a few photos and videos she had accumulated from the scenes around her.

Lacey and her family were already well on their way out of the city by now, sending across her condolences upon news of Terry's decision.

'He's not as bad as you made him out to be really :)', Lacey stated.

'I guess... ' Ria replied.

'I hope they both get back to you okay, really sorry to hear that :(. You guys can come with us if you want, we're heading down to Canterbury until this all blows over, my nan lives there'.

'We'll see, have to get outta this shit hole before we decide what to do next'.

'Who is with you?'

'Lil bro and that Charlotte woman, she's driving'.

'She's still with you?! :o'

'Yeah, she's not bad either, pretty cool actually. Dunno what we would have done without her'.

'Is she pretty?'

'Why? There's nothing going on between her and my dad if that's what you're implying'.

'No way. Just curious. You gonna update your Chirper and Myface? People will think you're dead again'.

'Yeah, doing it now'.

Ria switched over to Chirper and uploaded a few of the pictures with an update of her father's departure and their escape out of the city. Her followers, re-chirps and favourites were stacking up ridiculously by the second.

She was midway into her update on Myface when the three heard a loud scream and before Ria could even look up to see what it was, they hit something or more likely someone, widening the crack on the windscreen across the entire expanse, it was a miracle it hadn't shattered.

"Shit!" Charlotte yelped as she lost control of the car and careened off the road onto the sidewalk, hitting more pedestrians before smashing into a shop, after their screams, all went quiet and black.

Ria roused to the sounds of frantic shouting and a ticking sound, she was disorientated and the dust and darkness wasn't helping matters.

Shaken up, her hands would not stop trembling, that was the single most terrifying experience of her life, she was almost certain she would die.

Sluggishly, she gave herself the once over, a few bruises, very superficial. The car itself had taken quite the abuse, with dents and shattered glass absolutely everywhere. It was only as she tried to ease the ringing in her head with gentle massages did she suddenly remember her brother, but as she looked over towards his seat, she found it empty with the door besides it ajar, that alone was enough to spruce her up.

"George! George! Where are you?" She called out to him, her eyes and head darting to and fro, with hopes of spotting him somewhere nearby, but she couldn't see him and her calls for him received no answer.

She grabbed her phone and attempted to clamber out on his side, her door obstructed, suddenly remembering Charlotte as she did so.

"Charlotte!" She poked her head around to the front, only to gasp and drop back, covering her mouth with her trembling hands in horror at the sight of Charlotte lying motionless on the steering wheel.

The danger of these old vehicles and probably the exact reason Aradin as a car manufacturer was always in the fire pit, the airbag hadn't ejected.

Once she was able to pluck up the courage, fearing that a real dead person now lay just in front of her, Ria stretched forward and grabbed Charlotte's shoulder to lightly shake her, but she didn't respond.

Was she dead or just unconscious? Ria prayed the latter was the case. Charlotte's legs were wedged between the wreckage, so there was no telling what condition she was in.

Ria didn't really want an answer to question of Charlotte's condition, for fear of having to confront the harsh reality of mortality, so as heartless as it may have seemed, she prioritised her brother, she would ask someone else to help Charlotte.

She stepped out of the car on her brother's side and glanced around. They were in what looked to be a DIY store and at the front was the gaping hole their crash had created, surrounded by curious spectators clearly too stupid or cowardice to help instead of just stand there and stare.

George was nowhere in sight. Had he left the store?

"Help me!" Ria cried. "There's a woman in that car that needs your help and did you see a little boy leave here?"

A man nodded and pointed her in his direction, adding that he and others would do what they could to help Charlotte. With assurance that Charlotte would be okay in their care, she went in pursuit of her brother.

CHAPTER 14 - DANIEL

4:53pm - 5 Hours, 8 Minutes since outbreak

. . .

FACT FILE #6:

The International Network & Broadcasting or **INBC** as it is more commonly known, is responsible for the gathering and broadcasting of news and current affairs. The network and department is the world's largest broadcast news organisation and generates about 120 hours of radio and television output each day, as well as online news coverage.

Supplying news to many countries around the world, if not most, INBC is a quasi-autonomous corporation operationally independent of any government, as such its global branch is expected and required to report impartially. It does however have subsidiaries reporting from more biased perspectives.

As with all major media outlets, it has been accused of political bias from across the political spectrum.

. . .

God only knew how, but somehow Daniel had made it out of that car alive, a combination of very quick thinking and sharp reflexes kept him alive as psychopaths with some kind of death wish, lunged in at him through the car windows.

It had taken nothing short of the fight of his life to get out of that situation alive and here he was, still running as fast as his legs could carry him, if the drooling mindless didn't get him, those gunners in the helicopters certainty would.

This had gone past the point of being classified as mere chaos, this was literally hell on Earth. Every direction he looked in was the same scene of death and destruction, shattered glass, flames engulfing cars and erupting from shop windows, the ground littered with the things fleeing people had left behind, blood trails leading to corpses and the cannibalistic psychopaths responsible for murdering them.

Daniel passed a man pleading for his help. He dragged himself across the ground, leaving behind a long blood trail from where one of his legs had once previously been.

Whilst he felt compelled to help the man, even if he could carry him on his back, the poor lad wouldn't last long with that much blood loss, or so Daniel told himself to justify his actions. It was a dog eat dog or human eat human world in this case and he was determined to keep all of his limbs intact.

Only a minute later he was confronted with yet another conundrum, a crying boy turned away from him who looked no more than about six or seven. He stood alone, crying and calling out for his mother.

"Mummy! Where is mummy?" He wailed.

"Kid, I can help, when did you last see her?" Daniel asked, but with the boy facing away from him, it was possible he didn't hear the question, since he didn't respond accordingly.

"I can't find her, I can't find mummy".

"Hey", Daniel called and placed his hand on the boy's shoulder.

The boy turned to him and lunged at him, biting into the finger of the hand he used to defend himself. The pain was indescribable and Daniel reacted by punching the little boy square in the face with the ferocity of as though he were facing a fully-grown adult in a bar brawl, but he didn't even have the time to feel ashamed at himself for striking a child, since the boy barely reacted to it, impossible! This little fucker didn't even flinch, in fact, he just bit even harder as though his teeth were locked down on Daniel's finger.

Daniel yelped in agony, panicking as the sheer bloodlust in this boy's eyes intensified. He struck the boy continuously, until he was almost certain he had done enough to break or at the very least fracture the boy's skull, yet still he did not flinch, but he did retract, his face covered in blood that didn't all belong to Daniel, but taking Daniel's finger along with him, right from the bone.

106

Daniel wailed in agony and clutched his injured hand as the boy stood there staring at him smugly and chewing on his finger, before swallowing.

"I just remembered what happened to mummy", he said with a menacing grin, "I ate her all up... and now I'll eat you". He lunged at Daniel again, but this time Daniel was prepared and ducked.

He took off, sprinting away from the boy, bobbing and weaving between cars in an attempt to lose the little bastard, but the boy leapt from car to car like a fucking chimp, keeping up with him.

Daniel dived between two cars, wedging himself slightly beneath them to squeeze his way through. Just then, Daniel noticed a smashed shop window with a crowbar resting next to it, didn't take a genius to work out what had transpired here.

The boy grabbed his leg, but Daniel kicked at him, freeing himself and scrambling to the other side.

"Are you playing hide and go seek? I like that game!" The boy screeched and hopped up onto the car, jumping down just behind him. Almost as though toying with him, the boy stopped and turned away.

"I'll count to ten and you can go and hide".

Was he fucking serious? Did he think this was a fucking game? Daniel suddenly felt stupid, fleeing from a fucking child, but if this was any ordinary child, we would never have even been in this pitiful position.

Wasting no more time, Daniel made a mad dash for the crowbar, grabbed it from the ground, dived into the shop and took hiding behind the counter. He clutched the crowbar tightly in his hands and braced himself, complacency would be the death of him.

"Nine... ten! I'm coming to find you!" The boy shouted and spun around to look for Daniel. He wandered about aimlessly, clearly looking for him, they were abnormally strong these psychopaths, what's to say they didn't possess superhuman senses too? Daniel could only pray that that wasn't the case, but who could blame him for thinking that way.

He glanced around once more and lost all sight of the boy, he could hear not a whimper from him either.

Daniel remained where he was for another minute or two, before deciding it safe to leave his hiding spot. Had the boy left? Was he in the clear? He couldn't justify hiding here for much longer if that was the case, it wouldn't be much longer before he was overwhelmed with more of them.

As he inched closer to the door, his injured hand began to tingle and he could feel a headache coming on. He thought nothing of it, the adrenaline that had made him forget about the pain was evidently beginning to wear off.

"Dammit", he murmured, trying to forget about it again. He pressed his back against the wall besides the front doors and glanced out to see if the coast was clear.

With no sign of the boy anywhere in sight, he deliberated using this opportunity to flee the scene.

Squeezing the crowbar in his hands and pressing it to his chest, he took a few deep breaths and just as he turned to run through the door, the boy leapt out at him.

"Found you!" He shrieked and Daniel's heart almost escaped his chest. Where had this little fucker popped out from?

Daniel fell backwards and scrambled to his feet as the boy climbed into the shop in pursuit of him.

Daniel tried the back door, but it appeared locked. Seeing nowhere else to run, Daniel threw anything he could reach at the boy, a few of which hit the boy, but didn't appear to faze him, instead he charged at Daniel, knocking him to the ground with tremendous force.

"I don't want to play anymore, I'm too hungry!"

"Fuck you!" Daniel shouted and swung at the boy with the crowbar, drawing blood the first time, but again not fazing the boy. Like what the fuck? Did the concept of pain not correspond at all?

The boy bore his teeth with intent to bite Daniel, but Daniel defended himself by wedging the crowbar between the boy's teeth. Together they tussled, a bloodlust and crazed glint in the boy's eyes, with the spray of his saliva and an erratic twitch.

Gaining the upper hand, Daniel managed to shove the boy off of him and subdue him upon the floor, where he pushed down on the crowbar wedged between the boy's mouth. Daniel poured the full extent of his power into pushing down that crowbar, breaking the boy's jaw and pushing it back into his skull, still the boy struggled, hissing and lashing out at him. Daniel retracted the crowbar and hit him with it repeatedly until he had cracked his skull and blood sprayed across Daniel's face, then he would wedge the crowbar between the boy's teeth as the boy begged, pleaded and screamed for forgiveness and repeat the process, every so often retracting it to continue his onslaught. It was at that point that Daniel realised he was no longer in control of his actions, it was as though his body had taken on a mind of its own and try as he might to stop this heart-wrenching senseless violence against a minor, his body simply would not listen to him.

'Stop it! Stop it, please!' He would scream at himself, but his arms continued to batter the boy, cracking open his skull and spilling its contents like a watermelon. Consumed with an unfamiliar and terrifying blind rage, it was only as the boy lay upon the ground a bloodied, twitching and gurgling mess, did Daniel stop.

Where had his humanity gone? He pondered staring at his bloodied hands, before gazing over at the flattened mass that was once a boy's face.

Why did he have such little control over himself? It was a strange phenomenon, like looking through one's own eyes as a spectator. He could think rationally, yes, but these fury driven actions were not his own. Bemused as to where this frightening anger had stemmed from, to not only kill a little boy, regardless of the fact the boy had attacked him, but to smash his face into nothing more than a bloody mess, Daniel tried to regain control of himself, but found he could not, his body was moving independently, muttering obscenities, venting anger towards everything and everyone, especially... Terry.

He stood up, clutching on to the blood covered crowbar, still seething with rage.

Just then, two more of those psychopaths stopped at the front and glared at him, twitching and foaming at the mouth.

Shit, he thought, realising that even with the crowbar, there was no way he would be able to take on two fully grown psychos when he had had that much difficulty with just a fucking child.

As though that wasn't enough, behind him came a sound and he turned to see the mutilated child impossibly stumbling to his feet without regard for his state.

But as Daniel had just about given up and was prepared to accept his fate, the two psychos at the door left, paying him no further attention and the headless child stumbled right on past him and out into the open.

Daniel was lost for words or thoughts and for a while he couldn't quite comprehend why they had disregarded him, until the headache worsened, the repetitive whispers in his head to kill Terry amplified and drowned out his own thoughts and his entire body began to twitch erratically. It had become clear, he was now one of *those* people and he knew why. His finger, his fucking finger. That fucking child had infected him.

Having come to this realisation, he accepted it, succumbed to the pain, the rage and the desire to kill anything that stood in his way.

Stumbling out of the shop, he stood there, surrounded by noise, the noise of screams, the noise of explosions, the noise of gunfire and the noise of people running past him, shouting, screaming and muttering under their breath.

He felt invigorated, stronger than ever before and consumed with this insatiable desire to eat and eat nothing but meat in all its forms.

A grin spread across his face as he finally knew what he had to do, kill Terry, kill those fucking insolent children of his and eat Natasha alive so that they would become one forever, this he would make a reality.

With that, he stepped out of the shop and broke into a sprint with one destination in mind, Natasha's workplace, he would unify them first, he would never let that fucking Terry have her.

CHAPTER 15 - GEORGE

5:02pm - 5 Hours, 17 Minutes since outbreak

. . .

. . .

George could vaguely recall in which direction they had dropped off his father and as he went in search of him, he couldn't help but oversee the destruction that had taken place here prior. People were fleeing in the opposite direction clearly spooked by something or another.

George suddenly didn't feel so confident, maybe it wasn't the best idea to leave his sister behind, but when he came to, he panicked, neither one of the girls was responding, were they dead? He *did* ask those people for help, before leaving to find his dad.

Did he even have a plan? If and when he did find his father, what then? What if his dad got angry, especially for leaving his sister? What if he only slowed his dad down in the process? What if he didn't even make it to his dad?

He shook his head, he couldn't think like that, it was scaring him.

As the streets emptied out, it became evident that most people had run away at this point and a few short seconds later it was clear to see why. Up ahead of him were several of those crazy people he had seen earlier. They seemed pretty preoccupied with the people they had killed and were eating, or at least the search for more people to kill.

He didn't think they had seen him, or at least he hoped they hadn't. Sneaking past them wasn't going to be easy, but at least he could use the cover of the cars to make it a possibility. Did he know the way to his mother's workplace at the very least? He could remember the road she worked on, but hadn't the slightest clue how to get there.

He ducked and kept low, using the cars as cover to slip by the crazy people. It certainly wasn't going to be an easy feat with so much debris scattered everywhere, but what other choice did he have? He just had to watch his footing.

Timing his moves before slipping between cars and constantly glancing over the cars or through the windows to see where the crazy people were, George's heart raced faster than it ever had in his entire life, he was terrified, one false move and those crazy people would be all over him, tearing him apart in the same horrific way that they had those other poor people.

George felt nauseous and his legs and hands were trembling uncontrollably, at this rate they'd most certainly find him. He kept his head low, slipping from the cover of one car to the next when two of those crazy people had left the area. There were bodies everywhere and the scenes were morbid, stomach-churningly so. Men, women, children and even animals all lying dead on the street in pools of their own blood.

There was no video game that compared to this, no amount of violence in games could weigh up to this horror unfolding before him.

There was a clearing ahead with an alleyway, if he could just slip out of the cover of these last few cars, he could probably make it over there unnoticed, but that was easier said than done.

Creeping along the side of the cars, remaining as silent as he possibly could, George waited for his moment to slip out into the exposed clearing and get into the alley.

Just then, as he was but a few short seconds from making the nerve-racking attempt, he heard a noise from behind and turned to see nothing. Just as he had begun to think nothing of it, the noise came again, closer this time.

Following the direction of the sound, he looked upwards, towards the top of the car he had taken refuge behind and there atop its roof was one of those crazy people glaring down at him.

George's heart skipped a beat and terror consumed him as he stared up at a monstrosity that was once a human being. Foaming at the mouth, menacing wide eyes, covered in her own blood or someone else's.

She twisted her head at an impossible angle to get a better look at him and he found he couldn't move, he was cemented to this spot and to make matters worse, he could feel his trousers getting damp beneath his bottom, a phenomenon that needed no explanation, shame was the last thing on his mind.

The crazy woman crawled on all fours like a lizard, twitching and gurgling.

"Well what do we have here? A fucking rodent. I hate rodents!" The woman spat.

Everything in George told him to run as she advanced towards him, but he just couldn't, he couldn't move.

"It does look fucking delicious though, doesn't it Earl?" She continued. Who was she talking to?

"Oh... that's right, Earl is dead. I tore out his fucking guts and ate it all like spaghetti, it was delicious. Now I want dessert".

Her mouth began to tremble, as saliva seeped down the sides. She crawled closer to George and finally stood over him, baring her teeth and licking her lips.

George began to cry, he was so terrified that he couldn't even control his own body. What did it matter even if he did find the courage to run, he'd only get caught and killed before he had the chance to get anywhere meaningful.

Why didn't he just listen to his dad and stay where he was? Why didn't he stay with Charlotte?

"Daddy!" He screamed, as tears streamed down his face, but his pathetic cries only served to entertain the disturbed woman arching over him, as she laughed hysterically and drew the attention of three more of those things. He was dead, it was over.

"Don't devour him all yourself, you selfish bitch, we are hungry too!" One of them snapped.

George suddenly felt tiny, they towered over him and that alone was overwhelming enough without the added pressure of life threatening aggression from them.

He huddled as small as he could be into a ball and braced himself for the worst, but before he should hand himself over to his fate, a voice he couldn't have been happier to hear, cut through the silence.

"Get the fuck away from my boy or I'll shoot!" He dad snapped. George turned to see his father standing there with a gun in hand, although which type, George couldn't tell.

"Daddy!" He yelped out.

"Just stay there, kiddo, I won't let any of them touch you!"

"You'll what, cocksucker? Shoot us?" The one standing over George replied and burst into hysterical laughter.

"Get the fuck back!" His father warned again.

"Belligerent twat, fuck you! You won't do shit! Know why? Because you're a piece of shit cowardice cunt!" The woman screamed back at him. George had never heard so many swear words in his life, far less stringed together in such a creative manner. Never had he wanted for anything more than to get away from these people and return to his father's embrace.

"Last warning! Get away from him!"

George's father had never physically harmed a thing in his life, far less killed anything, even the fight with Daniel was hard to be considered a fight, since only one of them had landed any punches, the other landed in a hospital bed, no awards for guessing which was which. It was because of this that it would be understandable he would be so reluctant to shoot without a second thought, even if his enemies were mindless now, they were still human.

"Who? Him?" The female creature asked, pointing towards George, "My prey?"

Terry took aim and tightened his finger on the trigger.

"Okay, you can have him", it obliged, taking steps backwards. Its suspicious behaviour was soon explained with the appearance of another one of them creeping up behind George's father.

"Daddy! Behind you!" George screamed. His father swung around and pulled the trigger just as it launched at him, blasting it backwards into a car. The surprising recoil also ejected the guns from his hands.

"Shit!" His father shouted, scrambling for it, before more crazy people pounced in his direction. He fired another shot from the ground this time, blasting the two assailants backwards, before taking aim at the remaining woman besides George.

She hissed at his father and lunged at George, just managing to scratch his face with her nails, before shotgun shells blasted her back

The shot was desperate, but reckless, having the potential to hit George in the process or even infect him with the splattering blood. Fortunately, the blood only reached his clothes and neck.

George was left frozen with terror, so it was not until his father ran over to him and cuddled him, did he snap out of his state of shock. He couldn't remove the image of that woman's eyes from his head, a madness masking sorrow and pain.

His father pulled him to his feet.

"I'm here now, it's okay, I won't let anyone or anything harm my kids. We need to go, lad. Climb onto my back and hold on tight". His father ordered and George, still trembling, complied.

No sooner did George mount his father's back, those he had shot down began to rise again, despite sustained injuries that would render any normal person immobilized or even kill them, yet there they were, standing as though nothing had ever happened. If that weren't already enough to deal with, the gunfire had attracted more attention and his father wasn't prepared to stand around and find out the outcome of all that.

They tore through the streets, into alleyways and through shops, whilst being pursued by those with sole intent to kill them. Those crazed people flung themselves through windows and doors without regard for their bodies, ripping off skin and breaking bones in in the process, but getting right back up in order to continue the chase.

As they dashed into a Forward clothing retail outlet - for those who love high quality brands and reasonable prices -, George spotted an elevator, it wasn't much, but it could at least buy them some time.

"Daddy! In there!" George pointed. His father pivoted in place and made for the elevator. Pushing down clothing racks to slow down their pursuers, they stopped before the elevator doors to hammer at the button.

"Come on, God dammit!" George's father shouted.

Behind them their pursuers, having smashed through the front glass panels, ran through the aisles, knocking down shelves and leaping over displays.

Finally, the elevator arrived and the doors parted to allow them entry. They dived in and his father slammed on the buttons to ascend the elevator, shutting the doors seconds before the crazy people slammed into them.

"What now, daddy?" George asked, a tremble in his voice. *That* was far too close for comfort and George wasn't sure how much longer they could keep this up. His heart was pounding and he wasn't even doing the running.

His father slammed the alarm button, halting the elevator in place and ringing a low tone bell. He then put George down and turned to him.

"Do you realise just how foolish that was? Do you realise just how close I was to losing you back there? Had your sister not called me in time and told me you ran off, I wouldn't have known you came to look for me and return for you, you would be dead, George! I told you to leave with your sister!"

"But daddy, I was scared and Charlotte crashed and…" George begun to reply.

"You should have stayed with your sister, made sure she was okay and got out together. I wanted to trust you could do that, now I have to worry about your safety with me. Your sister has her phone, she could have kept me informed as to what was going on and I would have told you both what to do. It's only by chance I found this shotgun on a CEU enforcer, if I hadn't, how would I have rescued you? We'd both be dead!"

"I'm sorry daddy", George replied weakly. His father sighed and ran his fingers through his hair.

"Thank god you are both okay after that accident. Do you know if Charlotte is okay?" George shook his head. "God, I hope she is… but I'm glad you two are okay. Poor thing, you've experienced two traumatising crashes in a single day. Your sister was trying to run after you when she called, thank God she called, otherwise she could probably be killed coming after you".

"Is she okay?" George asked.

"Shaken up, but she's fine. I told her to leave by any means necessary and to keep well away from dangerous situations and suspicious characters, she will keep me updated by text. I also assured her I would find you and by stroke of fortune I did, healthy and alive, but the outcome could have been very different if I were even a minute later than I was. I should probably put her mind at ease". He pulled out Charlotte's mobile and texted Ria.

"Dammit, reception…" He muttered under his breath and glanced around their metal confines. "It'll send automatically when we get out of here. We should probably take our chances escaping from a different floor, those things are almost as intelligent as they were as humans, unless they have no head, somehow, they still move, but without direction or purpose… God only knows why I'm telling you this. The ones chasing us probably already ran up to the floor they saw the elevator going to, so we should outsmart them, escape this elevator and take a back way out. We have no other option, I don't have many shells left and I have a feeling we'll need them later. We're going to make a move, I'll need both my hands free, so I can't carry you on my back, you'll have to stay close".

"Okay daddy". His father glanced upwards and began pushing at the elevator roof emergency hatch. Once he had pushed it aside, he hoisted George up.

"Do you see a ladder anywhere?" He whispered.

George glanced around the unnerving elevator shaft and spotted a small ladder leading up alongside the doorways to each floor.

"I see one", he whispered back down to his father.

"Good, good", his father replied and hoisted himself up onto the top of the elevator. This was the first time George had seen the top of an elevator and it was somewhat disconcerting, but no more than what he had already seen and experienced today.

"I'm going to lead the way, stay right behind me. I'll open a door and help you in", his father instructed and proceeded to climb the ladder, encouraging George to do the same quickly. George grabbed the bars of the dirt caked ladder and began climbing up behind his father.

When they finally reached a floor his father was satisfied with, listening for any noise behind it first, his father attempted to prise the door apart, using the gun as his wedge. With time and energy, he managed to prise the door apart enough to allow leeway onto the floor.

Poking his head out first to ensure the coast was clear, he climbed on through and then turned to help George up.

They found themselves surrounded by lingerie, most of which lay on the floor, likely as a result of the mad rush of people fleeing, the moment word of danger reached them. The floor was completely deserted and the soft department store music was still playing.

George's father glanced around the floor looking for a way out besides the main escalators. They could hear disturbances below them, likely it was those people looking for them.

"Keep low, follow me, I think I see something", his father whispered and led the way. George followed closely behind, as they made their way between the aisle over to the cashier till. Just behind it was a door that led to the staff only section and storage.

Using the key card left on the till counter, his father hurried him into the new section and they made their way through a series of narrow corridors, passing a locker room, storage room and lounging area on their way to a staff staircase. Taking it all the way down, they eventually came to a door leading to an exit, with a metal push down bar.

Pushing it down and stepping out, they found themselves standing in an alley at the back of the department store with four large trash containers beside them.

"We just need to make it to your mother's workplace now. Stay close and don't make a sound, can you do that?" His father asked, to which George nodded briskly.

"Good", he replied and he lowered himself to almost a crouch and led the way once again. George already dreaded it, what if they heard him? He didn't want to be responsible for getting them both killed.

They soon found themselves back on the main road, except his father had picked up a few items he could use as distractions and weapons along the way, bottles and a jagged pole amongst other things.

George had noticed there was a clear difference in his behaviour since shooting those people, his sentences were short and snappy, his entire demeanour seemed somewhat hostile compared to how he usually was. Those people didn't die, but maybe the guilt of shooting them at all weighed heavily on his mind.

All of this was changing them and not for the better, how would George ever return to the happy, bubbly, playful little boy he once was when he had endured so much. The simple act of smiling felt like such a distant concept. Vividly reliving the stains of this day on his memory over and over, what kind of future would that be? The most he could hope for now was just the simple peace of mind that came with being with his father.

They surveyed the area, taking note of where all threats or potential threats were and made their way through the jungle of mostly open doored, smashed and or covered with blood, cars. Sprawled across, besides, beneath and inside cars were corpses, so many, more than George's mind could comprehend. To see a dead person was a wretched sight alone without the added trauma of witnessing dead children and babies still strapped to the baby seats of which they were left.

One scene in particular would never leave George's mind, a dead mother visibly in the process of trying to shield her baby when she was attacked and killed, *killed* used loosely, since nobody seemed to stay dead for long from what he had seen so far. The baby itself was beyond the point of being rescued, hissing, spitting and twitching with the same ferocity as the others.

George had seen enough and looked away quickly, following behind his father quietly.

His father proved resourceful in the face of danger, averting every possible negative encounter up to the front of the building. Where they planned to go from here was another question, the entrance was swarming with those crazed people.

They hid behind a car on the opposite side of the road.

"Doesn't look like the entrance is an option, we are going to have to go around the back and enter through the basement parking bay. We can take the stairway up from there, assuming it isn't crawling with those things", he turned to George, "Ready, kiddo?"

George nodded. *Ready* was an interesting word, a vast contrast to how he felt about anything at that moment in time, things were happening all over the place and the situation could change at any given moment, who could possibly be ready for anything he had already encountered?

They took the long way around to the back alley, only to find more half eaten corpses littering the ground, along with those responsible.

As they hid behind the dustbin, George's father looked down at the mobile phone.

"Your sister is okay, she said some people kindly helped get Charlotte out of the car. Charlotte seems to be in a bad way, she can't move her legs, it's quite possible she may remain that way. They've been offered a ride out of the city and to take Charlotte immediately to the nearest hospital outside of London", his father whispered. "Honestly, I would rather her stay there, then go off with strangers, but it doesn't seem they had much option. Charlotte will probably die if they don't tend to her soon and I want Ria out of the city. I am going to check on your mother".

He dialled her number, brought the phone to his ear and waited, soon enough she picked up, always a relief.

"Natasha? Are you okay?" He went silent in order to listen to her. George couldn't hear what she was saying, but the concerned expression on his face was more than enough to determine the state of the situation, they had to hurry.

After he hung up, his change in attitude once more confirmed George's fears, he became short and anxious.

"We need to hurry, they don't have long left", he whispered, "Let's go".

"What about them?" George asked, pointing towards the crazed people standing at the door.

"I'll throw this bottle, hopefully it distracts the twitchers and if they move, we move, stay close behind", he instructed.

Twitchers? Was that what they were called now? It made sense considering their strange erratic twitching was probably their most distinguishing and common feature.

"Okay", George replied.

"Good, here we go", his father replied. Taking aim and reaching back to get a good swing, he lobbed the bottle high into the air, over them and far to the other end of the alley.

As the bottle smashed, the twitchers propped their heads up in curiosity, but initially didn't move from their spot, leaving the two wondering if they would have to reconsider the plan, but with good fortune, the twitchers went to investigate, giving George and his father a chance to slip by, beneath the ticket barrier and into the basement parking bay.

Whilst many of the cars were gone, there remained a large majority, telling of either a change of plans and the decision made to run, by their respective owners or a case of misfortune, much like that of his mother.

Stories could be told with what remained behind however, two cars appeared to have collided in a hapless attempt to ascend the ramp slopes at the same time and their owners simply abandoned them. A series of abandoned cars unable to get pass, formed a conga line all the way to God only knew where and these were the storytelling scenes that met the two at every turn.

The two made their way quickly across the parking bay and over to the doors leading upstairs, since the grisly massacre of mutilated corpses blocking the elevator door made that a none option.

So common had these awful depictions of death become, that it proved senseless for his father to still attempt to shield him from it all, especially when so much more was at stake, instead he grabbed George's wrist and led him towards the stairway. The door was broken off of its hinges, something had clearly hit it with some force.

Each step up was as unnerving as the last, the tense feeling of what may lurk on the flight of steps just one level above, was unlike anything George could describe.

Doors sat ajar on almost every level, exposing them to the dangers which lay beyond and forcing them to slowly and cautiously sneak by, as opposed to picking up the pace as his father would have much preferred. For every possible encounter they were forced to wait out until the coast was clear once again, his mother drew closer to death. They only need reach the eighth floor and just getting that far was taxing enough, it would be hard to imagine how long it would take to ascend any further. The screams of people infected or not, echoing up and down the stairway were more than enough to send chills down George's spine. There wasn't a single shred of him curious enough to know where those screams had come from.

Before entering the door to the eighth floor, his father placed his finger on his lips and brought his face closer to George's ear.

"We go in quietly and you take hiding, I'll check out what's happening and try to figure out a way to deal with it. I only have three or four shells left I think, so I need to get those guys out whilst at the same time trying to avoid drawing too much attention to ourselves from the twitchers downstairs".

George nodded, what could be argued? Even the slightest mistake could end horribly and he himself was too weak to help his father should that happen, there were no words.

"Let's go", his father instructed and gently opened the door. They found themselves in a small corridor which led around to the toilets where they found an emptied fire extinguisher and a grisly scene of body parts scattered across the bloodied ground.

The fire extinguisher gave his father an idea of some sort, for he immediately went in search of the nearest full one.

"Hide in the toilets", he instructed, "Don't come out until I say so".

"Okay daddy", George replied.

"I'll be back soon, promise me you'll stay here, don't move regardless of what you hear, okay?" His father insisted.

"Okay daddy".

"Lock yourself in a cubicle and remain as silent as a mouse, only if I call you come out". The repetition was a clear sign of distrust, but who could blame him, George may have been agreeable for the sake of appeasing his father, but truth be told, his affection for his father surpassed his obedience to him and he would far sooner disobey an instruction and put his life at risk than let his daddy die and in this case his mummy too, so even as they temporarily parted ways, George was more than prepared to disobey his father.

He entered the toilets and waited there for a few minutes, refusing to hide in the cubicle. He caught a glimpse of himself in the mirror and was hit with a shocking reality, blood, both dry and recent covered him from head to toe, he could barely make out his own face. The sight scared him more than he would think it would, likely because it was the first glimpse of himself in the thick of this disaster. He hadn't looked at himself since this morning whilst brushing his teeth and the boy staring back at him now wasn't the same excitable boy gazing back at him from the mirror this morning.

His attention was averted to a loud noise from the office and he couldn't help but take a look, he needed to ensure it wasn't his father.

Leaning outside of the door ever so slightly, he couldn't see very much, so he crept further out in order to get a better view of the entire office, or at least what the tops of the cubicles weren't blocking him from seeing.

His father was nowhere in sight, but he could hear the twitchers towards the other end of the office, even if he couldn't see them. They were ramming themselves against something and shouting obscenities.

On all fours, George crept a little further, moving from desk to desk to get a better view. Soon enough he spotted his father, but not wanting his father to spot him and know that he had left the toilets, he remained out of sight. His heart raced, one slight mistake and he'd probably give away his position and get himself right back into trouble again.

His father pulled out the jagged pole he had been carrying along with him and held the shotgun steady in the other hand. He got up in order to make a move, but frustratingly brushed his bag against a stupid overhanging clipboard and it dropped to the floor, making quite the racket. He ducked and took cover, but as three twitchers ran out to investigate, George wasn't certain he would be able to evade them and he wouldn't last long against three of those people.

Panicking, George quickly glanced around for something to use as a distraction and found a stapler. As they encroached on his father, George threw the stapler in an entirely different direction and was rewarded with the crashing sound of it hitting something solid, stopping the twitchers in their tracks and averting their interest.

His father took full advantage of the situation, dashing out of his hiding place the very moment the opportunity arose.

Distracted and divided, the twitchers had inadvertently made themselves weaker, but no less threatening. As one passed by his father, still hunting the source of the original sound, he crept out from his hiding place, approaching it from behind with the sharpest end of the pole poised towards it. With a gentle tap on the desk besides it, the twitcher spun around to face him just as he pounced on it, driving the pole into its eye socket.

To think George had reverted to simply calling them *it* now, for a being with not a shred of humanity left in them could neither be referred to as a he or she, merely a creature acting on its primal instincts.

As his father and the twitcher went down, George could see nothing more, which didn't bode well, for the fuss had drawn unwanted attention from the other two again and George couldn't tell if his father was finished and out of the way.

George picked up a ruler a flung it in another direction with hopes that it would achieve what the stapler had, but this time they appeared less susceptible to the attempt at distractions, merely glancing in the direction that the noise had come from, but instead, making their way towards him. That's all he needed, danger to come directly his way.

He had to think fast, for every second was a second closer to him than they were, but his mind drew blanks. He might be able to hide beneath the desks, but maybe that idea was a little ambitious, since the desks didn't conceal much. Before he could consider possibly using a chair to finish the job of hiding him away the desk failed to do and the twitchers could locate him, he heard a loud pitched shriek and poked his head out to investigate. His father had attacked one of the encroaching twitchers from behind, impaling it through the head with the pole, but it seemed he was having trouble retracting the pole to defend himself against the other one, so before the other could react, George acted on his protective instincts, dashing towards the twitcher and throwing himself onto its back.

It shrieked and began hurling abuse, but he clung on as hard as he could. His father managed to retract the pole, leaving that twitcher writhing on the floor in order to attack the one George clung to and he did so without a moment's hesitation, piercing its forehead with the pole and knocking it down temporarily.

He shoved George out of the way as it got back to its feet and attacked again. These people either had a high pain threshold or no feeling of pain whatsoever, no matter what was done to them, they just scrambled back to their feet after some time.

The scuffle intensified as it lunged towards him and he jumped out of the way, sending it crashing into a cubicle and the surrounding desk. His father grabbed a screen monitor and threw it.

"George, get the hell out of here!" He snapped. George refused, given the situation, he had no intention of leaving his father's side.

"Don't make me repeat myself, god dammit!"

"No!" George screamed, back at him. Their ruckus drew the attention of more twitchers. How many of these infected people were there? They seemed endless.

Things didn't look good. His father resorted to desperate measures and pulled out the shotgun, firing one of his remaining bullets at the immediate aggressor, sending it crashing back into the tables behind, before grabbing George in one arm and running towards the other end of the office.

That blast just opened a great big hell sized can of worms, the noise it created probably attracting every twitcher far and wide.

Twitchers, both the ones his father had already taken down and more still, came after them, jumping over cubicles as though they were never there to begin with and knocking things out of the way.

His father dodged obstacles he had hoped would slow the twitchers down, but obstacles didn't appear to do very much for the two of them, least of all faze the twitchers.

They dashed down a corridor and his father kicked over a bin, which of course did nothing to slow down their rage fuelled rampage. It was at that point that his father knew he had to act fast, for it was merely a matter of time before they were caught and killed, so with that his father threw him out of harm's way.

"Get to your mother! Don't you dare disobey me!" He snapped and spun around to fire a shot at the pursuing twitchers. George had never seen such a serious expression on his father's face, but after what they had already been through today, it was fair to say that his father was an entirely different man to the one he was this morning. He was scary, but George couldn't have possibly felt safer, this was a new, stronger, more forthright version of himself, the version that would save their family.

With that he stood up and ran, calling out for his mother.

CHAPTER 16 - TERRY, TODD & KERRY

6:22pm - 6 Hours, 37 Minutes since outbreak

. . .

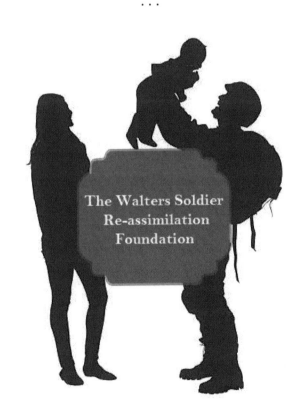

The Walters Soldier
Re-assimilation
Foundation

. . .

Terry's shot had at the very least slowed down their pursuers. Shotguns were supposed to be destructive at close range, so when a person stood up again and act as though taking the mother of all shots to the torso were little more than *inconvenience*, you knew you were royally fucked. If matters weren't already pretty shit, twitchers were pouring out of every nook and cranny like a traumatising case of diarrhoea. He lunged at another with the bloodied pole, narrowly avoiding its teeth and rupturing its eye socket, spraying blood everywhere. He then used the twitcher to defend himself against the others, others that by all measure should have been dead. Weren't you supposed to aim for the head? Wasn't that the universal method to stop a zombie? So why wouldn't they just stay fucking dead? Why were the headless still getting back up? This was nothing like the movies, what the shit was this?

Shaken, Terry let his guard down, just long enough for one of the headless to pounce on top of him, but without teeth to bite him with, the most it could do was scratch at him. Terry grabbed the headless twitcher and threw it over his shoulder and on top of another assailant, he then took another shot into the swarm of twitchers dashing towards him and almost immediately after taking that shot, there was a terrifying series of shrieks not only from the twitchers in front of him, but many in unison that seemed to come from anywhere and everywhere, almost as though every twitcher in the building had reacted to the sound of his gunfire. If that wasn't enough to convince Terry to make like a dancer and get to two stepping, nothing would.

"Shit! Shit! Shit!"

He abandoned the attempts to buy time and dashed down the corridor in pursuit of his son. As he ran, he couldn't stop thinking about how traumatised his kids would be by all of this, most notably his son, but he was a little trooper, a little stubborn trooper who still had the mind to risk his life in order to rescue his father, rather than follow his father's strict instructions to hide.

With perspective, it was probably for the best, had he followed that instruction, Terry would be dead and the poor lad would probably be stuck in there for who only knew how long, his stubbornness had given the both of them a second chance. That kid was braver than he ever was, if he had even a shred of the courage that boy had, his marriage wouldn't have been a train. He'll grow to be a great man someday.

"George! Natasha!" He shouted out at the top of his voice and initially heard nothing, but venturing further down the corridor and repeating their names was rewarded with the reassuring sound of his ex-wife, he couldn't have been happier to hear her voice if he tried.

"Terry!"

"Natasha?" He followed her voice and was led to a damaged door with clear signs of attempted forced intrusion. The door was cracked right down the middle from top to bottom and there was a gaping hole in the middle. The only thing preventing further entry was an equally heavily damaged metal cabinet behind it.

"Hurry, let him in! Shift it out of the way! That's Terry!" Natasha ordered.

"What if he's infected?" Someone replied. "Ain't no fucking way he made it all the way up here without getting infected".

"I'm clean, is my son in there with you? We both made it up here together and if you let him in, you have nothing to fear from me, but speed it up, I can't guarantee that that will be the case in another few seconds".

They pushed the heavy cabinet out of the way and parts of the door in front of it fell apart.

Terry stepped into the room and helped them push the cabinet back into place, before finding himself surrounded by Natasha's colleagues with makeshift weapons.

"Didn't you hear me say I *wasn't* infected?"

"Can't be too careful", one of them replied.

Natasha and his son pushed through into the centre of the circle the others had formed around him.

George leapt into his arms and Natasha briefly hugged him, before turning to the others.

"For Christ sake, put those down, he's not infected!"

"How the hell would you know?" Another asked.

"It's fine", Terry interrupted, "Your suspicions are completely reasonable, keep your weapons on me for however long it takes for you to trust me, but in the meantime, I think we should plan our way of escape, I think we should expect to be confronted with every one of those crazies in the building".

"Yeah, no thanks to you", one of them replied, referencing the shotgun in his hands.

"I had no other choice".

"And you brought them all right to our door, giving us no other choice either".

"We're going to get out of here".

"And that's based on your sound judgement I'm guessing. How do we know you won't use us as bait just to save Natasha? You're the one with the gun".

"Never mind all of that, what I want to know is why the hell George is with you?" Natasha interrupted.

"He wasn't supposed to be, I sent him out of the city and he managed to find his way back to me, I couldn't leave him where he was and ensuring he got out would mean leaving you to your fate".

"You probably should have done that!"

"Look, Natasha, I don't want to argue with you now. You won't believe what we've been through today, I'm not in the mood right about now, I just want to get out of here".

"Where is Ria?"

"Safe, she's leaving the city, like we should be. Can we get moving? Now? Please?"

A loud bang at the door and cabinet, followed by screaming, swearing and scratching, signalled the unwelcomed arrival of the twitchers.

Abandoning their interrogation of Terry, they rushed over to keep the cabinet from toppling over and Terry did what he could to help.

"Fuck! We are screwed!" One of the females replied.

"Fucking understatement", one of the males replied.

"Shut the fuck up, Todd!" Another female snapped.

"We haven't got much time, we have to think of a way out of this place, every one of those crazies will be up here wanting for our blood soon and we can't hold this cabinet up forever", Terry replied.

"We might have to fight our way out, it's the only way", Natasha replied.

"Then that is what we will have to do".

"Wait, what? What makes you think we are going anywhere with you? You just come in here giving fucking orders. Do you know how long we've been stuck in here praying for our lives and holding off those fuckers? We've seen our entire office turn into those psychotic cannibals! There's a city out there filled with those things, where the hell do you think we can go in these conditions? On top of that, what about you? You still haven't given us one good fucking reason why we should trust you?" Todd spat. He was a douchebag about it, but Terry couldn't argue with the logic.

"I've been out there, I've ran from, snuck around and fought those crazies just to get here. I don't know anything about this infection other than the vague and frankly useless information the CEU gave me, but if you have any better ideas, be my guest to take over. I'm just trying to get us all out of here alive and since death or suffering the same fate as those others is just beyond this cabinet we are struggling to keep in place, I don't think your options right now are brimming, just an observation. I'll be honest with you, I'm here to save Natasha and my son, but I'm suggesting that our chances of survival, *all* of us, increase if we work as a group".

"What is the plan? We won't get out of here easily", Elmira replied, the only one of Natasha's colleagues Terry knew.

"It's safe to assume that the main stairway isn't an option, neither is the elevator. Elevator was out of commission and stairway is probably crawling with those twitchers now", Terry replied.

"Twitchers?" Natasha asked.

"Easier to call them that, you'll understand why".

"The fire exit stairway", another male suggested, "it should be relatively empty, it requires a key card to get into and is only used in emergencies, but I'm a fire marshal for this floor, so I can get us in. I can't guarantee it'll be safer, especially given to circumstances, but I'm willing to bet that less people thought about using it to get down before shit hit the fan".

"Good call, Bishop", someone else replied.

"Okay, that's our best bet, you should lead the way".

"How do we get out though?" Elmira asked.

Terry looked around and remembered something.

"When I say push that cabinet out of the way, do it!" Terry ordered.

"What have you got in mind?" Natasha asked.

"Fire extinguishers, I have one on me and it seems you already have a few in here too, I can't guarantee it will work, but maybe we can create some sort of smoke screen. It's our best bet besides taking each of them on and trust me, we want to do as little of that as possible".

"That's your fucking idea? Fucking hell! No! I'm not going anywhere with you! I'm staying right here! Fuck that! You'll get us all fucking killed! Who the hell do you think you are? Rambo?"

"Fuck you, Todd!" A young woman shouted at him. She had been silent up until that point. "I'm going! Stay here and fucking die! I'm taking my chances! I'm so sick of fucking listening to your shit and if we never have to work together again, if I never have to hear your insistent rambling, your fucking self-righteousness, file your fucking reports and listen to how much you hate this and that, it'll be way too motherfucking soon!"

"You said it, Kerry", Elmira replied.

Todd stood there in shock. For a small Chinese girl, she could certainly make an incredible point and had it not been for the circumstances, she would have likely received a round of applause right there.

Terry set his fire extinguisher down besides the doorway.

"Okay, so those with me, I think I have like one shell remaining, so remove the cabinet, I'll fire, extinguisher explodes, we charge, aim for the face, preferably the eyes, keep moving! Bishop, you lead the way once we have a clearing. Stay close and tight everyone, *don't* get bitten. This will be one hell of a fight, use every resource available to you and protect each other, the moment we fall apart is the moment our hopes of getting out of here are dashed. We've only got one shot at this, it's all or nothing".

Elmira and another woman stood ready behind.

"I'm with Lizzy, we'll cover your rear", Elmira declared.

"Fuck this shit, feel free to walk into the embrace of death by yourselves", Todd snapped, but they ignored him.

"Three... two... one! Now!" Terry shouted. With a powerful thrust, they pushed or pulled the cabinet out of the way and jumped back as the twitchers poured in. Terry fired, praying for the best and almost immediately there was an explosion, as the pressure in the extinguisher expelled, shrouding the entire room and knocking several of the twitchers to the ground.

The group poured through the door, hitting and stabbing in the face any twitchers that stood in their way, leaving Todd behind.

The corridor was swarmed with twitchers, it took everything in their arsenal - extinguishers, kitchen knives, keyboards and more - just to battle their way through and it wasn't without loss, as four of their own were ripped to shreds.

Suddenly the blaring sound of the building alarm commenced and Terry turned to see that Elmira had smashed and set off the nearest fire alarm. Smart thinking, the sound would distract the twitchers and mask any noise they themselves made.

Finally, they made it out into open area of the office where they could use the cubicles to lose their assailants.

"This way!" Bishop shouted, taking lead.

Easier though it may have been easier to traverse the open floor as opposed to the choke of the corridor, it wasn't without a battle of survival and two more, despite everything the others did to help, were tackled to the ground and torn apart like deers to a pack of wolves, leaving only seven of them remaining.

They scrambled towards the fire exit and Bishop hurriedly flashed his card against the little scanner. It flashed green, allowing him access to the emergency exit stairway and he pushed through, with the rest of them following behind.

Todd who had remained behind, took to hiding in the remaining cabinet and praying that he wasn't seen or heard. He was prepared to stay there as long as it took. Those fuckers could go and get themselves killed if they wished, he wasn't about to be a part of that suicide pact. He would wait this out and then make his way up to the roof once it was all clear, from there he would hopefully wave down a helicopter and be rescued, if all else failed, he would just use the window cleaning lift to get down.

Stupid bitch Kerry, who the hell did she think she was showing him up like that? She made him look a right fucking tool, when all he wanted was to point out the ludicrousness of their plan. Up until that sonovabitch came marching in like the big boss around town, they didn't have the entire building worth of crazies to deal with and the plan was simple, make it to the roof and work out what to do from there. That guy, Terry fucking ruined everything. Well, they were entitled to do as they pleased, good fucking luck to em all, he thought.

Terry and the others ran down the stairway leaping most of them with sheer determination to just get out of the building and get to safety, but just as they were coming to the last two floors Bishop stopped abruptly.

"Why did you s...?" Terry stopped mid-sentence when he spotted who stood at the bottom of the next flight of stairs grinning up at them and he wasn't the only one, Natasha too couldn't believe her eyes.

"My good man, Terry, where are you rushing off to? The party is only just beginning. What's more, taking my woman along with you? It must be one hell of a motherfucking ball, otherwise you've obviously lost your fucking mind". Daniel stood before them covered from head to toe in blood.

"Daniel! You're alive", Natasha yelped with happiness and relief, but before she could approach him, Terry prevented her. She glared at him.

"It's not what it looks like, I'm not trying to stop you for the sake of it. That's not him", Terry said simply, glancing at her with a serious expression.

"What are you talking about? It's definitely him", she replied.

"Look at his eyes", Terry replied.

His eyes were alight with the raging infernos of sheer hatred, a look that far exceeded the usual disdain he had for him.

Natasha didn't contest, maybe for a change she trusted him.

"He's infected", Terry explained.

"But he's..."

"I know".

"What are you saying up there about me, Terry? Are you trying to convince her to stay with you? You sly fuck. The moment I'm not around you're bad mouthing me and trying to steal my woman. Don't you get it? You're a fucking failure, something the cycle of life puked up. A piece of shit like you doesn't deserve to be with a woman like Natasha, accept your fucking lane, you maggot", Daniel snapped.

"How did you find us?" Terry replied, ignoring the remarks.

"Security cameras. Credit where credit is due, you've managed to stay alive this long and even find Natasha, I was almost certain you'd already be dead or at least out of the city by now like the coward you are". Terry once again ignored the remark, instead looking for the entry of infection wound, a feat made a challenge due to all the blood. In his hands he clutched onto a crowbar soaked in his blood.

"You've been busy", Terry replied.

"What can I say? Circumstances demanded it".

"That blood, it doesn't just belong to you and the infected does it?"

"It's surprisingly invigorating, Terry. It's a great stress reliever. Besides, doesn't look like you've been much of a pacifist yourself".

"I haven't killed anyone... technically and I haven't hurt anyone innocent".

"What is innocence anyway? Who decides what constitutes innocence? Fuck that! There's nothing quite like the thrill of having someone's life in your hands and taking it away as they fucking beg, you'll feel like a fucking god!"

"I always thought you were something of a narcissist, but I realise now that you weren't even scraping the surface of what you had the potential to be".

The thought occurred to Terry, that maybe there was the possibility personality traits remained intact for the infected, he might even go one step further and say they were amplified, but he still had no concrete evidence of Daniel having been infected to confirm that theory, even if his behaviour led him to believe it so. If, however the personality of an infected person did in fact remain intact, did that mean some semblance of their conscience still existed, trapped in their own bodies? If so, then maybe he too was already a murderer. Shit, he was overthinking, this was way too philosophical a thought for this moment in time.

"Aw come on, Terry, for once in your pathetic life, don't be such a fucking pussy", Daniel replied. As he said that, they each glanced upwards to the sound of twitchers above storming down the stairway.

"We have to go!" Bishop shouted.

"Why don't you, this is between Terry, Natasha and I, the rest of you can fuck off", Daniel replied. Bishop looked over towards Terry.

"Sorry guys, I can't stay here, I have a daughter".

"Go, Bishop. Be safe", Terry replied. Bishop nodded and turned to the others.

"Are you coming?" He asked. Kerry slipped out to join him, but Elmira and another woman held back.

"I'm staying with them", Elmira insisted, glancing over at her colleague next to her, "Lizzy?"

Lizzy sighed, before replying with, "So am I".

"Good luck all of you and if I don't see you again, it has been the greatest pleasure working with you all", Bishop declared and with that, he and Kerry began their descent of the stairs. As they drew closer to Daniel, they slowed down a little, maintaining eye contact with him, but his unwavering glare remained fixed on Terry and Natasha. Believing themselves to not be the focus of Daniel's interest, they made the fatal mistake of taking their eyes off him and he reacted with swift, brutal judgement, swinging the hooked end of the crowbar right into Bishop's face, impaling his eye socket and slamming him into the wall. It all happened so quick and sudden that the others didn't even see it coming. Kerry screamed.

"Bishop!" Terry shouted.

"Really thought I'd just let you stroll the fuck out? I said you could fuck off, I didn't specify how!" Daniel shouted and withdrew the crowbar to repeatedly hit Bishop in the face with it, splattering blood everywhere.

"Fuck... you... stupid... fuck!" Daniel shouted with every blow. Kerry stood there in shock, too terrified to attempt to run and when she finally did muster up the courage to make a break for it, Daniel took a swing at her, rupturing the skin above her collarbone and using her bone to slam her to the ground. She yelped in unbearable agony.

As Terry braced himself to attack, his son and Natasha held him back. Daniel left Kerry writhing and weeping on the floor and returned his attention to Terry.

"What's wrong Terry? Aren't you the little hero anymore? Are you just going to watch her die and do nothing? Are you just going to let her down? Too much of a fucking coward to take me on again? We all know what happened last time, don't we? That's right, I beat your motherfucking ass!"

"Stop it!" Natasha screamed.

"I'm doing this for us, Natasha, don't you see? This is *all* for us. I'm paving us a future, with me your security and wellbeing are assured, join me".

"This isn't you! The Daniel I knew was sweet and considerate, he'd never hurt a soul outside of boxing. He was never needlessly violent or filled with rage".

"I'm the same fucking man, I haven't changed, I'm just stronger, more capable and I did it all for us. Or would you prefer me a weak and unreliable fuck of man like Terry?"

"No, you're not the same Daniel I fell in love with, you're a monster! You killed Bishop for no fucking reason! You're hurting Kerry!"

"The weak have no place in this world", Daniel replied, placing his foot on Kerry's head and pushing it down as she screamed in agony.

"Stop it!"

"I'm making the world a better place one weakling dead at a time. Once I'm done, it'll be a utopia for the strong, you and I together".

"You and I will never happen!"

"Oh?" He removed his foot and kicked Kerry several times on the floor, torturing her rather than killing her, as she tried to crawl away. More twitchers arrived from above, stopping only a single flight of stairs short, etching closer, but unusually taking their time about it. Did Daniel have influence over them? How?

Terry was itching to help Kerry, to kill Daniel for what he did, but Natasha continued to hold him back.

"Terry, you know what I hate? Handicaps. Don't you just hate handicaps? Anything that holds you back from achieving greatness, people like Terry! Allow me to demonstrate. Subject A, this Asian bitch here may be injured, but I think we can all agree she's a little better for wear than our Bishop over there, he's definitely going nowhere. I haven't done anything yet she can't recover from, therefore it's not a handicap. This..." He swung the crowbar and pierced the back of her leg with the hooked end of the crowbar once again, resulting in a scream from her that echoed throughout the entire stairway and from the amount of blood loss in a short span of time, ruptured an artery.

"... Is a fucking handicap", he concluded.

"Daniel! You fucking heartless bastard!" Natasha screamed. Terry's rage had hit peak point, he had never hated his man so much in his entire life.

"Yes! That's it! That's the reaction I fucking want! See, this Asian bitch is nothing more than food now! There's no chance she'll survive out there on her own and that's more satisfying than killing her myself!" Daniel shouted.

Kerry, in tears crawled desperately away, slipping down the stairway and leaving a trail of blood behind her.

"Leave her alone!" Lizzy snapped.

"I'm not interested in her anymore, she's already dead. See, that's the thing about handicaps and weaknesses, the world eats you alive, though in her case quite literally".

"What do we do?" Elmira asked, panicking as they were boxed in, twitchers above, Daniel equipped with a crowbar below.

"When I say go, run. I'll hold him off", Terry whispered.

"I'm not letting you fight him alone, he'll kill you", Natasha whispered back.

"You have George to worry about, you two have to get out of here". She glared at him with disapproval, but what could she say? She knew he was right.

"I'll fight", Lizzy chimed in.

"Are you kidding me?" Elmira replied.

"I'm the only one with at least a remotely full fire extinguisher, I can at least distract him momentarily".

"That's a point, but don't look for a fight, as soon as you get the chance, run".

"I'll be with Terry, don't worry. I'll make sure we both make it out alive".

"On my say so", Terry instructed.

Just leaving the exit downstairs was Kerry, tears streaming down her face, blood pouring down her leg and shoulder. She couldn't move very fast, limping was about as much as she could manage.

She made it out into an alley, took a moment to recover, before spotting her first twitcher.

"Shit", she muttered. It hadn't spotted her, but she didn't want to wait around long enough for it to do so. She limped off in the opposite direction and eventually ended up on the main road.

She stopped before a scene of chaos and looked around in shock. This was the first she had seen of the anarchy on the streets. Cars were piled up, some on fire, bodies or at least what remained of them, littered the ground and not a single direction was there not a twitcher. Smashed windows, smoke billowing high into the air, discarded items swept up and around by the breeze, sirens and alarms blaring everywhere, this was literally hell. Kerry had never seen anything like this, never in all of her life and she had seen riots in both London and her second home, Hong Kong.

Her thoughts were primarily on her parents, they lived in Clapham and last she had communicated with them they were grabbing last bits in the house with intention of evacuating London. They were an elderly couple, but at least they were out of the vicinity of danger.

They had hoped and prayed for her safe return, but things didn't look as though they were shaping out that way.

She didn't want to die, she really didn't want to die, she had so much she wanted to do, so many things she wanted to achieve, so many places she wanted to visit. She wanted to find her prince charming and get married, she wanted to be a beautiful bride, have a wonderful honeymoon, give birth to a gorgeous child and become a mother. She was only twenty-six, this wasn't fair, all she wanted was a normal life, was that too much to fucking ask?

She took cover behind a car as a twitcher lumbered past. Maybe there was still a chance, maybe God was still looking down on her. She slipped behind another car as the twitcher passed her by and made her way up the road, limping as fast as she could.

Fuck, the pain was unimaginable, how could it hurt so fucking much? The agony from her leg was just about bearable, but her shoulder was a pain unlike anything she could have imagined. How did it come to this? She was just a normal girl seeking a normal life, how the hell had it come to this?

She passed more cars by and prayed for a miracle, someone to save her, someone to come and help her out of this situation alive. The others were probably dead by now, slaughtered in a horrifically brutal fashion the way Bishop was, so there was no relying on them. Was she alone now? Was she entirely on her own?

It didn't seem as though driving was an option, as much as she wished it was, for even if the keys were left in an ignition, the cars were far too jam packed together to make any headway. The moment she'd start the engine, every motherfucker in the area would be on her like a magnet.

She didn't want to die, she didn't want to die! Not like this, not so young. She was terrified, her heart was racing, pure adrenaline was keeping her upright.

Shit, shit, shit, she thought as she rounded a corner and came face to face with a fucking twitcher, a child twitcher. She had done so well, she didn't want to die now, but why couldn't she move, why wouldn't her body fucking move?

The twitcher drew closer, its eyes wide and menacing, blood combined with saliva dripping from its mouth, the skin on its arm ripped to shreds clearly from an earlier incidence, blood trickling down its legs. This was once a little boy who was probably going to the cinema, the park, or shopping and seeing him in this state was a grim reality of the situation that Kerry had to face, London was fucked and she didn't want to be anything like that... that... thing.

Mustering up the courage to run, she spun around and limped as fast as she could in the opposite direction, expecting it to pursue her, but much to her bewilderment, it didn't, instead remaining transfixed to its spot, watching her pathetically flee for her life and for a moment she honestly believed there was a chance for her to escape, she could live to see another day... until it screamed, or more akin to a high pitched shriek and an overwhelming sense of dread washed over her like the powerful waves of an ocean.

If she wasn't fucked before, she was most definitely fucked now. Twitchers arrived from everywhere like fucking ants, seemingly popping up from every hole and space imaginable. Her heart raced as she limped away as fast as she could, knowing that impending doom loomed over her, shrouding her in its ominous shadow.

She didn't want to die, she didn't want to die, she didn't want to die!

She tripped over and compelled herself to get back up, but before she could, something grabbed at her leg. She turned to find one of the twitchers clinging on to her, a fat man glaring at her with insatiable hunger in his eyes. It was the psychopathic look of a rapist or serial killer and it frightened the life out of her. Fuck this fat bastard, he wasn't getting his fast food today without working for it.

"Let go of me!" She screamed and tried to kick out at him with her good leg.

"You look delicious... like a juicy steak", he groaned.

"Get off of me, you fat fuck!" She lashed out at him, but the more she struggled was the more energy she expended. To make matters worse, more twitchers arrived, holding her down. She shouted for help, praying that someone would come, praying to God to help her, praying to anyone who would listen as tears streamed down her cheeks.

"I can't resist... I need to eat", the fat twitcher replied and with that he pulled her thrashing leg to his mouth and sunk his teeth into her. She let out an agonised scream, as a combination of tears and sheer pain blinded her, but the full extent of her suffering had yet to be realised. More of them ripped away at her flesh, digging into and tearing open her lacerations with their fingers. She couldn't breathe, the pain was blinding and she was forced to endure every excruciating second of it, confronting every bit of the pain until it all seamlessly merged into one. Slowly she slipped into a dark place of which there was no redemption, watching them tear open her stomach, smother their faces in her blood, pull her muscles from arms and legs, feast on her spilling insides and after pain had peaked, it began to dissipate, with it, her screaming died down, her prayers went unanswered, visions of her past and her family flashed through her mind and then all pain was replaced with just a cold, endless, but somewhat peaceful darkness.

"What the fuck are you guys plotting over there?" Daniel asked from the bottom of the steps, but the group above didn't answer.

Terry gazed down at the hollow shell of the second man his ex had fallen in love with. He was all but gone now, nothing more of him remained and his all too familiar twitch confirmed that, she had only him to rely on now and he didn't want to let her down again, not now, they were getting out of London alive, one way or another.

"Go!" Terry shouted and with that, together they charged down the stairs towards Daniel. The other twitchers bounded after them, jumping from the highest steps to the level below and breaking bones in the process they seemed to give little regard to.

Terry charged right at Daniel with the jagged pole, not simply content with just creating an opportunity for the others to pass by, but with intent to pay Daniel back tenfold for all he had done.

Daniel blocked the attack and pushed Terry back with relative ease.

"Terry!" Natasha yelped.

"Go!" He snapped at her. She hesitated, but didn't wait for him to say it again, she grabbed George's wrist and dashed down the stairs along with Elmira, whilst Lizzy stayed to fight.

"Where are you going?" Daniel shouted after Natasha as she fled. He turned to Terry. "Fuck off, you weak piece of shit! I won't let Natasha escape from me! I won't let you have her!"

"No, fuck you, Daniel"" Terry shouted back and swung at him again, only to have his attack blocked once more.

Once Natasha was out of sight and with Lizzy at his rear blasting the twitcher swarm with the fire extinguisher, Terry put in his all, swinging endlessly at Daniel, not giving him a chance to retaliate.

"What?" Daniel shouted in his face, "You think you're a fucking man now? You feel like you could take me on now! Fuck you! You're still a spineless pussy! Know your fucking place, you worthless piece of shit! I'll fucking kill you this time!"

"Come on then!" Terry shouted back.

"You think I won't, you cocky motherfucker?"

"You'll pay for what you did".

"Look at you. Give you a fucking pole and you think you're a big man suddenly. Why don't you stop pretending you give a shit about those scum, this is about you and I! This has always been about you and I! I took what you loved from you because you were too pathetic to hold on to it, now you want revenge!" Daniel swung at Terry with so much force that the pole flew from Terry's hands. "What are you now? Nothing! That's what you are! Fucking nothing! Fuck you, you weak ass fucking motherfucker!"

Daniel raised the crowbar to deal the final blow, but before he could do so, Lizzy spun around and unleashed a blast from the extinguisher on him, forcing him to retract in an attempt to cover his face.

"No! Fuck you!" She screamed.

Terry didn't need to be told what to do, he reached for the pole, stood up and drove the sharper end of the pole right into Daniel's eye. He thrust it further, ensuring it penetrated right into the fucker's skull. It was only after Daniel slumped to the floor did Terry step back. He stood staring in pity at Daniel, somewhat relieved that he would no longer have to deal with the sorry son of a bitch.

Lizzy emptied what remained of the canister on the encroaching twitchers above, before dropping it to the floor and the two fled for their lives.

Terry kicked open the back door of the building and they ran, taking a left. Without knowing which direction Natasha had taken, he would have to wait until he had reached safety before attempting to contact her, assuming and praying that she was okay. *Safe* was an idealist word to use in these circumstances as twitchers poured out of the exit into the alley and gave chase.

"Fuck this!" Lizzy shouted and took off her expensive low heels, tossing them aside. "Expensive pair of fucking shoes gone!"

It was any wonder how she had made it this far in them. She was better off barefoot, they were only going to slow her down and no value exceeded the value of her life.

"We need to lose them", Terry replied.

Terry and Lizzy exited out onto a side road and sprinted down it as fast as their legs could carry them.

They clambered over the bonnets of cars.

"Over here!" Lizzy shouted as they ran, pointing towards a hotel.

They barged through the rotating entrance doors and hopped over the scattered luggage that guests had abandoned. Terry jumped over and Lizzy rounded the reception desk towards the back of the lobby and entered an open staff room where they found an exit. Bursting out into an opening at the rear of the building, still pursued by the twitchers and more they had inadvertently attracted the attention of, they cut across White Lion Street and continued eastwards until they came to the Regents Canal, where they spent all of a few seconds deciding whether or not to take the plunge. The problem was in the fact that Lizzy wasn't a great swimmer and that murky green water didn't look the most inviting, but death at the hands of twitchers beat it to claim the trophy of unpleasantries hands down. They dived into the water, with Terry making every possible attempt to keep his phone above it, water resilient sales jargon or not.

He'd be lying if he had claimed to have believed that the twitchers would jump in after them, but then it shouldn't have come as too much of a surprise given that some of them were former swimmers and *all* of them were reckless now.

The two swam as far as they could and came out just behind London Lexicon leading on to City road. Panting and drenched, they at least had the bask in the fact they had evaded their pursuers.

Terry's phone had been ringing off the hook since midway through that swim and up until now he hadn't been able to answer it. It was tremendously reassuring to hear Natasha's very much alive voice on the line.

"Oh, thank God", she sighed, "Every thought possible was racing through my head, Daniel killed you, those twitchers killed you, something else killed you. I'm glad you are okay".

"Did every thought you have about me involve my tragic demise?"

"More or less, yes, but you know what I mean".

"Sorry, we were a little... occupied. How are you? Are you and George safe?" Terry asked.

"Not exactly safe, but we're okay for the time being, we're on Exmouth Market, next to Spa Fields Park".

"You're quite some distance away from us, we're further north east, City Road. We should decide on a place to meet and work our way there".

"Old Street?"

"Okay, remember that club we went to several years back for Louise's birthday? Golden Wasp?"

"I vaguely remember, I should remember my bearings when I get there".

"Use Soba-maps if you get lost".

"I don't have much battery life left".

"Use your phone sparingly then". She went silent for a few minutes and sighed.

"It's six fifty-five... the kids would have been home safe almost half an hour ago..."

Terry didn't know how to reply, what she sought was comfort, the type of comfort and reassurance he could not provide, not when their lives were still on the line and so much had already happened.

"Let's just try and get out of this situation alive, we'll figure out next steps when we are safe".

"Terry... about Daniel... did he...?" She begun, heading in a direction of conversation he wasn't comfortable with, but to his relief a call came in on the other line.

"I'm getting a call, Natasha, I'll text you. Let's not ring each other without texting first, just to be on the safe side. We'll meet at the Golden Wasp".

"Okay, be safe", she replied and hung up. Terry switched to the other line and heard sobbing.

"Hello?"

"Daddy? Help me! Please come and help me quickly!" Ria cried, sheer terror in her voice.

CHAPTER 17 - RIA

4:57pm - 5 Hours, 12 Minutes since outbreak

. . .

FACT FILE #7:

The **Walters Soldier Re-assimilation Foundation (WSRF)** was set up with the ambition of reintegrating soldiers into everyday life after being on the battlefield.

Dr. Marlen Walters, formerly a soldier and medic, set up the foundation to tackle the severe lack of attention given to those who have returned from the horrors of war. The foundation, funded by the public and private military institutions, aims to facilitate soldier re-integration into society with medical funding for any injuries sustained in battle, psychologists and other forms of counselling to tackle various forms of PTSD and more.

Dr. Marlen Walters himself lost a number of comrades and witnessed horrific tragedies. He hopes that the foundation will help soldiers re-assimilate easier and connect with their families and friends in a way that was previously a challenge.

. . .

Long before the events that led to Ria calling her father in tears, she had just given up pursuing her brother, realising that the two of them running around without any clear aim of where they were going would only lead to them both endangering their lives, besides, the dispersing crowds and people fleeing in the opposite direction left her feeling uneasy.

Panting from having already run a marathon, she picked up her mobile and called Terry.

"Dad!"

"Ria? What's happened?"

"Oh my God, we were on our way out and then there was a crash and we were unconscious for a bit, and..."

"Slow down, Ria, explain again".

"We were in a crash".

"What? How? When?"

"Not long ago, someone stepped out in front of the car, Charlotte hit them, swerved into a shop and crashed".

"My God, is everyone okay, is your brother okay?"

"I'm fine, just some bruises, mostly superficial, Charlotte looks in a bad way and George... erm..."

"What happened to George, Ria?"

"He ran off while we were unconscious, I think he's coming to look for you".

"Shit! Shit! Shit! Okay... okay, I'll backtrack and keep an eye out for him. Go back to Charlotte and if you can't do anything about her, get to safety yourself".

"What about Charlotte?"

"Your life is my priority, Ria. Of course I'm concerned about Charlotte, but I'd rather your life not be in jeopardy for her sake".

"Okay dad".

"Head east and wait outside of the city by any means necessary, do you hear me?"

"I hear you".

"Good girl, we'll talk later. Text me if you need anything". Terry hung up.

Ria spun around on the spot unsure of what to do next. Charlotte was the only thing that came to mind, but before that... she spotted shops to the side and had an idea.

She stepped forth from the shops equipped with a few new batteries, a charger, a pen knife, snacks, a flashlight, other little bits that might come in handy and a guilty conscience. The situation didn't make it okay to steal, regardless of how incremental these things would become in her attempt to escape.

She spent no more than about five minutes scouring for the items in the shop and already she was beginning to spot suspicious characters in the direction George and her father had ventured. Not suspicious in the sense that they were up to something, but that something was up with them. Twitching erratically, standing on top of cars and appearing as though they were sniffing the air.

Pulling out her phone, she used the camera to zoom in. Closer inspection revealed their blood-soaked clothes, hands filled with what could only be left to the imagination to interpret.

A shudder passed down her spine.

She took a few photos and decided it best to make a hasty exit before they drew close enough to spot her. As she ran, in the opposite direction back to Charlotte, she uploaded the photos to all her social feeds using her tag #riasinlondon and much to her surprise, not only was the tag trending, so too was she, but in spite of it all, she felt as though her reasons for documenting everything now were more with regard to mortality rather than profit, she was faced with danger after danger, each one bringing her a little closer to death's doorstep and since she had faced this all mostly by herself today, she didn't want to die with no one to notice, she didn't want to die feeling as though she had achieved very little in life, she didn't want to die full stop.

She could imagine what the naysayers would have to remark about, but they weren't here, they weren't in her shoes, stricken with nausea induced dread. Fame was the last thing on her mind now, she had a responsibility to share this with the world. Whether they believed it to be authentic or not, people needed to know what was going on here, what she and her family were experiencing and in the event they didn't make it, at least people knew who they were.

Upon returning to the scene of the crash, she found the streets to be emptier than they previously were, the aftermath of their presence all that was left behind, the scene of what looked to have been a riot.

She approached the shop they had crashed into and outside sprawled across the ground was Charlotte, discarded like a used rag, a complete lack of empathy shown towards her, invoking anger in Ria. How could they treat her like that? How could they treat another human like that? What had people become?

Ria rushed to Charlotte's side and checked her over. Miraculously, she was still alive, but only just. Every breath she took seemed a struggle, her life hanging in the balance.

"Hang in there, Charlotte, I'll get you out of here, I promise. I won't let you die".

Ria looked around for someone or something useful. If only she could drive and knew how to break into and hotwire cars like Charlotte, she could maybe just speed right on out of here.

A noise from the tool store besides her caught her interests, she turned to look and it stopped, only to start again. She stood up, maybe it was help, someone who could assist her in carrying Charlotte out of here. She approached the store with caution, paying mind to the fact that she could be setting herself up to fall into someone's trap.

She stepped inside the shop and looked around, feeling compelled to shout out to someone, but also not to, for fear that it might be one of those people she zoomed into earlier.

Quietly she crept around the car and fallen shelves to investigate. She could hear a series of whispers and louder shuffling. As she crept forward, she noticed movement towards the back of the store. She crouched down and peered between the gaps in the shelves. Three individuals, rummaging around for things, likely tools.

"Do we have enough, L.N?" One of suspicious characters asked another, a male voice.

"We'll need about two of everything, chuck in some of those Allen keys, they'll prove useful", another male replied.

"The fifth container?"

"Nails".

"Does it matter which?"

"No, once it goes off, they'll all do the same job".

"What do we need for the mufflers?" The third male asked, but before L.N or the other male could reply, Ria, in attempt to get a better view, knocked a box of screws to the floor. Dammit, just what she needed. The three men spun around with a start.

"Who is there?" One of them demanded.

Ria ducked and covered her mouth, but it was a reflex rather than necessity, immediately feeling stupid for doing so afterwards.

"Come out, we know you are there".

Ria stood up and stepped out to where they could see her.

"Who are you?" They asked.

"Hi... err... I was just... err... looking for someone to help me carry my friend", Ria replied.

"Who's your friend?" L.N replied.

"The woman laying out at the front".

"Is she with you?" One of them asked.

"Yeah, we were in a car crash".

They stood upright and turned to her, holding items they were clearly in the process of stealing from the store before she interrupted.

"What did you see and hear?" They asked?

She waved her hands submissively.

"Nothing, barely anything. I just got here, you totally don't need to worry about me, I took some things from a shop I was in before here, so I wouldn't judge you. I'm not here to spy on you, my friend is just in a really bad way and I wanted someone to help get us out of London and her to a hospital".

"No, we haven't got time for kids and she's a lost cause", one of them replied.

"Hey, don't be like that to the young lady, didn't your parents teach you manners?" L.N shut him down. He then turned to her, "We will help, but under the condition you keep what you've seen here today to yourself".

"You've got a deal, secrets reeled, I'll never squeal, my lips are sealed".

They stared at her blankly for a second, before L.N chuckled.

"I like this girl. Don't worry, we'll give you a lift out of London and get your friend to a hospital, we have a vehicle".

Finally leaving the darkness of the store, Ria was able to get a better look at them.

L.N was particularly good looking, enough so to make her heart flutter.

He smiled and suddenly, she didn't know what to say or how to react and she was certain that if she could flush red, she probably would. How was it even possible to be that good looking? And that smile was most definitely criminal!

She felt as though she had seen him before somewhere, though couldn't recall ever having met him before, she definitely would have remembered that heart-melting smile.

L.N suddenly felt compelled to question her.

"Why did you leave her side?"

"I went to look for my brother, he ran away when we crashed".

"Is he okay?"

"My dad is going after him, I called him just now and I came back for her", Ria replied, pointing towards Charlotte.

"Are you two related? Is she your sister or something?"

Ria shook her head.

"No, no. I only met her today, but she's been helping us, so I guess we are together. Is it okay with you if I just let my dad know that I'm okay? He'll be worried about me".

"Yeah, as long as you don't..."

"Don't worry, I won't say anything. I stole stuff too, remember?"

The guy smiled.

"We need to hurry a little, I don't think we have much time. Radio says the army has lost control of the situation and can't contain it, might mean they are considering more extreme measures. We don't want to be around if and when that happens".

"Okay", Ria replied, following behind them.

She pulled out her mobile and texted her father.

'Dad, found some help for Charlotte an old couple', she lied, 'her legs look really bad, she might not make it without medical help soon, so they offered to take her to hospital outside of the city. They offered me a ride, I don't have any other option, everyone else is gone and we can see those people coming our way, so I guess I'll go with them, but I'll let you know if anything happens. I'll talk to you later'.

A few short minutes later she received a reply.

'Be careful, princess, let me know if something happens. Be vigilant, opportunists and twitchers everywhere'. Twitchers? Was he referring to the crazy people? What a weird nickname.

They came to a people carrier family vehicle, where upon they opened the doors to dump their loot, carefully place Charlotte and allow for Ria to sit down.

Ria took the middle seat, propping Charlotte's head up onto her lap, whilst one of the men took the seat next to her.

Once they were all in the car and Ria felt a little more at ease about finally making a move and leaving this hellhole behind, she thought she might update Lacey, because she was sure to be worrying about her, but if the aim was to quell Lacey's concerns with news that she had not only been rescued, but rescued by three strange men, she was sorely mistaken. Lacey was not most pleased with her nonchalant attitude towards the situation and seemed dismissive of the fact that she was short of options, they seemed nice, Charlotte was perilously close to death's door and that one of them was cute... although she did return to that last point after her lecture, evidently weak to the power of good looks. Lacey requested a photo, but with the guy sitting next to her, glancing over at her phone every so often, that was going to be no easy feat. He was probably just paranoid that she'd out them all, but it was annoying as all hell.

She felt a little guilty for not having put more thought or feelings into prior events, the crash, who they had hit, those people she had seen, where her brother had gotten to and whether or not he was safe, the wellbeing of her parents, but with everything converging on her all at once and mentally dismantling her little by little, the pathetic little distractions like how cute L.N was, was a nice *normal* distraction, at least for the meantime.

She put her phone down as though disregarding it, keeping it out of the line of sight and fumbled for the camera button. Once she was fairly certain she had it, she made conversation in order to get their attention.

"So, where were you when all of this started happening?"

"Home, shit's unreal, still can't believe this is all happening", the driver replied. L.N sat quietly in the passenger seat, but it was him she wanted a reply from.

"So why were you with that woman?" The driver asked. "Where's your parents, kid?"

"I'm not sure", Ria replied, refraining from giving away too much information. It was a good thing she had that pen knife, not that she was expecting anything per se, but you could never be too cautious.

"Your dad didn't tell you? You spoke to him, didn't you?"

"He's rescuing my mum from her office in the centre and then coming for me".

"Ah, okay. Pretty brave, not even the ol' bill is taking a chance with that shit".

"Yeah..." Ria replied half-heartedly, softly stroking Charlotte's hair. "Do you know anyone who was in the middle of it all?"

"No, fortunately".

None of this was working, L.N wouldn't even glance at her, she needed to be more direct.

"So, what are your names?"

Maybe that question was a little too direct, because they responded to it with radio silence.

"You don't have to tell me, I was just making conversation, my name is Ria". That was about the most they were going to get out of her and it would prove to work, because L.N glanced back.

"I suppose we can share with you. My name is Barry and these two here with me are Ross and Jason.

He was lying. There was no way *he* was a Barry and she specifically heard the others refer to him with the abbreviation L.N, so whether or not those were his real initials, was yet to be discovered. If he *was* lying about his name, it was safe to assume he was also lying about theirs. It was understandable that they'd want to keep their identities secret, if only to avoid implicating themselves in anything.

She missed an opportunity to capture him with her camera the first time around, but she was ready for him the second time and snapped away, praying she had captured his best side.

"Pleasure to meet you, Barry, Ross and Jason", she replied, to which L.N shot her a reassuring smile.

Keeping her phone out of the line of sight, she sent a photo over to Lacey. It was a little blurry, but that was probably the best she was going to get under these circumstances.

Within seconds Lacey replied and the feelings were shared, cute but frustratingly familiar.

'Do you want me to post his picture? Find out who he is?' She asked in a message.

'It's okay, I'll ask', she replied and reverted over to Chirper to upload the picture with the words.

'My handsome hero! Who is he?' Followed by a series of love hearts.

The replies were most definitely not what she was expecting and within seconds, everything changed.

"I'm putting on the radio", L.N declared, "We need the updates".

Meanwhile, Ria scrolled through the messages, her stomach feeling heavier and her mind spinning a little more with each one.

Llisaluv @ria_riley<3 Darling! Don't go with him, he looks like the leader of that massacre not so long ago.

Gerrybitts @Llisaluv @ria_riley<3 The Walters Foundation massacre. If that's who we think it is, that's Lugo Neil, the leader and ******* scum of the human race.

Kiki1 @Gerrybitts @ria_riley<3 Lugo? Holy ****! OMGOMGOMG! Of all the people to be stuck in a car with. Jump out if you have to!

RachelHeart @ria_riley<3 Get the hell outta there babe, fuck that shit

And the torrent of messages kept coming in, each one sending her mind further into a tizzy. Her mouth dried, as panic overwhelmed her.

L.N was Lugo Neil, it all made sense now. It explained why they had lied about their names, why they were so concerned about her leaking information, fuck... this whole thing was probably their plan, they were terrorists after all.

She needed to get out now, why the hell did she even get in? Her dad told her explicitly not to go off with any strange people and not only did she do so, she ended up in the car of the very worst possible people and now they were going to kill her and Charlotte, kill her and dump her corpse in a shallow grave where her family would probably never find her. She couldn't bear to think about it. She couldn't breathe, she couldn't think straight. She was better off taking her chances on her own. Why hadn't she just tried to escape by herself, why did she have to be so reckless and stupid? So much for nice *normal* distraction, this couldn't be further from normal if she tried.

Just as the car had begun to feel as though it was crushing in on her, they came to an abrupt stop.

"Why are we stopping here?" Ria asked nervously.

"Picking up something", the driver replied and stepped out of the car.

"Shouldn't we keep going? Those twitchers are not far behind us".

"Don't mind, don't mind, chill your socks, sweetie, I won't be long", Lugo replied, stepping out and shutting the door behind him.

Sweetie? Who were they calling sweetie?

Why were they stalling? What were they up to? Ria's mind went into overdrive, every little thing since hearing of their identities only served to elevate her already heightened sense of paranoia. If her own life weren't enough to worry about, there was Charlotte too, to think about and since Charlotte was about her only saving grace for the moment, this was not the time for her to be out cold.

She sought solace in the sound of the voices on the radio - not that panicked voices frantically updating listeners about the tragic state of their city was a source of comfort, but anything to distract her right about now was welcome - and tried to come up with a plan of escape.

"... Reports that fires have broken out in the city centre, you can see the smoke billowing high above the buildings. I can only be thankful that we were moved so quickly. Three helicopters have mysteriously gone down today, was it the crazed? We still have no word on the origins of this outbreak, the rumour mill is working overtime and the government's only officially released statement still stands at *we are doing everything within our power to contain this outbreak*, they have warned everyone to remain inside and not to panic. We still have no solid idea of just what it is we are looking at and dealing with, so it is difficult to ascertain what we should be doing. The government's lax attitude leads many to wonder if we are being shielded from them reality of dire situation. Is the word to evacuate the city simply scaremongering or genuine foresight for the sake of our wellbeing? If there is one thing that can be assured, the sheer speed of spread, the failure to contain and suppress it so far, downed helicopters, rumours that the army, CEU and police have been ordered to shoot on sight, indiscriminately might I add only adds fuel to the infernos of existing hysteria. We still have no word on colleagues Valerie and Richard who were at the London office today, we can only pray that they are okay, and personal experiences and accounts of the events have been pouring in".

Ria thought of a plan of escape that would require a certain degree of tact, but wasn't impossible. The only remaining issue was escaping with Charlotte... or at least that's what she thought, for as the radio host cycled through various personal accounts of the events taking place in London, he eventually - and at the worst possible time - came to the subject matter of her and her escapades. Why now?

"... also, one of the more followed personal accounts documenting the events is that of the young sixteen-year-old, Ria Riley".

Ria instantly began to regret telling these men her real name. Why was she so stupid? Why hadn't she just lied and made up something?

Keeping a low profile now was only going to cast the spotlight on her, so instead she decided to talk over the report, distract them as best she could. They seemingly hadn't concluded that the Ria being talked about and she in the car with them were the same people yet, she wanted to keep it that way.

"Isn't it crazy what people are going through, it's like everyone will have a story for the rest of their lives now. There are probably people like literally dying all over the place. I have never *personally* seen a dead body, unless TV counts, I don't think it does, anyway that's probably for the best. There are also those infected people, have any of you seen them? I saw them... or at least I think I did... for just a moment and it was more than enough to make me shudder", she declared at the top of her voice, just making conversation about anything and everything at this point.

"... Brave little girl. She's even finding the time every so often to update us on her tribulations, despite how scared she must be. We have reason to believe the twitcher nickname originated from her. Brave people like her have been more of a news source today than even news stations".

Her futile attempts to distract the men only served to stall, but eventually the driver hushed her and there was little she could do to stop things from taking their course, short of stretching across and just switching the radio off. Taking desperate measures, she yelped out, surprising the two men.

"Whoa, what happened?" The driver replied, stretching back.

"She's not breathing", Ria replied.

"What the fuck? Check on her for me, Jason".

So-called Jason stretched over to check on Charlotte, but quickly discovered that she was fine.

"She's still with us", he assured them.

"Oh phew, I thought she had stopped breathing there for a second, I just panicked", she replied with a nervous laugh.

"Well no need, we'll be off again in just a second".

Believing she had created enough of a distraction to avoid being exposed as the host went onto other topics, she sighed with relief and sank back into her seat.

"The circumstances continue to develop as time goes on and with or without word, people have taken it upon themselves to evacuate the city centre and head for the outskirts, even as far reaching as Croydon and Romford. Public transport is sparse and most if not all means of transport out of the city has been terminated in order to prevent further spread of the infection to the outer reaches of the city. I repeat, look for the symptoms, twitching is a major giveaway, as well as any other displays of erratic behaviour. Also, if you are planning to leave the city, I'd suggest doing so as soon as possible, not to frighten you, this is just because the roads are jam-packed with abandoned vehicles and traffic. Caution whilst driving, the roads are filled with people".

Just what she needed, a reminder of what got them into this mess to begin with.

"Also, I really couldn't stress more", the host continued, "as much as I'd like to blindly put my faith in humanity, apply all of those precautions you normally would, but to a higher degree. We have reason to believe that our last personal account, Ria Riley, may have unsuspectingly jumped into a car with none other than Lugo Neil, suspected leader of the Walters Foundation Massacre and possible instigator of other heinous terrorist attacks who has not been seen or heard from publicly since the case against him was dropped. Now this is not confirmed, but if you see or hear from Ria, please contact..."

Fuck! That was sly! There was absolutely no way she could have foreseen that coming. She had gotten complacent thinking she was safe and that host just pushed her right into the fire. What the actual fuck?

The two men in the car turned to look at her almost immediately. That's it, she was *so* screwed now.

"It's her... fuck! It's fucking her!" The driver shouted, "Little fucking nigger bitch! You let them know everything?"

"I knew we couldn't trust you. Give me your phone!" The one next to her demanded and reached for her phone, only to retract as she lashed out at him with slaps and scratches.

"No!" She yelped.

"We were actually going to help you two out of the city!"

"Fuck that! I never planned to let these bitches go! Knew one of em would fucking squawk! Lugo was right, nab em, get their hands dirty instead of ours and cut their motherfucking throats!" The driver snapped.

As she fought off the guy next to her, she didn't even realise when the driver stepped out of the car until the door on Charlotte's side flew open and the driver grabbed her by her hair.

Ria screamed and thrashed, but it didn't seem to faze him, as he tugged with an aggression she had never personally experienced.

She was dragged out of the car along with Charlotte and slammed down on the ground. The same man then snatched the mobile from her hands and attempted to grab the pouch she had too. Everything she needed was in that pouch, including the knife, she couldn't let him have it.

Caught in a very short tug of war for the pouch, he ripped it from her fingers with ease and threw it aside. Defenceless and terrified, Ria attempted to flee, but once again, his brutish strength won out easily when he grabbed both her ankles and dragged her back

"Leave me alone!" She screamed.

"Take a long nap nigger bitch!" He snarled and the last thing she saw was the man who had been sitting beside her step out of the car, before she struck to the face with a blow so hard, that she passed out in an instant.

CHAPTER 18 - RIA

6:08pm - 6 Hours, 23 Minutes since outbreak

. . .

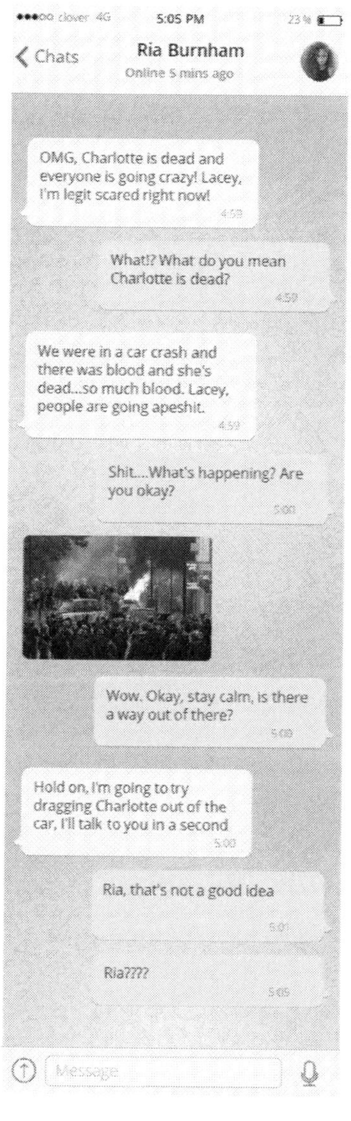

. . .

Ria was brought crashing back to reality with an unpleasantly cold splash of water, leaving her spluttering and gasping for air.

What the hell?

Her heart pounding for a multitude of different reasons, no less being soaked with cold water, her eyes darted two and fro, looking for the perpetrator. She found him standing next to her with a small bin in his hands and in her terror, tried to shuffle away from him, only to bump into Charlotte propped up against the wall besides her, her groans a positive indication she was still alive, even if the amount of blood she had already lost seemed worrisome.

"Was that really necessary?" Came another voice. She found the man who had been sitting next to her propped up on a table opposite her.

"Little bitch outed us like beached whales, what makes you think *she* deserves respect?"

Ria glanced around, where the heck was she? It looked as though they were in an office of some kind, this being one of many cubicles, but where computers should have been were empty desks with laptop stands.

Her head was throbbing, as was the spot on her face of which she had been punched, but she found she couldn't nurse them, for surprise surprise, her hands were tied behind her back.

Panic set in and all she could think was that she was going to die, or be raped or both. She didn't want to go out like this, not like this.

"Can't we just leave them here?" The back-seat passenger replied, "It's not as though they can get very far like that".

"This one saw our faces; do you want this coming back to bite you in the ass?"

"She only knows Lugo's name".

"That's all they need, you fucking moron! Did you miss the part where I said she had seen our faces?"

"I won't say anything, I promise. Please let me go, I just want my parents and brother, that's all", Ria blurted out.

"Sorry, but that's a no no. People know you now, you'll be all over the place if we let you go and you survive", driver replied.

Lugo returned, the first she had seen of him since he stepped out of the car.

"So, you're awake", he said simply, "And now you know who I am. Quite the little detective. Needless to say, we can no longer release you as we had intended, you have seen and heard too much already and I can't have you becoming a nuisance once this all blows over. Simply put, no loose ends".

"Please, I won't say a thing. I'm good at keeping secrets, just ask my friends. My lips are sealed, I promise", she pleaded, but her words went on deaf ears.

"Those crazies are coming, we should make a move soonish", Lugo suggested, lighting up a cigarette.

"What to do about the bitches?" Driver asked.

"Whatever the fuck you want, as long as this doesn't wind up coming back to us. Should be easier to cover up their deaths with shit going down. Just make it look like crazies got to them, better yet, let the crazies rip them apart. Blood is off our hands".

"What about the plan?"

"Screw the plan. Let's keep a low profile for now. Wait till all this shit blows over. Nothing we can do now anyway. We don't need them anymore".

"Wait! What?", Backseat passenger interjected.

"No crumbs, you heard Lugo", driver replied.

"Are you fucking serious? You're talking murder. Just tie them up and leave them here".

"Oh, come off it, that's the same damn thing as just straight up handing them over to the crazies. Besides, you talk as though you didn't know what this was about, you're working for the Walter's Foundation Massacre instigator, of course there was going to be murder".

"Lugo approached me and while yes we share mutual beliefs about the state of our country, what we don't share is that the murder of innocents is the only way to get that message across. I only agreed to help under the condition we could create chaos without endangering innocent people, only the targets, otherwise my skills stay to myself".

"Is he serious?" Driver asked, looking over towards Lugo, who had remained silent throughout this conversation.

"I'm afraid he is, unless you know anyone else who can build remote bombs like he can", Lugo replied.

"Exactly", back seat passenger replied. Did that mean she and Charlotte were safe?

"So, what now?" Driver asked.

"You kill them", Lugo answered. Ria's heart sank again.

"Why?" Back seat passenger demanded.

"I don't think there is anything we can do that'll make a statement as big as NOMA did today. This whole epidemic thing has us beat, none of the targets will be stupid enough to still be around for a while and the message would be lost, so I'm thinking we cut our losses and focus on living to see another day, which means ditching the excess baggage and making sure they don't talk, otherwise you too will find yourself under the microscope like I already am, or worse, jailed for kidnapping and intent to use them as hostages".

"No, fuck that, this wasn't what we agreed to, no one said anything about getting my hands bloodied".

"Don't be a pussy", driver replied. Whilst they argued, Ria desperately looked for a means of which to escape.

"Get off the fucking high horse!"

"Enough bitchin'", driver replied. He dug into his pocket, pulled out the pen knife, approached Ria and Charlotte and stopped before them. He glared down at Ria, whose heart pounded in her chest and turned his attention to Charlotte. He then crouched down before her, raising the pen knife to her neck.

"What the fuck are you planning to do?" Back-seat passenger demanded, stepping up to him. Driver spun around and pointed the knife at him.

"Calm down, I ain't done nothing yet, but get too hot on your heels and I might just cut you too". He turned back to Charlotte. "Fucking waste if you ask me, she has a tight body on 'er". He raised his free hand and groped her. "Stonking titties".

"What the fuck man!"

"She gets me fucking hard, wish we had more time so I could play with her".

"Get away from her!"

Ria stared in horror, too scared to move or say a word for fear he would do something to her instead, but guilty and frustrated she could do nothing to help Charlotte.

"I said get away from her!" Back seat passenger snapped.

"Okay", driver replied, but before he stood up, a quick swipe of his hand and had slit her throat in one fell swoop.

"No!" Ria screamed, as blood sprayed everywhere, including over her.

"Motherfucker!" Back seat passenger shouted and approached driver, but he pointed the knife at him.

"Come at me, see what I'll do".

Ria began hyperventilating with crippling fear, finding it suddenly difficult to breathe, shudders passed down her spine, her body trembled like a leaf, all the horrors of today converging on her in this one moment. Was this really happening? No, she had to be having a nightmare, this was all too much.

"You're a fucking psycho! What the fuck do you get from killing a severely injured woman and a child!"

"Man the fuck up. It's a dog eat dog world now, we look after numero uno, fuck everyone else!"

"It's a fucking outbreak, not a killing spree free for all!"

Charlotte's death was slow and painful; with her hands tied, she couldn't even prevent the loss of blood if she had the consciousness to do so.

Ria began screaming and crying, unable to hold back the overwhelming surge of emotions welling up inside her any longer. This only angered the driver and he approached her, striking her again knocking her down and startling her, but not hard enough to knock her out.

"Know what, I'll be outside when you two want to come find me, but remember, I made it explicitly clear that time is not on our side, so do whatever you need to do fast, otherwise I'm leaving your assess behind", Lugo declared and left.

"You keep quiet, little monkey, this ain't the jungle! You'll bring those fuckers outside right to our doorstep!"

Ria lay there crying and bleeding, having bitten her lip when punched.

Charlotte's choking died down and Ria didn't need an explanation for what that meant, she just wanted her mum and dad.

"Fuck, she's dead. Say, have you ever had a nigger chick?"

"What the fuck are you asking?" Back seat passenger replied.

"I'm thinking I should try one just this once, seeing as we definitely killing her now, since she can implicate both of us, accomplice. No one will know about it".

"Except me!"

"And you won't say a thing. I mean, we'll need to bleach down afterwards, don't wanna catch nothing, but pussy is pussy".

"She's a kid!"

"Like I said".

"No, I'm not letting this happen! You already killed that woman! You are scum! This was never about the narrative with you, you just have a sick bloodlust!"

"Fuck the narrative, what the fuck has ever been done for me? I've been screwed over at every turn and now I get to reclaim that. The WFM was glorious, fucking wish I was there".

"You know what? I'm not going to be here for whatever bullshit you have planned next, I'm fucking gone".

"Where do you think you're going, Jack Hemmingway?" Driver demanded.

"Bastard..."

"Now that she knows at least your name, you have no other choice but to kill her, right? Who do you think she'll remember and lead the police to if she lives now? Word of advice, never give people you don't know your full name. Mine was an alias, so even if you told her, it would never lead to me. Needless to say, your choices right now are sparse, whilst you're gone, I'll be having fun and who knows, I might just release her afterwards, if only to see you go down for it".

"You'd fucking implicate Lugo too".

"Fuck Lugo, his reputation means shit now, you heard him yourself, everything he and we did might as well be a hopeless cause now".

Ria used the opportunity whilst they were distracted to flee to a corner, but driver was back at her ankles before she had a chance to get away.

"Where are you going little one, don't run from me now".

"No! No! Leave me alone!" She screamed, tears streaming down her face, "Daddy! Help me!"

"Your daddy ain't here. it's just me and you, baby girl. I'm going to have my way with you, then cut you up and post it all on your social media, how's that for a status update?" The grin on his face was spine chilling and Ria had never been more scared. Suddenly she felt her shorts slip from beneath her skirt and down her legs, but she couldn't fight it with her arms tied and this man's strength far exceeding her own.

"Get the fuck off of her!" Back seat passenger snapped, jumping onto the driver's back and pounding the living daylights out of him.

The two tussled, slamming into cubicle separators, desks and walls, all the while, Jack refused to release driver.

She didn't want to die, she didn't want to die like Charlotte, not like that, but she couldn't escape, not with these two. Consumed with regrets of not having made up with her father, her dismay that she'd never be able to see her stupid brother again, her mother's voice, she hated herself for briefly making her social status a priority. Why did she have to post all that on her social? Why didn't she just keep quiet?

The driver put Jack through a desk with a toss over his shoulders and left Jack there reeling.

"I see how it is motherfucker, you just lay there for a moment, I'll kill you next, you worthless piece of shit!"

Driver returned to her.

"No, please no", Ria begged.

"Shut the fuck up". He took her hair and slammed her head against the back of the desk. Ria yelped and with teary eyes looked up into her killer's eyes as he whipped out the pen knife and brought it to her neck.

"Make it slow and painful. Make her fucking suffer", front seat passenger demanded.

As Ria's eyes widened, her body shook like a new born puppy and she wet herself from sheer terror.

Without warning, Jack reached around and grabbed the knife.

"Get your motherfucking hands off me!" driver snapped, wrestling with Jack for the knife.

They fell to the ground, Ria being released in the process and Jack, unable to pull the knife free of driver's hands, slammed his hand against the ground until he released it.

"Go! Grab the knife and get the fuck out of here!" Jack demanded. Ria was initially too stunned to move, her emotions far too discombobulated to make sense of anything that was going on.

"Go or they'll fucking kill you!" Jack snapped at her.

She didn't have to be told another time.

She pulled up her shorts, bent down in a way she could grab the knife and fled the cubicle, passing her pouch on the way out. She returned to it, rummaging through for her phone and fled once it was in her hands, leaving the pouch and everything else behind.

Ria didn't know where she was going, she still didn't even know where she was, but she didn't want to be here, she knew that much. These men wanted to kill her in a brutal fashion and not without tormenting her first. What kind of animal would behave that way?

She still couldn't get the horrific images of Charlotte's death out of her head, it replayed over and over. She was still trembling. She came to a storage cupboard and passed it by, there had to be an exit somewhere in this office-like.

Running aimlessly, panic consumed her with every second that went by without finding an exit, just windows and she looked pretty high up, at least five floors.

She eventually found a doorway that led out to a corridor and followed it around, coming to some elevators. She repeatedly hammered the elevator call button, praying for it to move faster and from the ground floor it begun its slow ascension upwards, going past the ground floor, the first floor and the second, but before it could make it to the top, she could hear the running footsteps of one of the men drawing closer. She disregarded the elevator and continued on down the corridor, eventually reaching a point where it split off into two directions, providing no clear indication of where each led. She had to pick one fast because the person behind her was gaining on her, so she picked left and soon regretted it when she came to a dead end with the male and female toilets. It was too late to go back now, so she ran into the female toilets and locked herself in a cubicle.

This was probably the stupidest decision she had ever made, of course he was going to know she was in here, she ran down the wrong way, she entered the females subconsciously instead of the males and she stupidly locked herself in a cubicle, the only locked cubicle in the toilets. Hands trembling and trying hard to think of what to do next, she began cutting away at the zip-tie around her wrists with the pen knife.

It eventually snapped loose and fell to the floor, freeing her wrists. One less concern. She rubbed her wrists and put her phone into her pocket, before trying to steady her nerves enough to think of something. Her thoughts were cut short as there was a loud slam from what could only be the main toilet door.

"Come out, come out wherever you are. Don't make this difficult. I promise I'll make it quick and painless". It was the driver's voice, toying with her, getting sadistic pleasure from slowly tormenting her. She sat down on the toilet lid and pushed against the door with her feet to keep it shut.

He stopped in front of her cubicle.

"Hey little piggy, why don't you let me in, don't make me huff and don't make me puff, because I don't know what I'll do once I begin". He followed up his terrible rhyming with a malicious laugh.

"Come on, don't make me stain those porcelain sinks red with your cracked skull or better yet, drown you in that toilet bowl you're hiding on", he snapped, kicking at the door.

Ria didn't reply, she was far too terrified. She had to find a way out of here and the only way she could think of was over the top of the cubicle, it was stupid and it most likely wouldn't work, but what other option did she have?

She got to her feet, climbed up onto the toilet lid and attempted to clamber over the top, but just as she had managed to get some footing, the door to the cubicle slammed open and the driver grabbed at her ankles.

"No! Let go of me!" She screamed.

"Stupid bitch! I gave you a fucking chance, now you die!" He roared, punching her in the back and legs with all his might.

As his strength overpowered her own and pain forced her to give up her attempts to fight, she realised that there was only one way out of this situation alive, the alternative was a brutal death. She turned without warning, catching him off guard for a second and stabbed him in the eye with the pen knife. He let out a room echoing scream and they tumbled down to the ground together, her falling on top of him. She scrambled to her feet and made a run for it, leaving the pen knife behind.

"Bitch! Bitch! You fucking stabbed me in the fucking eye! Stupid fucking, piece of shit, cunt motherfucking bitch!" He screamed at the top of his lungs, holding his eye.

Limping from the full-strength punch to the back of her leg, she scampered out of the toilets and back into the corridor. As the pain overwhelmed her, the only thought going through her mind was survival.

This time she took the other corridor which led down to a staircase leading downstairs. Slowly she descended the stairs, tears from both terror and pain blurring her vision and making it difficult to see where she was going. She was a mess; battered, bruised and emotionally traumatised, whether she would ever recover from this was a question unto itself.

As she made her way down, she heard a male voice coming from above. Familiar, but not that of the driver or Jack, she peered up to spot Lugo glaring back down at her. Shit! Had he come back?

"Hey kiddo! Wanna make my life easier? Don't really want to chase you, that's effort".

"No catch and kill that fucking nigger bitch! I'm gonna smash her fucking skull into the fucking ground! She'll fucking pay for this!" She heard the driver scream with rage from somewhere behind him.

Lugo pulled out what looked to be a gun and before Ria even had a chance to jump back, he fired, hitting her shoulder.

Searing pain akin to an electric jolt passed right through her body, making her yelp out and grab her shoulder, before falling back. It was a pain unlike anything she had ever felt, but just a few more inches to the left and it would have been a shot to the skull, instant death.

She wept, blood trickling down her chest

They stormed down the stairs after her and her adrenaline kicked into gear, side-lining the pain to focus everything purely on survival.

Touching down on the bottom floor, Ria made for the door, which led her out to the lobby of the building and there before her was an exit.

CHAPTER 19 - RIA & TERRY

6:48pm - 7 Hours, 3 Minutes since outbreak

. . .

FACT FILE #8:

Lugo Neil was a former soldier and lieutenant. He comes from a family of five, with his two parents and two older sisters. He joined the army with hopes of defending his nation, freedom and fighting for what he believed to be right, but over time he became disillusioned with what he once believed was true, instead becoming indoctrinated with a new and growing philosophy similar to that of NOMA. He believed his enemies were being aided and abetted by his own home nations, that war was for profit and that so called innocents were only the momentarily pacified terrorists of tomorrow.

He, fuelled with rage, joined a small group of others with intent to stir up an uprising, a revolt against both sides, their enemies far away and their enemies right at home.

His first target was the Walters Foundation for more than one reason, which he was accused of instigating, but not actively participating in, in order to keep his hands clean, his second was to target political figures he believed national traitors, but this fell through with the outbreak.

. . .

An exit though it may have been, a means of escape it most definitely was not, for there to greet any daring individuals stood several blood covered people glaring at her with a seething madness and frightening bloodlust in their eyes.

Shit, these people were among the infected, the erratic twitch and heavy breathing a tell-tale sign.

Her mind went blank as she slowly backed off the way she came, her heart racing uncontrollably. This was too much, out of a pot and straight into a fire. The only thing worse than being caught by those men was being torn apart and eaten alive by twitchers.

Why weren't they moving? Why were they just standing there glaring at her?

Just when she thought she could make it back to the door without them launching at her, her pursuers burst through the door

Lugo spotted her first, but no sooner did he take aim at her, he noticed the twitchers.

"Fuck!" He exclaimed and without warning, took a pot shot at them.

Oh boy, why did he do that? What the fuck was he thinking?

Almost making her heart burst out from her chest, the twitchers shrieked and bolted towards them.

Ria turned and ran past the two men, threat though they were, they were the lesser of two dangers right now. She ran to another door in the lobby and entered into a corridor. Curse those heartless monsters, curse them for the agony she was forced to endure for the sake of survival.

The two men weren't far behind her and behind them twitchers poured through the doorway into the corridor, tumbling over each other and violently smashing against walls in an attempt to reach the three.

Ria could see few means of escape as they drew closer to the end of the corridor, there were closed doors besides her, but did she want to take a chance after what had happened upstairs?

Running out of options as she drew closer to the end of the corridor, she stopped and tried one of the doors. Locked, dammit. She tried a different one and this time had more success, she found herself in a room filled with laundry, which for a brief moment she thought was a dead end, but there were steps at the opposite end.

She ran over to them and ascended, just as her two pursuers dived in. Leaving them behind attempting to barricade the door with a washing machine, she came to the top of the steps and exited through a door into the stairway she was in before. She was going in circles and this was tremendously frustrating. Best to avoid going back down after what happened before, she'd go up instead.

She climbed the steps and her heart skipped a beat when she found herself confronted with Jack, beaten black and blue.

He started waving submissively when he noticed her backing off.

"It's okay, I mean you no harm. I helped get you into this mess and your friend was killed because of it, I'll help get you out. I won't let them hurt you again".

She didn't trust this guy by any means, but what other choice did she have, he was her only means of safe escape for now, especially with twitchers added to the mix.

"You're bleeding, those bastards shot you?"

Ria didn't reply.

"We should get out of here fast", he said, approaching her.

"No..." Ria replied, "can't go that way, twitchers... and those two others".

"Okay, err, let's find a different route, quick, follow me". He turned and made his way up a single flight of steps, before taking a doorway on the next floor leading to another corridor.

They ran across that office floor, filled with more cubicles, passed through a storage room and came to a double doored exit towards the back, their pursuers hot on their tail once again.

They descended a set of steps right the way to the ground floor, passed through yet another corridor and double doors to find themselves in a loading bay, behind which was an unrelated construction yard for what looked to be the beginnings of what would soon become another complex.

"Quick, over that fence", Jack instructed, hoisting her up, "Be careful, there are tunnels and uneven surfaces, it's dangerous".

She clambered over, glancing back at him once, before dropping down onto the other side.

"Run, hide, do whatever you must. I can hear the other two coming, I'll try to find another exit. Be safe", he said through a gap in the fence and with that, he took off.

Was he doing this because he genuinely cared or was it simply to clear his consciousness? It honestly felt a little like both. In the pursuit of self-preservation, a person could make a selfish cause look like valiant selflessness.

No sooner did she start running towards the scaffolds of an incomplete construction, she heard the other two men shouting after her. Lugo climbed up the fence and took a shot at her, narrowly missing her, but making her stumble and fall in her panic. Covered in construction yard mud and grazing her knees, she scrambled back to her feet and ducked inside the walls of the building through an open door, as another bullet ricocheted right by her face.

Out of breath, she ran up the stairs and clambered up onto another level without any stairs, ascending the dangerous structure.

She peered down and spotted Lugo coming up after her alone. If she didn't do something, she'd have nowhere left to flee too, there were only so many floors finished and she was halfway up already. She came to a floor with the steps still being constructed and nowhere left to go besides a temporary elevator. Naturally she didn't need to think it over, she jumped in, jabbing at the button to ascend the two remaining floors, stepped out and slammed on the emergency stop button. That would suffice for now, neither he nor she would be able to restart it without the key.

She could hear him thumping on the metal elevator doors and shouting obscenities with threats up at her, but she was at least safe for a while. Unless he had some hidden gymnastic abilities, there was no way he was making it up here.

In agony, exhausted, shaken and weeping, she inspected her bullet wound, before reaching into her pocket and pulling out her mobile. Shit, only ten percent battery life left. Without those batteries she had left behind, she would have to use what she had very sparingly.

She went through her contacts and attempted to call her father, but her heart sank, tears welled up and panic set in for every unsuccessful attempt. It would ring endlessly, serving only to kick her imagination into overdrive. What if he was dead? What if he and her brother had been ripped apart by twitchers when she had been so nonchalantly updating her fucking status? What if they hadn't managed to reach her mum and now she too was dead?

"Please..." She whimpered, and with trembling, blood covered hands, tried one more time, before she would attempt her mother and as a last-ditch effort, Daniel.

It rang twice without an answer and she screamed at her phone.

"Please!"

Three more unanswered rings and her hopes began to dwindle.

"Please, daddy! Pick up! Please pick up!"

Just as the answering machine came on again, it stopped midway, then came a click and finally the most wonderful voice she could ever hear in the world, so wonderful that she choked up, her words stuck in her throat.

"Hello? Ria?"

"Daddy? Help me! Please come and help me quickly!" Ria replied, blubbering like a baby over the phone, with snot running down her face and choking on her own words as she tried to explain everything that had happened to her to him in a single sentence.

"... They killed Charlotte, daddy... they cut her neck and there was blood and they tried... they tried to...me... they..."

"Ria, slow down, where are you?"

"I... I don't know, I climbed to the top of... an unfinished building and... and... daddy, help me", she burst into tears, everything that had happened overwhelming her.

"I need to know where you are, princess, find something you recognise and give me a clue".

"I... I don't know... wait... I can send my location on babbadoo, do you have that?"

"I believe so. Okay, try that and call me back", he replied, so reluctantly - for fear she wouldn't be able to hear his voice again - she hung up, sent him through her location and called him again, with her battery power dropping to eight percent.

"I've got it, you're some distance from me, princess, but I'll be there, I promise. I won't let you down".

"Come quickly, daddy".

"I will *not* let you down! Wait for me!"

"Okay…" Before he could put down the phone, she stopped him. "Daddy…"

"Yes, princess".

"I love you".

"I love you too. Stay there if you can. If not run, I *will* find you".

She hung up. She hated hanging up on him, she wanted to remain on the phone, to hear his reassuring voice at a time when she felt as though the world were closing in around her.

Her hands still trembling, she used the remainder of her battery life posting her ordeal to her social and a parting message, just in case she didn't survive. She didn't even wait to see the answers before putting her phone down, clutching it tightly in her hands as she huddled into a ball against an iron beam, holding her gunshot wound.

"Daddy… don't let me down", she whispered to herself.

"Change of plan", Terry announced, turning to Lizzy, "My daughter is in danger and I have to reach her fast".

"What are your intentions? The roads are jam-packed with cars and there are twitchers everywhere".

"Run".

"Are you serious? Run where?"

"She's not far from Bethnal Green".

"Bethnal fucking green? Are you serious? You want to run all the way there?"

"My daughter's life is at stake, I'm not about to let her die, not on my watch. I'll fucking run all the way to West Ham if I have to".

"Don't be ridiculous, you'll never make it and even if you do you'll be so out of energy you'll be useless".

"Well what do you suggest?"

She glanced around and pointed towards a bike rack, bikes supplied by the city council years ago as an initiative to get more people riding around London as opposed to driving.

"Bike it? You'll get there faster and with more energy to spare".

"Good idea. Okay, I'll lure as many away as possible, use that opportunity to go find a car, get to my wife, explain what happened and I'll tell you where to pick us up".

"Okay, get going. She's waiting for you". Terry nodded and took off, leaving Lizzy behind.

He rummaged through his pocket for his clam card and flashed it over the scanner pad to charge him for bike usage, releasing it from the security rack.

He grabbed the handle bars, perched himself upon the seat and pedalled his way to his daughter.

The sun was beginning to go down as seven thirty rolled on, beginning to shroud

London in darkness. Given the circumstances, Ria didn't want to be in the city during the night, not with a dead phone and no idea of where she needed to go. Where was her dad already?

Her mind wandered for a moment, she never got to ask her dad if her mum and brother were okay... stupid, she should have asked, but did her father prioritising her mean that they were safe now? She could only hope. She glanced down at her phone, five percent, calling them now would only kill her battery.

She placed her phone down and huddled back into a ball, hugging her knees tightly. Charlotte was dead, those men tried to rape and kill her, she didn't know where her family were and if they were okay, she had no idea where Lacey was or why she hadn't replied to her last message and the icing on the cake was that London was more than likely crawling with the infected, these were the realities she had to face and in top of that, she had been shot, a pain that refused to fade, but only the worst of many pains around her body.

Was she meant to survive? Was this the night she would die? Was this the last time she could inhale the fresh air, gaze up at the skies, feel the breeze caress her face?

This morning her only worry was whether her father would disappoint her again and waste her time; that felt like so long ago, a trivial perspective and almost laughable in contrast to now.

If she listened, she could still hear a convergence of different sounds seemingly coming from all around, none of them reassuring, but the one thing she could no longer hear were the voices of the two men.

She never should have trusted those monsters, she probably would have been better off just dragging Charlotte to safety herself. Charlotte... how Ria wished she could apologise to her for prejudging. Had it not been for Charlotte, they would probably be dead already. The memory of her choking on her own blood was so vivid, Ria could almost still hear her shudder-worthy choking on her own blood.

Smoke rose up into the skies and the smell carried through the breeze. Helicopters whizzed overhead, but none paid her any mind regardless of how much she waved and called out to them. Ember filled the skies and the scene she was presented with was the very depiction of hell.

She sat back down and there she remained huddled for what felt like another five minutes, before something disturbed the solitude.

Ria propped her head up as the sound of hushed voices commanded her attention.

She peered around an iron beam and spotted the two men on her floor approaching her direction.

"She's here somewhere, I heard her a minute ago".

"Just find that bitch, she stabbed me in the motherfucking eye! I'll see that she pays ten times over for this shit".

"You mean half see".

"Fuck off! Do you think this is a fucking joke?"

"No, I'm sure it's a bastard, but you've been bitching about it none-stop. Men have died for the cause and you're fucking whining about an eye".

"What the fuck have you lost then?"

What were they doing here? How the hell had they managed to get up without the escalator? They had every opportunity to escape London by now, why were they so persistent?

Panic stricken once more, she stood up and looked around. There wasn't much in the way of hiding places.

She ran behind a doorway which led out to the exposed scaffolding and hid behind it. The two men drew closer

"We are wasting time on this brat", Lugo insisted.

"Fuck that, I won't be satisfied until I've checked every last fucking corner, found her and skinned her alive!"

Ria's heart was pounding again. Why did she matter so much to them? If there was a God, did he want her to suffer?

She turned and looked down from what was intended to be a room, possibly an office and saw the expanse of the construction yard laid out below her, filled with machinery and vehicles and open underground walkways. This height was quite intimidating, but she might just be able to make it down to the lower level. If she managed to get down unnoticed, maybe they would find nothing and eventually leave.

She found a point of which to get down, but she had to be careful, one false move could see her plummet to a grisly death. Deliberating over the idea, she eventually decided to take the chance, it was now or never.

She slipped her legs over the edge and carefully tried to lower herself down, but as though the god of misfortune were toying with her again, five fighter jets roared overhead, followed by a deafening series of explosions, the darkening skies lit up as flames extended high into the air.

Startled, she dropped harder than she had planned, knocking down a bucket to the side she had been trying to avoid and cutting herself on exposed bricks upon her fall.

She didn't have time to pine over her cut, for the men above had heard the noise and run over to investigate, spotting her on the lower floor.

"There she is! I knew that bitch was here!" The driver snapped, looking down at her, "Shoot her!"

Lugo aimed, but Ria dived out of the way before he could fire, so instead he began lowering himself down, whilst his driver companion took off in the opposite direction.

Ria didn't wait to see what would happen, she was up and running, circumnavigating the peculiar layout to find a way down to the next floor.

She ran to what looked to be a ledge down to the bottom, but before she could jump down, the driver seemingly popped out of nowhere and grabbed her by her hair.

"Caught you, little bitch!"

Ria screamed and flailed her arms as Lugo came running to join them. If he got his hands on her, their combined strength would eclipse any strength she had remaining, or any she would have had even without the handicaps. She had to break free and now, before they had a chance to work together.

She attempted to keep the driver between them, stopping Lugo from grabbing her and as the driver managed to get the pen knife from his pocket, she lashed out at his arm, knocking the knife out of his grip and sending it sailing through the air to the ground far below.

"Dammit!" The driver snapped and reverted to hitting her instead.

Feeling the aura of death looming over her like the weight of a sandbag, she was determined to stay alive long enough for her father to get to her.

Lugo grabbed one of her kicking ankles and held on tight, bringing her to the ground, but lost his grip as she fell.

Suddenly, Ria remembered something as the driver held on tightly to her hair, if there was one thing that Daniel had taught her well, it was how to defend herself and she knew exactly where to strike. She raised her fist and with all her might, punched the driver in the groin, knocking the wind out of him and forcing him to let go as he crumpled to the floor in agony.

Ria was up and before Lugo could grab her, she dropped down onto the level below with a thud, landing hard on to her uninjured arm.

The pain was seething and it was only as she stood up did she realise that she may have inflicted more damage to it than she had first thought. She could barely move her hand as tears welled up in her eyes. Had she fractured it? No, this was all she needed, more injuries.

"Fucking whore! Kill her, shoot her in the fucking face!" She heard the driver snap with venomous rage. Ria got up and begun running just as Lugo had begun climbing down. She ran through some open doors and scrambled down flight of steps towards the ground floor and ran across the construction yard, but not far before Lugo caught up to and lunged at her, grabbing her ankle, forcing her to the ground. He tried to pin her down, but she kicked at him, kicking him in the face and using the split-second opportunity to run. It was then that she just about heard her name being called and turned to see her father behind a mesh fence, the best face she had seen all day.

A few minutes prior to that, Terry had arrived in the general location sent to him by his daughter, but with less light available to him and twitchers prowling at every turn, finding her was going to be no easy task. To make matters worse, he had brought along a swarm of twitchers that he simply couldn't afford to waste time evading, with the hopes that he might be able to lose them along the way, to no avail, up at least until a few short minutes ago, but it was only a matter of time before they found him. He was only too fortunate it was summer, so sunlight still lingered and probably would remain so for another few hours, but he couldn't bet on that. If it got too dark to see, he was screwed.

Having ditched the bikes, he took cover behind cars, observing the movements of the twitchers in the vicinity. He had to keep his wits about him, for the ambition was to avoid further detection.

The twitchers muttered to one another, mostly appearing distracted by a series of very concerning explosions he and they had heard in the distance, shortly after jets flew overhead. Terry could only pray that those explosions weren't the beginning of some crazy sanction to level the city.

The desire to call out for his daughter was overwhelming, but if he did so, he'd be swarmed and killed before he even got the chance to reach her. He could only pray that she was alright.

Using debris as distractions to divert the twitchers away from him, he slipped into a side street and ran up towards the pointer on the maps. He came to a stop next to a building and a construction yard, just like his daughter had described, but where was she? Was she still at the top?

He circled the fenced off construction yard, looking for an easy way in and heard a scream. Was that Ria?

These safety fence obstructed him and his view, so he ran around until he found a mesh fence and spotted two figures up on the construction itself. He called out to them, hoping that one of them was Ria, but neither of them seemed to hear him.

He looked up and above the mesh fence and wooden panels was barbed wire. He certainly wasn't going to get in that way, but for the others to have managed to get in, there had to be a point of entry.

He followed the fence around and stopped as the figures reached the ground, running across the construction yard. It was then that he recognised his daughter and she was running from someone, before being tackled to the ground. Terry witnessed the scuffle and his blood boiled. What were they trying to do to or with his daughter? He needed to find a way in and quickly.

She managed to break free and he called out to her.

"Ria!"

She only noticed him after the third call and the look of desperation in her eyes was unlike anything he had ever seen, fear beyond all fear and her yellow dress stained crimson red with blood.

"Daddy!" She screamed out to him.

"I'm here, Ria! Run to safety! I'll get around to you!" Terry shouted through the mesh fence, trying his damndest to reassure his daughter.

"Help me!"

"I'm coming!"

Suddenly a gun was fired in his direction and the sound was more than loud enough to attract every motherfucker in the vicinity.

The bullet missed him, but the point was made clear, this assailant meant business.

He ducked back and Ria continued running as her pursuer fired off two more bullets one in his direction and another in hers.

That son of a bitch had tried to kill his daughter! He was going to make the fucker pay, he was going to rip his lungs out from him mouth and fucking strangle him with it. Terry had never felt so much rage, so much blind determination to risk his life for a cause, but this was his precious daughter, scared, alone and vulnerable, he was prepared to do what it took to protect her from those fuckers.

Getting up once the pursuer had disregarded him in favour of chasing after his daughter, Terry desperately began looking around for either a means to cut through the mesh or the way in. He would sooner die trying, then to let those opportunistic fucks lay a finger on his daughter.

He tried hitting the mesh fence with a disregarded metal shell of an extractor to his side to no avail, desperation wasn't making him think clearly. He continued making his way around the side of the construction yard looking for a way to get in.

Ria dashed down into a pit with an open space that led to what looked to be an underground car park in the process of being built. Close behind her was Lugo, the next shot he took could be the fatal one.

She ran into the pitch darkness of the unfinished car park and outstretched her gunshot wounded arm to feel around for obstacles. It would take her eyes some time to adjust to the darkness, but until then, she was vulnerable to the dangers of the terrain.

"Where are you?" Lugo sang, his voice echoing throughout the empty space. "Are we playing hide and seek?"

Ria hid behind a pillar, if she ventured any further, who knew what she would encounter. She didn't want to lose sight of the exit, nor injure herself trying to get away, but she would soon regret that decision if Lugo managed to grab hold of her in the midst of her risk aversion.

As his footsteps drew closer, her heart pounded harder. Where was she going to go? He'd find her and kill her, but just as his footsteps reached a metre or so behind her, she heard a second pair of footsteps running towards her. Was it her father? Was it the driver? Who was it?

"There you are!" Lugo shouted, spinning around and fired a shot in the direction, but missed. "Fuck!" He cried as the gunfire for a second lit up the face of Jack, who lunged at him and punched him in the face. They landed hard on the ground next to her.

"Ria! Go, get out of here!" Jack shouted and lunged for Lugo again. Where the hell had he come from and why did he come back? He could have been long gone by now.

"You wanna kill me? You wanna fucking kill *me*? Should have fucking joined us, Jack, now I'll kill you along with her!" Lugo shouted. Ria ran towards the only exit she could see and for a second believed she was home free, but as her luck would fare, there blocking her way out stood the driver.

"Leaving so soon? You can't leave, I haven't repaid you for what you did to me", he snarled.

The remaining light from outside shimmered on the pen knife blade he held. He found it? How?

"Just leave me alone, please", she begged, "I really won't tell anyone anything, I didn't even see what you were doing".

"I don't fucking care about that anymore! This is personal! You took my fucking eye, I take your fucking life!"

Ria turned and ran back in the opposite direction, back into the depths of the abyss, praying that there was another exit. Her eyes having become a little more accustomed to the darkness made it slightly easier to manoeuvre around. She navigated around obstacles, listening out for the driver's footsteps and leaving Lugo and Jack far behind. She jumped down to a lower level, but the noise was probably only alerting the driver to where she was.

Eventually she came to a ramp leading up to what she could only assume was the road, with a barrier and ticket machine, as well as a booth besides them. Beyond the barrier was a metal shutter, the last remaining obstruction between her and freedom.

Ria ran over to the shutter and attempted to open it, only to discover that it was padlocked.

"Oh, come on, come on!" She yelled in panic induced frustration, but quickly realised her efforts were futile.

She slumped down against the shutters and wept, feeling hope slipping away quicker than the sand of an hourglass. The sound of footsteps approaching her made her stand up and paste her back against the metal shutters. As the figure drew closer and she prayed that it was Jack or her father, her heart sank when she realised it was the driver.

"Nowhere to go, little piggy. What will you do now?" He mocked and to make matters worse, who should join him? None other than Lugo.

"Did you kill Jack?" The driver asked.

"Two bullets left in the chamber and he slipped away, if he turns up, he gets shot".

"You should have fucking killed him, now he'll become a liability".

"Don't worry about him, he could barely move. He won't have the energy to take us both on. If he shows his face, we put a bullet in it. I'm more concerned about some guy that was calling out to her from beyond the security fences, so kill her first and then we'll hunt them down before the crazy brigade arrives", Lugo replied.

Ria wept and pleaded with them, but her words went on deaf ears.

"Don't you get it? Getting rid of you is doing the world a tremendous favour. I call it sterilisation. Just cleansing the world of the scum that infected it", the driver replied.

"I didn't care to get you involved in this, but you made it a necessity. There are some things that simply have to be done and this cause superseded everything else, collateral damages. You were part of that".

She hopelessly tried to run past them, but they grabbed her and shoved her back into the metal shutters. She wept harder as the driver approached her and kicked her in the stomach. She keeled over, gasping for air, but he grabbed her hair and punched her in the face, fracturing her nose, before rubbing her face into the ground.

"Fucking disrespect me! I gave you a fucking easy way out and how did you fucking repay me? By stabbing me in the eye! You should have taken both my eyes out because I'm making sure the last one sees you to your fucking grave, you little fucking worm!"

He raised her head, punched her again and slammed her head on the ground.

Ria couldn't even cry, the pain was blurring her vision, her eyes were drooping and she found herself simply gasping for air. She could see it... the doors of death creaking open before her and getting closer with each blow he gave her, every cut he made to her flesh with the knife. The world was slowly slipping away and as he brought her head up one more time to quote, cut her fucking head off.

"Stop the torture bullshit and kill her already, I'm growing impatient", Lugo complained.

"I want her to suffer, I want her to feel as though there is no more hope. I want her to experience the kind of pain that I'm experiencing".

Lugo sighed.

As the torture continued, Ria could just about hear running footsteps, before seeing Lugo go down.

The driver dropped her to the ground and stood upright.

Wincing, through teary eyes, she could just about see her father with a pole in hand unleashing a torrent of unhindered rage-filled hurt upon Lugo, the sort of violence she never thought her father capable of.

The driver lunged at him with the knife poised, but her father struck him to the face with the pole, knocking him to the ground. Lugo stumbled to his feet, but her father punched him back down and hit him again with the pole repeatedly, until Lugo grabbed it and fought back. The pole flew to the ground, punches were thrown left and right, the driver joined the scuffle, stabbing her father in the shoulder to make him cry out in agony.

He didn't subdue, if anything, that only fuelled his rage further, this was a different man, a man she hardly recognised, a man protecting his family like a lion a man she wanted so desperately to win.

"Daddy!" She weakly cried, barely able to move.

Her father, withdrew the blade from his shoulder and swiped at Lugo, cutting him, but not severely. Lugo drew the gun, but before he could fire, her father grabbed his wrist and knocked the gun out of his hand. The driver stormed at her father, tackling him to the ground and Lugo lunged for the gun in the meantime, but couldn't fire without clear aim, the driver was in his way.

Fury driving him, her father stabbed the driver multiple times in the arm, waist, shoulder, neck and back, using him as a shield against Lugo. The driver screamed and tried to release himself from her father's vice grip, but he wouldn't let go, stabbing him over and over and over again until blood was everywhere and the man stopped moving.

"Fucker!" Lugo roared and fired the gun towards her father, regardless as to whether the driver lay on top or not, hitting the driver in the back. Her father, shoved the driver's lifeless corpse off of him and flung the blade at Lugo, using the split second that Lugo took to dodge the blade to get up and pounce at him before he could fire again.

He slammed Lugo up against the wall and repeatedly punched him in the stomach until he dropped the gun once more, then unleashing all his rage, her father grabbed him by the scruff of his collar and shoved him into the metal shutters.

"You fucking lay a hand on *my* daughter? I'll kill you, you motherfucking son of a bitch!"

Lugo threw punches back and the exchange lasted some time, before they both went down. Lugo was seething with rage, a madness in his eyes only superseded by her father's own.

Her father was never a fighter, he had never fought for anything, but now he was fighting for everything and she could feel the impact of his every punch, packed with determination, with fury for what those men had done to her, with rectification for all the mistakes he had ever made. This man was her pride and joy, this man was the man she adored more than anyone in the world, this man was *her* dad.

Lugo temporarily managed to gain the upper hand, slamming her father's head into the ground, but he grabbed Lugo in a head lock and held him like that, taking all the punches to the gut, as Lugo attempted to free himself, until in one go he released Lugo and landed a punch square in the face, dazing him. Her father threw him over and climbed on top, showering him with punches, grabbing him by his head and slamming it against the ground, shoving his arms out of the way so that he couldn't fight back or defend himself and then punching him again until Lugo lay groaning and almost motionless. His face had seen better days, her father had beaten him until his teeth lay on the ground besides them, until he couldn't see through one of his eyes, until his nose bridge had shattered and twisted, until his jaw hung broken.

Out of breath, her father stood up and slowly went over to pick up the gun.

"Daddy..." Ria croaked.

He temporarily dismissed Lugo and came over and check on her. Slumping down beside her covered head to toe in blood, he took one look at her and burst into tears.

"What did they do to you? What did they do to my angel".

"They tried... to rape and kill me. They... sh... shot me and cut me and punched me".

"I'm sorry, I'm so sorry, princess. I failed you. I let those monsters lay their hands on you. I could have lost you and I wouldn't have been able to live with myself if that happened. I'm so, so, *so* sorry I didn't get to you fast enough to protect you". He took her in his arms and embraced her tightly. She winced from the pain, but tried to endure it.

"No..." she murmured, "You came. That's enough".

"No, it isn't, it's inexcusable, if I had come faster..." He gritted his teeth. "I'm going to put a bullet through both their fucking heads for what they did to you!".

She sat up and glared at the two men, especially the dead driver who had brutalised her and rage begun to well up inside her, she wanted vengeance, she needed to vent this grief somehow.

Pushing her father aside momentarily and dragging herself over to where the pen knife had landed, she grabbed it and crawled over to the dead driver.

"Honey, what are you doing? Don't move", her father insisted, but she disregarded him, stopping next to the dead man and driving the pen knife into his other eye, different parts of his face, his neck, his chest, his groin over and over again, releasing all the repressed rage and frustration that had built up inside her. This was for all the times she had begged and pleaded with them to let her go and they ignored her, mocked her, tortured her, wounded her. She screamed with rage and the blood splattered everywhere, across the ground, across her clothes, across her face.

"Die! Die! Fucking die!"

He father had to abandon Lugo again and grab her in tight embrace to get her to calm down again. Panting, she released the knife to her father's possession and wept into his chest as he cooed her, wept until she could weep no more.

"Daddy".

"I know, it's okay now, I'm here. I won't let them touch you".

Their moment was interrupted by footsteps. Her father stood up and pointed the gun in the direction they came from.

"Whoa, whoa, whoa, no problem man, we're good, I saved your daughter, I came here to help", Jack said, stopping short and raising his hands submissively. He turned to Ria, "Tell him, tell him we're good".

Ria stared at him coldly. Yes, he had helped her, but he was one of them, they were *his* buddies.

"He's one of them..." She replied.

"What? No! I saved you, if it wasn't for me you wouldn't be alive now", he turned back to her father, "Please, think about this, I'm no threat, honestly. I just want to go home like you guys, I swear it. Come on man, please don't do this! I have a family, I have..." He didn't finish his sentence before her father put a bullet through his skull, splattering the walls and floor behind him with his brain matter. He slumped to the ground, dead.

As Lugo stirred and groaned in pain, her father pointed the gun at him, ready to take the next shot, but that's when they heard the shriek and thundering running footsteps of twitchers echoing throughout the car park.

"Shit!" Her father snapped and left Lugo. He ran back over to the shutters, noticed the padlock and fired a shot at it to release it. He pulled free the broken remnants and grabbed the bottom of the metal shutters, pulling them up just high enough for them both to slide beneath.

"Let's go, princess", he insisted, scooping her up in his arms despite his own injuries and carried her beneath the shutters.

Safely on the other side and looking up at the open exit to the carpark, Ria finally felt like there was hope again.

Lugo rolled over and spotted them leaving.

"H... help... me! D... don't leave... me!" He murmured.

"Go to hell!" Ria screamed at him, as her father slammed the shutters down. They stood back to the sound of Lugo's shrill screams.

Her father propped her up onto his back and they made their way to safety.

CHAPTER 20 - TERRY & RIA

8:02pm - 8 Hours, 17 Minutes since outbreak

. . .

. . .

They took shelter in a nearby ransacked shop and her father took some time to reach her mother, but not before wrapping her in one of the coats hanging from the shop racks.

Ria was exhausted and emotionally drained, but at the very least, she was glad that that chapter was done with.

She couldn't wait to get out of this city and hopefully soon, given how the sound of explosions seemed to be drawing perilously closer, as more jets roared across the skies.

It didn't take very long for her mother to pick up the phone and after a minute or two of speaking, her father turned to her and reassured her that her mother and brother were okay, that they were with two of her female colleagues, Lizzy and Elmira and they had found a car. Her father arranged to meet them at Stepney Green where they would make their way out of the city together.

In order to avoid them hanging around too long and being attacked by lingering twitchers, her father instructed them to get to the Stepney Green station entrance by 8:20, that he would be waving the illuminated phone to be seen.

Once he put down the phone, he picked her up on his back and they left the shop together.

Initially they were silent as they attempted to get past the twitchers in Bethnal Green Gardens and the back roads, using the noise of alarms and explosions to mask the sound of their own movement. Globe Road however, was more or less quiet, though it had certainly seen its fair share of events. Doors hung open and all manner of disregarded items littered the ground. Clearly the flats and houses along this road had been looted for all they were worth and Ria was willing to bet there were dead people inside those houses too, not all of them the victims of twitchers.

When Ria felt it was safe to talk, she did so.

"Daddy..." She said, clutching on to his neck and resting her head on his back.

"Yes Ria?"

"Forgive me".

"Whatever for?"

"For being spoilt. For being a brat. For not respecting you".

"I'm to blame for that, I was pathetic".

"And I was really mean to you, you didn't deserve that".

"I won't deny that it hurt, but I can't deny that I was weak, unreliable and a mess. I can't imagine how ashamed you must have been of me".

"That's not true, I've never been ashamed of you... it just... made me angry when you stopped making an effort and I guess not fighting for mum, not fighting for *us* when Daniel came along, I got frustrated".

"I was in... a bad place, but that's no excuse. I was a bad father and I want to make it up to you both, all of you, including Natasha".

"Well I was a bad daughter, so I guess like father, like daughter". Her father chuckled.

"It's in our blood, princess. Say, do you remember when I used to give you piggybacks as a kid".

"Of course, not", she replied, wincing as each bump reminded her of the pain she was in. Everything hurt.

"You used to call me your magical horse and I said magical horses were for *real* princesses and you said, you must be a princess then and that's how you earned that nickname".

"Come on, dad. I'm not a kid anymore, you're embarrassing me".

"Ria".

"Yes?"

"I'm sorry for being an asshole. I just want you to know that you, your brother and your mum mean everything and more to me. To lose either of you would be to lose my very soul". Ria smiled and embraced him tighter.

"I know I said the museum was lame before, but if I ever got another chance to go with you and George, I would", she replied. Her father smiled and said no more.

They passed beneath a bridge, but as they emerged from the other side, a large figure dropped down from above, blocking their path. Initially they thought it to be another twitcher, but as it turned to face them, the horrific truth revealed itself. There before them stood Daniel, except this was more than just Daniel, it was Daniel merged together with someone and something else, almost like conjoined twins.

"What the fuck?" Terry murmured, stepping back. How had that bastard survived, found them all the way out here and become this... grotesque thing? Was there even a creative mind who could conjure up such a being?

He pointed the gun towards the monstrosity and pulled the trigger, but much to his horror, nothing happened, nothing but the click of an empty magazine. Dammit, now would have been the time to have that shotgun from earlier. What were they going to do now? He had only the pen knife at his disposal and that wasn't going to be anywhere near enough to bring this lumbering nightmare down. On top of that, he had also his daughter's wellbeing to consider.

The houses, maybe they had something useful; it was a stab at the dark, but what other choice did he have.

"Daddy..." Ria whispered, panicking.

"Hold on tight, princess", Terry replied. He spun around and bolted in the opposite direction, with her clinging onto him.

They ran into an open doored house with clothes scattered across the drive. The windows were smashed inwards and the house was vacant. Upon further inspection, they realised that blood covered the walls and floor. There had most certainly been quite a scuffle here.

That aside, Terry ran into the kitchen, where he put Ria down. The back door leading out into the small garden with a shed hung open and in the middle of the lawn was what looked to be a dead animal, most likely a dog.

After inspecting his surroundings, he hurried back over in her direction to access drawers and shelves behind her.

"Ria, I need you to get out of here. Climb the fences, make your way to the front and get to Stepney Green station", he instructed, as he rummaged through drawers and cupboards looking for anything he could use as a weapon, but all he could find was matches, a rack of knives and a kitchen gas lighter.

"Without you?" Ria replied.

"Without me. I'm almost convinced that Daniel is coming after me specifically and if that's the case, then no matter where we go, he'll be right there behind us. I need to deal with this once and for all".

"How do you know that? Why would he do that? How can you be so sure that that is even him?"

"Because we met him when we were trying to escape your mother's office and he attacked us. He was infected. There's nothing left of him, he just wants to finish me off and kill you three. I'm an obstacle and he hates me the most".

"But how would he have even found us all the way here?"

"I have no idea. You need to get to safety, get out of the city".

"No, I'm not going anywhere without you, dad".

"Ria!" He snapped and just then, they were interrupted by the sounds of Daniel lumbering in through the front door.

"Ria, I won't tell you again! Get out of here!" He turned to her with scorn in his eyes, as though to intimidate her, but behind them she could see his genuine paternal concerns for her wellbeing and it made her heart hurt. She was going to say goodbye to her dad again and she really didn't want to, so instead she said nothing and slipped out of the back door.

Not until she was safely over the fence did he turn to face his greatest enemy standing at the kitchen door. A towering, lumbering, grotesque creature that not even his worst nightmares could hold a candle to.

The twitcher stood there glaring him down with the head that did not belong to Daniel. It twitched like all others, but appeared more aggressive despite its slower mannerism. The aura coming from it was intensely ominous and its speechless approach only increased the gravity of its menacing presence.

As it slowly approached him heavily breathing, wheezing and twitching, not saying a word, Terry felt as though his feet were glued to the ground. He began to wonder if there was any semblance of Daniel in there whatsoever or was this just another twitcher that had somehow combined itself with Daniel and in doing so, adopted Daniel's gripes against him.

Attached to its bottom half was what looked to be a dog, but it was so horribly disfigured, it could have been anything.

There wasn't much room to move in this kitchen, so Terry had no clue how he was going to get out of this alive, but he wasn't going to let this thing do any harm to his family.

It gurgled before launching an attack on him. He ducked, about the only thing he could possibly do in that instance and just as it smashed the counter behind him to bits, but just as he had believed he had gotten by, the fucking mutilated dog attachment took a massive bite into his leg, drawing blood. Terry had to fight it off by repeatedly stabbing it with the pen knife before the twitcher had a chance to recover and launch another attack on him. It eventually let him go, but even freed of its jaws, Terry knew that it was all over, he had been infected and it was only a matter of time before he became one of these monsters.

Still, now that he had nothing to lose, he also had nothing to fear. This house would be the location of his and Daniel's final confrontation and only one of them was walking out of here alive.

There had to be something in this house he could use to take down this fucker once and for all. The very moment he clambered to his feet, it launched another attack, smashing shelves and flinging kitchen utensils everywhere. It swung at him, sending pots and pans hurtling across the kitchen, cupboards fell apart, plates poured onto the floor and shattered beneath their feet.

Terry ran out into the corridor and dashed up the stairs, doing his best to disregard the pain from the bite in his leg. As he reached the top, he ran into the bathroom just opposite and opened up the drawers. There were lots of things here he could use, but whether or not they'd be effective was another question. He grabbed bleach, sanitizers and just about anything he could find, opened them and threw them down at the twitcher ascending the steps.

"Come on then, motherfucker! Let's finish this!" Terry shouted, but it didn't appear fazed by the poisonous chemicals, its empty angry eyes remained fixed on him as it slowly walked up the stairs. It was almost as though it were taunting him, moving slowly as though it knew it wouldn't have to overexert itself to kill him. Fucker, it was underestimating him, Daniel was fucking underestimating him again.

Terry ran into a bedroom and slammed the door close behind him, knowing not what he would find in here that would be of any use.

He hopelessly rummaged through the drawers not expecting to find anything, but to his joy found exactly what he needed. Thank God for Venelisse Eau de Parfum! The Maude branded perfume couldn't have been a more welcome sight. Game on, motherfucker!

He pulled the kitchen lighter from his pockets, placed the tip a little away from where the spray would eject and braced himself for the lumbering fuck to walk right into hell.

He heard it approaching, but somehow still expected it to walk into the bedroom normally, forgetting that these were the same things that had flung themselves through doors and window panes that entire day, so when the door flew off its hinges, debris almost hitting him in the process, it caught him completely off guard and knocked the lighter out of his hand.

The twitcher lunged at him and he dived out of the way as it crashed into the chest of drawers behind him, smashing it to pieces.

Fuck! Where did the lighter go?

He scoured the floor looking for it. It had to be somewhere close by. He flung things across the room at the twitcher, which of course did nothing and it lunged at him again. He rolled beneath the bed and it got to its feet, lifted the bed with one hand and threw it aside as though it were nothing.

Terry spotted the lighter just beneath the desk chair. He dived across the room to grab it, but didn't have a chance just yet stage a counter attack, for the twitcher charged at him, crashing into the desk and turning it into splinters.

Terry knew of only one way he might be able to slow it down. Getting to his feet, he pulled the bed sheets from the overturned bed and threw it over the twitcher, before toppling down a wardrobe on top of it. Neither of these would hold it down, but he only needed to suppress it long enough for him to attack. Arming himself with the lighter and perfume, he blasted small jets of flames at the twitcher, setting it, the sheets and the wardrobe on fire, but he didn't stop there, he continued spraying, covering everything in the spray and in doing so, turning the room into one big flammable hellhole.

Initially the twitcher didn't appear fazed by the flames, but not long afterwards its movement became more frantic as though trying to escape and it let out anear-piercing screech. Terry momentarily had to block his ears, before continuing his attack.

"Huh, don't like that do you, you ugly motherfucker? Burn! Fucking burn!"

Its burning flesh filled the air and it lashed out at him, trying to prevent Terry from burning it any more.

Terry blasted it with fire until he could blast it no more and the spray emptied. The room was ablaze with flames and the twitcher was right at the heart of it, flailing its arms and trying to escape.

Terry knew that that wasn't going to be enough, he needed more flammable liquids and he knew a few places they were likely to be. He ran out of the room and checked the other rooms, gathering hairsprays and throwing them back into the burning room. He backed off towards the stairs, spraying everything with either perfume, hairspray or deodorant.

The twitcher followed him out of the room, but so too did the flames.

"Where are you going, motherfucker? Don't you like it? I thought you wanted to watch the world burn!" Terry opened a bottle of nail polish remover and threw that at it, before making his way back downstairs, where he found alcohol in a cabinet of the front room. What a waste of good whiskey.

He returned to the staircase to find the twitcher of Daniel slowly making his way back down the steps in pursuit of him. Terry opened as many bottles of alcohol as he could and doused the twitcher in them, engulfing it in explosive flames and knocking Terry back.

He scrambled to his feet and backed off, as it slowed down and eventually collapsed down the last remaining steps to the floor below, where it would remain, unmoving and burning to crisp. No more twitching, no more raspy breathing, no more shrieks, just perfectly still to the sound of crackling flames.

He slumped down next to the front door staring at it, half expecting it to get up at any moment. It was over, he was rid of that arrogant son of a bitch, not that throughout it all he ever wanted Daniel dead, but at least he could say look at this as a plus. His sense of relief and accomplishment was marred by the bitter fact that he too would miss out on the happy ending, so maybe this was karma at work again.

His attention was averted to a sound behind him and there stood Ria at the doorway panting.

"You... killed it... you actually killed it", she mumbled.

"Ria, what are you doing here? I specifically told you to leave".

"I came back because I was really worried, but you killed it, so it's okay. We can go now, we can leave London together as a family".

Terry went silent for a moment; his revelation would shatter her little heart. While mustering up the courage to tell her the truth, he made idle conversation.

"I thought of a name for this one, how does the Siamese twitcher sound?"

Ria sighed and sat down beside him.

"Princess... I don't think I'll be going anywhere. Looks like you'll have to go on without me".

"What? What are you talking about? There's no time for jokes, dad, it's almost time".

He glanced towards her and saw the expression of concern written all over her face. Rolling up his trouser leg, he revealed the puncture wounds to his leg. Not only were they deep and still bleeding, the blood vessels surrounding the area of the wound had swollen, certainly not a normal sign.

"What happened?" She asked, staring at the wound.

"Got bitten, guess wanting to kill it and get away without a scratch was too much to ask for".

"No, no, no..." She repeated, shaking her head and refusing to believe what she was hearing.

"I guess things didn't go quite as I had planned, darling".

"No, no, you'll be fine, come on get up, we have to get to the others, we have to..." She began, getting up and tugging at his arm.

"Ria, if I go with you, I'll be a danger to both you and the others and I don't want that, it would be irresponsible".

"So, I'm just supposed to leave you here and go? I can't! I won't leave you behind! You're my dad, I can't do that, I just can't! I won't let those things find and kill you like they did everyone else!" She began shouting with anger as tears began to stream down her little blood-stained cheeks.

"You won't have to, I won't let that happen".

"So, what will you do?"

"Well I certainly don't want to become one of those things either, I guess I have no other choice", he replied, lifting the lighter.

"What? No! I won't let you do it! I won't let you kill yourself!"

"This isn't your choice to make, Ria! I have to do this to protect you all. The same way Daniel tracked me down is the same way I might track you down, you have to leave me behind, you have to forget about me".

"But you promised!"

He pulled her to his chest as she wept.

"I know... I know. I'm disappointing you guys again".

She pulled away.

"If you know that, why are you doing this? Why are you trying to make me cry? Why are you trying to break my heart?"

"Believe me, if I could find another means, I would. The last thing I want to ever be responsible for is making my princess, both my beloved children upset".

"Maybe there will be medicine, maybe it can be cured, maybe..."

"Ria, you saw what happened today. I'm not the first and I certainly won't be the last".

She stared at him helplessly, before collapsing to her knees once more. Looking down at her lap, as tears dropped onto her knees, she shook her head.

"Then... then what am I supposed to do?"

"Run, get out of here, be safe and protect your family".

"But that's what *you're* supposed to do, *you're* supposed to be our dad, *you're* supposed to be there as I grow up and encourage me and stuff. That's what *you're* supposed to do".

"I know, I'm constantly a let-down... if it's any consolation, you two are all grown up and stronger than I could have ever imagined, today you both demonstrated that to me more than any day before. George is stubborn and protective of those he cares about and you are headstrong and compassionate. Whether or not I played a part in any of that, you both found yourselves and the people you wanted to become, I couldn't be prouder of you two". He pulled her forward and kissed her forehead.

"Tell your mother I'm sorry for letting her down in the past and that I wish I could have had the chance to make it up to her someday. Tell your brother I love him, I always have and I always will. Tell him he's a brave little boy and he'll grow up to be a great man and tell him... forget it. He won't want to hear my excuses and apologies and knowing him, he'd probably never forgive me regardless", Terry sighed, then whispered, "I'm so sorry".

Ria's tears dropped onto his lap as she lost the fight holding them back.

"I can feel it... or at least I think I can. Get going, Ria, before the house explodes, I change or your mother doesn't see you on time", Terry instructed.

She pulled back from him reluctantly, her little face soaked with tears and the tissues stuck up her nose to stop the bleeding from the fracture. She stared at him, even with all the bruises and blood, as beautiful as the day she was born. He smiled.

"Get that nose seen to. Be safe. Don't let your brother boss you about, don't boss him about either. Look after your mum... oh, and take this". He placed his phone in her hands.

Ria stood up, her mouth trembling.

"Go..." Terry said once more and she stared at him for another minute.

"I love you, dad", were her last words before she ran out of the house, out of the drive and down the road, crying harder than she had ever cried in her life.

Terry's chest felt tight as he stood up, stepped outside of the house and watched her disappear down the road, a type of tightness he had never felt before. Was this because of the infection coursing through his veins or the tremendous guilt of letting his daughter down? Maybe it was a combination of the two.

How he wished things could have been different and they were so close to being so, but as fate would have it, once again he was thrown a curveball he couldn't catch. The pain of making his daughter shed tears on his behalf was unbearable and the effects of the infection only amplified the feelings of guilt.

He was beginning to feel hot and a little disorientated. Even without having ever experienced the symptoms personally, he knew he didn't have very long left, so with that, he turned and stepped back into the house, using every bit of what remained of his consciousness just to maintain control of his body. He ventured into the kitchen and switched on the gas from the cooker hubs.

His hands trembled as he lifted the kitchen lighter to his face and ignited it. He stared aimlessly at the flickering flame for a moment, losing himself in its simplicity. For all of its intricacies and complexities, the simplicity of igniting and extinguishing was not a far scope reflection of life itself.

How many lives had been extinguished in but a single day? Just like that?

In his final moments he was beginning to understand that maybe he *could* be considered a murderer if the twitchers he had killed or at least attempted to kill were subconsciously *still human*.

"I guess I'm going to hell if there is one... then again, given what's happened today, maybe there isn't even room there anymore. Ha, look at me getting all philosophical", he murmured and smiled to himself.

Just before the explosion, he twitched.

FINAL CHAPTER - EVERYONE

8:30pm - 8 Hours, 45 Minutes since outbreak

. . .

SOBA - TECH

FACT FILE #9:

Soba-Tech is an American multinational technology company with headquarters in Silicon Valley, California. It was founded by Johnathan and Lincoln Soba in 1972 under the name Soba Technologies, developing, manufacturing, licensing, supporting and selling computer software and hardware.

Having developed the intuitive and easy to use operating system, Dawn 1, and affordable hardware, Takomi series, Soba-Tech quickly garnered positive reception and the company went on to dominate the consumer electronics market with smart technologies and as of 20██, the world's first commercial augmented reality units.

In 1999, Soba-Tech expanded upon its catalog with internet-related services and products, which include online advertising technologies, search engine, cloud computing, software, and hardware.

As of 20██, it is the world's largest and most valuable company, owning brands **Myface, Vyou, Babbadoo, CINdy (Computer Intelligence Network), tPhone (Takko) Series, Dawn Operating Systems, Dawn Cloud Computing Systems** and **Takoma Series of PCs, Laptops, Tablets and flat surfaces.**

. . .

Ria turned as she heard the explosion and knew almost immediately that it was her dad.

She stood there sobbing and watching the flames billow high into the night skies.

The entire day's events flashed through her memories and she wished it had just been a normal lame day at the museums, looking at exhibits and eventually stuffing her face angrily with lunch. She wished it had just been a normal day spent bickering with her little brother, updating her measly 112 followers Chirper account about how boring and normal her day was and wanting to be spending time with Lacey and the guy she had a crush on.

Never in all of her wildest dreams and nightmares would she have ever foreseen a day as horrible and heart-breaking as today. She was battered and bruised, she had seen death right before her eyes, she could *still* see it vividly in her head and it made her shudder every time, she had been separated from her family members and forced to run from people or creatures that had developed a voracious cannibalistic appetite and to top it off, she had lost someone she cared deeply about just when they were about to escape and rebuild their lives.

Ria broke down, she couldn't contain it anymore, it was all too much. How much more of this was she going to have to withstand? Would she ever recover from the trauma induced experiences she had had today? Would she ever sleep another night without the nightmares haunting her? Would her father's face ever leave her mind?

Time ticked to two minutes past the half an hour, she was already 12 minutes later than planned, would her mother even be at the spot they agreed any longer?

She ran the rest of the way down Globe Road to Stepney Green sobbing and came to a stop close to the station. The place was swarming with twitchers.

What was she meant to do now and how on Earth would her mother know where she was? Had she left already?

Finding a secluded spot to avoid the light from the phone drawing attention to her, she checked the mobile and found a few texts from her mother asking where they were, followed by one last one a minute or two ago with the words, 'We are going to leave, it's getting dangerous. Let us know a better place to meet you'.

"No mum, don't move, I can't do this on my own, I can't", Ria whispered, fear induced tears welling up in her eyes.

What was she going to do? Where was she going to go?

Using her gunshot wounded arm, she texted her mother back, begging for her to stay in close proximity, that she was in the area and too terrified to move anywhere else, followed by a ping of her exact location.

Shortly afterwards her mother texted her back, 'when you hear the car horn, head as quickly as you can towards where you heard it from and head to the car with the headlights on, we'll have the door open for you. Move fast as it'll attract every one of those things in the area, if you can't make it fast enough, don't take risks, hide and we'll try again or something else'.

Five minutes passed and they felt like eons, Ria began to wonder if her mother would ever show. Suddenly, she heard the car horn.

Poking her head up, further down the road she could see the car headlights, but that also meant that the twitchers were seeing it too. She couldn't waste any more time, it was now or never, the one chance she had to get away.

She broke into a sprint, or at least the closest to it in her condition, sliding across the bonnet of cars and waving her phone in the air for them to see, but if they were seeing it, they certainly weren't the only ones, for every twitcher in the vicinity had also seen her running.

If the screams and shrieks of the twitchers bounding towards her, jumping from car to car, smashing out of windows, pouring out of houses and crawling out from every nook and cranny, weren't enough to motivate her to run faster, nothing would.

Her heart thumped as adrenaline and terror alone compelled her to keep moving, that track and field experience was proving its worth more than ever before.

The twitchers were drawing in on her now and she herself wasn't all that far away from the car. Did they see her? She couldn't hear them over all of the noise and she couldn't see them with the car lights beaming in her face. Did they see her? She couldn't tell, she could only pray they could, because if they didn't, the grisly alternative didn't bear thinking about.

Suddenly the car begun reversing away from her.

"No!" She screamed, they were going to drive away from her, they hadn't seen her! "Wait! Wait for me!" Could they even hear her? She could barely hear herself despite how loud and frantically she screamed out for them, hoping that by some miracle they could see her, hear her, but the car continued to reverse.

Much to her surprise the brakes of the car locked, sending it skidding backwards down the road, before the front spun out to face the opposite way. The back door opened and there she saw her mother calling out for her.

"Ria! Quick! Get in! Hurry, baby, hurry!"

The twitchers tore down the road behind her, closing in on her as she ran as fast as she could. She practically dived into the car.

"Okay! Drive! Drive now!" Her mother shouted and Lizzy, the designated driver, slammed her foot down on the accelerator, jerking them all forwards and speeding down the road.

Her mother embraced her tightly as Ria wept into her bosom.

"Ria... your father?"

Ria glanced up towards her mother and didn't need to say or do anything further for her mother to understand that Terry wasn't going to be joining them.

"You poor baby, what did they do to you?" Her mother asked, crying as well upon seeing the state of her.

Being in the car with her mother, finally leaving London after what would be the third or fourth attempt that long day, came with a sense of relief, but even that relief was short lived, for she would never forget what she had endured on this day and to this moment she still waited to wake up from the horrific nightmare, waiting for someone to release her from this horror.

If only she could take back everything she had said earlier that day about hating him and wishing for him to disappear, for karma was a bitch and she had claimed his life in the honour of penance.

She didn't even want to look at her brother, she could feel his eyes on her and she knew what he was thinking, she knew because she was feeling exactly the same thing. She wanted to scream, she wanted to punch something in frustration, but all she could do was cry and cling onto her mother like a new born.

George was confused, he couldn't help but wonder what had happened to his father as he kept peering back, half expecting his father, his idol, his best friend to pop out from somewhere and surprise them. His heart sank further and further into despair as the slow realisation that his father wasn't coming back began to settle.

Natasha could think of only one thing, protecting what remained of her family. In a single day she had lost both her husband and ex-husband to something she knew next to nothing about. She had seen the deaths of friends and colleagues and watched the city crumble right before her very eyes. To this moment she still didn't know what to think, but as she looked at the blood, wounds and bruises on her daughter, respect in her ex-husband was restored. Had he not acted as quickly and persistently as he had, she wouldn't be safely in her embrace right now. Wounds and bruises would heal, but she'd never be able to reclaim her children from the clutches of death, for that, she would never be able to thank Terry enough.

"Thank you, Terry..." She murmured under her breath and embraced Ria.

The five survivors, Natasha Riley, her two children Ria and George and her colleagues Elmira Dowling and Elizabeth Rowth, also known simply as Lizzy to her peers, made their way out of the city in a little car south eastwards towards the coastline. They had no clear idea where they were going or what their destinies would have in store for them, but what they did know was that London was no longer a safe place, no longer a place to call home, for now at least.

They stopped outside of the city once safe, to reflect on all that had occurred for a moment before progressing.

George was hysterical, refusing to get back in the car and determined to go and look for his father. Lizzy couldn't stop shaking, forcing Elmira to have to take over the driving and Natasha could only embrace her crying children as emotions erupted.

'How long is the recovery period for this sort of thing? How big is the universe? Two questions that would probably never get answers, but everything *will* change from now on, is *already* changing and nothing that once was will ever be'.

The last paragraph of Ria's last words uploaded to the internet would hold more weight than she could ever know, for throughout that night, tanks, jets, helicopters and soldiers besieged the city, attempting to contain the threat by applying the Ministry of Defence's contingency plan set aside specifically with the objective of tackling contagions on epidemic levels, including, but not limited to zombie-like threats, but what they could not have foreseen was anything quite like this one.

News quickly spread that those infected with the vora-virus were far from dead, by no means slow, strong, adaptable, semi-intelligent, able to communicate up to a certain degree and of course cannibalistic.

But those discoveries were only the beginning. Bullets to the skull didn't seem to faze the infected like they would the undead of fiction. Their ability to continue moving without vital ligaments, their keener senses, their inflated blind anger, lack of pain reception and perhaps most intriguing, their ability to assimilate in order to evolve, made them the single most problematic issues that government and army had had to deal with years, but they weren't to know just how problematic it could be until it was far too late and containment was slowly beginning to become impossible.

The speed, ferocity and unpredictability of its spread made it next to impossible to anticipate and prevent, for shortly after the outbreak in London, there were further outbreak reports in other cities and rural towns. Operation Phoenix - an initiative called upon by the government to first attempt to identify and contain, if that failed, shoot on sight and in the worst-case scenario fire bomb any and all compromised locations - had failed, serving only to claim the lives of uninfected innocents.

Information pertaining to the source of the outbreak remained undisclosed, a cure would not see the light of day until years later and the only short-term solution to eradicating those infected in the most efficient means possible was fire, but by the time this intelligence became common knowledge, the damage had already been done and the country fell apart.

All forms of transportation in and out of the country was suspended, the stock market crashed, food and medical shortages would become a rampant problem, crime rates would soar, information became sparse, leaders fled, abandoning their country, armies retreated, instead refocusing their efforts on protecting key strategic waypoints and leaving civilians to fend for themselves.

Wales fell in quick succession, Scotland attempted to ward off the threat with vast walls and electric fences, Ireland attempted to cut off all connections to the mainland and other surrounding European countries instigated and or participated in Operation Blackwater to prevent the vora-virus reaching French shores, this word coming shortly after news that the virus had somehow made it as far across the globe as Puerto Rico. The initiative would prove to hold out for a number of months, but would ultimately fail.

Then came black day, September 10th, the day that all went dark as telecommunications and electricity was cut indefinitely nationwide and with it all hope was crushed.

For London, one of the most powerful cities in the world, to buckle beneath the weight of its own conceited grandeur, it sent a powerful and long-lasting message to the rest of world, even the mightiest could be forced to kneel.

See, in mankind's relentless search for more, knowledge is power and they who know all, control all. Fear what the eyes don't see, what the ears do no hear and what the mind does not know, fear the unknown.

End

BONUS CHAPTER - ELLIE

12:45pm - 6 Days until outbreak

. . .

. . .

Ellie Branning was always a shrewd woman, she knew exactly how to get what she wanted when she wanted it. Everything was always about her and why shouldn't it be? She was a distinguished woman who had worked hard her entire life, she wasn't a layabout benefit scrounging leech, she never once asked anyone for anything and made it her mission in life to aim for the spotlight.

She could have been an Oscar winning actress, she was always told she was a brilliant performer. She could have been a multiple number 1 selling singer, she was always told she had the voice of a maiden. She could have been a model, she was always complimented on her beauty.

She could have been all those things and more, but she wanted an entirely different type of fame and admiration. She came from a long lineage of successful and ambitious people. Money and success flowed through her veins, where normal people only found blood.

She chose to become a reporter, a job she loved because it meant that she was always the focus of the camera.

More people watched the news then watched movies, the career of a reporter was more varied, stable and long lasting than a music artist's and she'd feel far more valued and respected as a reporter than a model strutting on the catwalk.

With this career she could flaunt herself and all her beauty at all and any times during the day. Her name and face would be ingrained into minds, she would never be forgotten. She would make friends in high places and be granted the opportunity to travel the world free of charge, what could be better?

Ellie took part in documentaries and was even an anchor for a few years on competitor news network SBC (Sun Broadcasting) News. She became a TV personality, highly recognised and established amongst the higher ups. Her determination to reach the clouds of success had no limitation, she certainly wasn't afraid of stepping on toes along the way, so for all the friends she had, she also had her fair share of enemies. She left disaster in her wake and her name alone struck fear into those who also sought the top.

But nothing could be said about her, she was amazing at her job, unmatched even. Three years ago, a disgruntled bitch made an attempt on her life and needless to say, like all other losers who had challenged Ellie to that point, she failed and was arrested and sentenced accordingly. Maybe next time someone wanted to break into her house, hide in her cupboard and jump out at her with a knife, they'd have the fucking intelligence to not leave evidence of their forced entry everywhere and do their fucking research, just a little bit went a long way and if they had, they would have discovered that she was a 1st dan taekwondo student, it would have saved her assailant the humiliation of ending up on her back... with a knife protruding from her thigh.

On the day of the outbreak, Ellie was due to exclusively cover the autobiography book signing of one of the greatest Olympic medallists in the world, it was a big day for her, a day she had fought hard for and in doing so, squashed bugs vying for the same position just 6 days before the outbreak.

3:45pm - 2 Days until outbreak

Two days before the outbreak, Ellie was more than prepared for the book signing, it was going to be an amazing day and she wasn't going to let the bitter ones ruin it for her with their insistent moaning, they would have to deal with it, she was better at this. You win some you lose some.

She was assigned this story along with cameraman Zachary Lincoln, the only cameraman she would agree to work with, for the others were imbeciles or amateurs. Zachery knew her inside from out, what she liked and what she didn't, as well as being a perfectionist at capturing her very essence of being on camera in such a way that she could only radiate.

6:45am - 5 Hours until outbreak

The morning of the book signing arrived and Ellie had her crew scrambled around like headless chickens. She wanted to look like a goddess on camera, outshining even the story subject, the athlete.

She had been here since 5, ready for the morning broadcast, but what the hell were the rest of her crew doing like this? If any one of those fuckers ruined this day for her, she'd make damn well sure they were fired.

Jesus fucking Christ, why did she had to work with brainless disorganised chimps half the time? A little bit of professionalism went a long fucking way.

12:12pm - 27 Minutes since outbreak

Ellie was at the scene of the book signing and it was all going fairly well; crowds were amassing, clearly recognising her face more so than the so-called Olympic celebrity she was interviewing.

Funny that, she didn't even need to have a gold medal around her neck to be respected, adored and admired, what a world she lived in.

It was midway into the interview that she noticed people around her behaving shiftily, something was awry and people were making their way out. Shortly into the interview, the Olympic medallist was also called aside, putting an abrupt halt to the book signing, an action that pissed Ellie right off. She had prepared 6 days for this, what the fuck was he doing? What could be so important that it couldn't wait until afterwards?

Pacing back and forth in a foul mood while she waited for his majesty to return - one stupid little gold medal and he thought he could behave like this -, she got a call from her

186

bosses who alerted her to the fact that a possible terror attack in London had occurred, was still occurring and they wanted her on it immediately. Of course, she jumped at the opportunity, anything to get away from this snooze-fest.

They sent a helicopter to retrieve she and Zachery, piloted by the one and only Steve Phillips, a man they had flown with before and who had racked up at least 20 years' worth of helicopter flying experience, an expert, just how she liked her men and co-workers.

They flew into the heart of the city, navigating around buildings, taking chances with no-fly zone without expressed permission, hovering dangerously low, for today was an exception, never before had anything quite like what they were seeing occurred., this was a scoop she couldn't afford to miss a single bit of detail on.

It was not until they reached the heart of the chaos did they realise the full extent of it. Below them, people chased other people, killed other people in the most horrific, barbaric and shocking manner, it was as though they were possessed. Ellie had seen some shit during the course of her career, more than any ordinary person would ever desire to see, from live beheadings, to massacres, to rape cases and even trafficking, she had even seen the aftermath of terror attacks, but nothing, absolutely nothing compared to what she was now witnessing. Humans were capable of some truly depraved things, but this shit right here made them all pale in comparison.

People were being ripped apart and eaten on the streets by other people. Cannibals were far from unheard of, but this... this was something entirely different, this genuinely scared the shit out of her and *that* was saying something coming from someone who didn't scare easily.

Zachery tried his utmost to keep track of the ongoings and she found herself becoming too distracted by everything to effectively report on what was happening below. It was all happening so quickly.

2:10pm - 2 Hours, 25 Minutes since outbreak

An hour later and they were still filming, still trying to comprehend just what was happening and the horrors showed absolutely no sign of slowing down.

Rare as it was, Ellie entirely forgot about how she looked, she forgot about what she was supposed to say, she forgot everything.

"Are you getting all of this?" Was about as much as she could muster. The question was directed at Zachery, but it could just about be extended to her audience, for it was without doubt the centrepiece of the broadcast.

Below, people waved up to the helicopter with hopes of being rescued, but alas, Steve could not and would not be performing any rescue stunts to put the lives of those on board in jeopardy, as painstaking as it was to overlook desperate cries for help.

Suddenly and startlingly, there was a loud slam towards the front of the helicopter, followed by a horrendous grating and clanging sound coming from the propeller above. Blood from an unknown source sprayed absolutely everywhere and the helicopter jerked backwards, throwing them all off their balance and the camera from Zachery's hands, plummeting to the ground below.

The helicopter went into a free-falling spiral of death with everyone on board clinging on to anything they could find and screaming. They lost altitude blisteringly fast and the last thing Ellie could recall before all went dark was her and the helicopter's reflection upon the windows of a shopping complex.

2:21pm - 2 Hours, 36 Minutes since outbreak

When Ellie finally came around, the smell of gas filled her nostrils, a fire alarm's insistent ringing filled her ears and she was soaked.

Absolutely everything ached, but what she couldn't determine just yet was the extent of the damage inflicted on her from that crash.

She glanced around, a little hazy and unsure of where she was, it took her some time to figure that out. Even as she stared at the wreckage of the helicopter, she couldn't ascertain how she had managed to survive.

With more investigation, she became aware that she was in the cafeteria section of a department store, but it was difficult to distinguish anything with so much dust and debris everywhere.

The water could be explained by the sprinklers above, preventing the flames from the helicopter burning wildly out of control, which was most certainly a good thing given the smell of gas lingering in the air. It was any wonder how the helicopter hadn't blown up yet, or blown something else up.

She coughed and returned her thoughts to the helicopter. Staring at it only brought the memories of the events prior back to her like a fucking punch to the face.

She gasped and scrambled away from the wreckage, wondering how on Earth she had survived. She checked herself over, but other than a few bruises and a gash to the head that a trip to the hospital and stitches could fix, she was fine.

What the fuck had knocked them out of the air like that? How had she survived? Maybe she was indeed lucky, maybe she was difficult to kill. She may have just thought it before, but now with the sheer amounts of scrapes with death she had had in her life, she had begun to genuinely believe that... but what about Zachery and Steve?

She got up and inspected the wreckage, being cautious around the unstable floor surrounding it.

Steve was a goner, she could only just about see his burning corpse in that mangled mess of metal and debris. She covered her mouth in abhorrence.

Agonised groaning tore her attention away and to the side of the wreckage she found Zachery, the lower half of his body lodged between a metal beam and the wreckage.

"Help me..." He murmured, coughing up blood. Choking smoke billowed out of the wreckage. They were probably more likely to die from asphyxiation than the flames or an explosion, neither of which was particularly preferable.

Hurrying to his aid, she attempted and failed to release him from his constraints. She had to face facts here, there was going to be no easy way of freeing him with just her hands alone and he was bleeding quite heavily.

"Ellie... I can't feel my leg, I think it's broken".

"Hold on, Zachery, I'm... I'm going to find something to free you with", she replied and clambered off of the wreckage. She stood upright and looked around helplessly, there had to be something she could use.

She wouldn't find the time to think about it though, for no sooner had she begun looking, high pitched shrieks gave cause to halt her search and investigate.

Carefully peering around a corner, she spotted a most unwelcomed sight. Running from the other side of the floor, several of those cannibalistic psychopaths that she had only been filming a few minutes prior.

As if that weren't enough, from behind the wreckage crawled another psycho, except this one lacked the entire lower half of her body.

How was she still alive with her innards dragging on the floor behind her?

Either out of habit or sheer desire to make sense of the unbelievable in some way, Ellie immediately pulled out her mobile. The glass had cracked, but it appeared to still be working, so she began filming, all whilst backing away.

"Ellie! Ellie, where are you? Have you found something yet?" Zachery begged.

Idiot! He was making a scene, he was sure to draw their attention right to this spot now. The crawler seemed curious to the noise too, deciding to ignore Ellie in favour of investigating the insides of the wreckage.

Ellie still had ample opportunity to attempt to save him, but what good would it do if she'd have to carry a guy twice her weight and decrease both their chances of making it out alive in the process. She'd been granted another shot at life and she sure as hell wasn't about to squander it, regardless of how bad she felt.

She disregarded his cries for help, moving out of the line of sight and only continued to back off when those cries for help became shrill screams.

All that noise was bound to attract the attention of more of those cannibalistic psychopaths and she didn't want to be a guest at *that* party, so with that, Ellie left Zachery to his demise and fled.

2:43pm - 2 Hours, 58 Minutes since outbreak

Having found a safe area to make a call for her retrieval, her superiors, who seemed delighted to hear she was okay, were saddened at the news of Zachery and Steve's deaths. She warned them that the building was swarming with the same people she had been filming and it was best to come equipped, or at least carrying someone who came equipped, she was taking no chances.

It was only upon further investigation of said department store to give them her exact location, did she discover that this was no ordinary department store, this was the most prestigious of them all, so prestigious in fact that it was the only one of its existence in the world and visitors came from far and wide to shop, this department store was none other than Lemara, the most expensive, most exclusive, most popular department store in the world. Could she be any luckier? Not only did the god of fortune want her to survive this, they wanted her to be surrounded by luxuries as an apology for the traumatising accident she had been forced to endure.

Her clothes were stained in blood and dirt. It was almost too compelling to grab and change into one of those limited-edition outfits, if it weren't for the fact danger lurked all around. Hell, there were items here worth thousands just sitting around, limited editions and even a few things that were the only one of their kind worldwide worth up to millions she'd bet. How frustrating it was to see them all sitting there enticing and unattended.

Fortunately, the frustration wouldn't have to eat away at her for very long, she spotted other survivors making a daring escape attempt and decided that her best bet was with them... probably.

2:53pm - 3 Hours, 08 Minutes since outbreak

Ellie soon established that these people were members of staff and a Tunisian family who had been visiting London and the department store that day when chaos erupted, many fled or attempted to flee the building when they were shoved and trampled upon, this before staff shut the doors to prevent thieves getting out and looters, as well as those cannibals getting in, but all that seemed to do was trap people inside and the psychopathic cannibals got in anyway, so now they were sitting sheep to the slaughter.

Survivors took to hiding in any spot they could find and waiting for things to blow over and rescue to come, but weren't sure how long that would take. There were probably countless others hiding around the store waiting for rescue, rescue that may never come.

The family with her consisted of a husband with his wife and their three children, the youngest just a baby.

They and the staff, likely others too, all hopelessly thought that her approaching helicopter was a sign of rescue, but when it went down, hope was dashed along with it.

They had seen someone jump from the top floor of another building, though whether they had jumped at the helicopter because they were one of the psychopathic cannibals or fleeing said psychopathic cannibals was something Ellie would probably never find out. Maybe the woman who had emerged from the wreckage without a lower half was the one responsible, but it didn't explain how she was able to still move in a condition like that.

The staff recognised her and automatically assumed they could use her fame to get rescued faster and in the spur of the moment, she stupidly entertained the idea as a means of reassuring them.

The news gave them hope they were already beginning to lose, it was the first sign of a positive development.

Good news eventually found its way to her in the form of a text, but in an ironic twist of fate, *only* her. Her merry band of survivors would not hear the news they were looking for and there was no easy way to reveal that too them.

The helicopter had been dispatched and would be arriving soon, but it had room for only one pickup, they had assumed she was the only one they need rescue.

Ellie's heart sank, she had genuinely hoped to rescue these people, especially since she couldn't rescue Zachery and Steve, but that wasn't going to be an option now.

She could have offered up her place, but with the noise the helicopter would inevitably draw, she'd be killed in the process and the gods had already bestowed her with one more shot at life, she wasn't about to give that up for anyone. Life was the most precious gift and she wasn't prepared to die just yet.

She needed to get to the roof, where they'd rescue her, but how was she going to escape this situation? They had all just seen her on the phone, so they knew she was talking to her rescue.

She made up an excuse about them being delayed and that she needed to pee, before standing up with every intention of leaving the others behind, but her silent departure wasn't going to be that simple, for someone in particular was suspicious.

"Where are you going, Ellie?" He asked. She turned to him and the curious stares of the others.

"Just... somewhere a little more private, I'm not going to pee in front of everyone", she replied with a nervous chuckle.

"On your own? With those things prowling about?"

"I'm not going far at all. 'll be fine".

"But what if they discover you? You'll draw them back to us, or worse, if you get killed, we'll have no means of communication with rescue".

"That won't happen".

"Surely you're not trying to leave us behind here and sneak off to be rescued by yourself?"

There was a series of gasps.

Shit! That little fucker! Was he suspicious of her this whole time?

"Of course not!"

"Oh, okay, it's just that I thought you'd have good news to tell us, but your expression changed when you read that last message, you looked solemn, so I assumed they probably said something along the lines of not being able to rescue us all and you figured you'd leave us all for fodder".

"That's not true! I wouldn't do that! I went solemn because the thought of having to wait longer made me anxious and scared, nothing else".

"Well okay, if you say so, can't blame me, I'm a little on edge at the moment".

191

Ellie sighed with relief.

"I don't, I'll be right back".

"Oh, just to calm us down, because we're pretty paranoid, why don't you show us the text you just got".

Shit! That was all she needed, why couldn't he just lay the fuck off and take her word for it?

They stood glaring at each other for an intense moment, as the others pushed her into quelling their insecurities. Her nervousness quickly switched to frustrated anger as she failed to come up with a good excuse.

"What do you people want from me? I owe you nothing!" She snapped, quickly realising the error in her words, as they stared at her in horror.

Slowly she backed off towards the door.

"She's trying to escape without us! Don't let her!" The man snapped and like an angry mob, not much different in their nature to that of the cannibalistic psychopaths, they all launched at her, pulling her to the ground as they pulled at her hair, reaching out for her phone.

"Get the fuck off me!" She screamed, raising her voice as loud as she could.

"Make for the roof! If she was going to be rescued, that's surely the place!" The man shouted, but he only served to stir the group into an angry rage of desperation and as soon as some saw the opportunity to make a break for the roof, they were gone without a moment's hesitation, soon followed by others. They ignored Ellie in favour of making a quick dash for the exit.

"Fuck!" The man shouted, realising he would be left behind, no thanks to his foolishness and so too tried to run. Ellie panicked, she couldn't let them all get to the top, the helicopter would never be able to reach her, she'd be stuck in this shithole as it flies overhead and leaves her behind.

She grabbed her mobile and lied through her teeth with a text.

'Those crazed people almost got me! They are running up to the roof to escape, shoot anyone that gets there on sight until you see me. I can't get out until they are all gone!'

They texted back moments later assuring her safety by any and all means and with that, Ellie got up and ran.

The noise had drawn the attention of the crazed from the ground below. Tearing across the aisle and smashing through obstacles, they lunged on top of fleeing survivors, ripping them to shreds right there on the ground.

Ellie ran straight past, disregarding them as they screamed out for help. Karma was a fucking psychotic bitch.

An old man grabbed her ankle, bringing her to the ground, on his back a crazed middle-aged woman ripped at his flesh, hissing at her.

"Get off of me!" She screamed, but the man refused, clinging on to her now with two hands.

"You have to save me!" He begged.

"No, I fucking don't!"

"Help me!"

"Get the fuck off of me!" She hit at his hands and face with her phone, but he refused to let go. It wasn't until another crazed man pounced on top of him and tore out his innards, spraying the old man's blood everywhere like a grisly fountain and drenching Ellie in it, did he finally release her.

Initially she was far too stunned and terrified to move, as blood dripped down her hair and face and what could only be kidneys and a bit of intestines fell onto her lap.

She screamed and swept the bits off as a chill ran right up her spine.

She scrambled to her feet covered from head to toe in blood. If that wasn't enough to spur her on, nothing would. She completely disregarded those calling out for her help in blind desperation, in order to save her own skin.

"Fuck you!" She yelled back. This was her future at stake here and she wasn't about to let it slip through her fingers for anyone. Nobody would take her future, fuck those bastards, fuck them all!

She came to a stop at the escalators, blocked by several crazed people. Those up ahead were pounced upon and torn apart as more crazed people appeared. Where were they all coming from? The entire fucking floor was swarming with them?

Ellie abandoned that route and made for the other side of the floor towards a fire exit, also swarming with the crazed. Along the way she encountered a pregnant woman and filled with rage, she shoved the woman into an aisle, knocking both she and the display down.

"Get outta my way, bitch!"

The woman hit the ground hard and whimpered as she held her stomach, struggling to get back up. Her whimpers quickly became shrill shrieks as she was pounced upon by a crazed person.

Ellie didn't even look back to see the outcome, her legs carried her all the way to the door and with her full body weight, she shoved it open, threw herself inside and slammed it shut behind her, in doing so, trapping the Tunisian family shortly behind her outside with the twitchers to the sounds of their cries for her to wait.

Ellie leaned up against the door, preventing them from getting through. She could hear them, husband, wife and children, thumping at the door, begging to be let in.

"You're not taking my future!" Ellie screamed.

"Open the fucking door!" The husband shouted, pushing on it.

"Go to hell!"

Stronger than her, he and the added pressure from his family, had almost managed to get in, when their haunting screams suggested the beginning of their demise.

She heard them being slammed against the door and the walls besides it, she heard the husband wailing out for his wife and children, she heard them weeping and screaming out for him, she heard him ordering them to run and their inevitable failure in doing so, she heard it all and could visualise every heart-breaking second of it in head, all the while convincing herself repeatedly that it was absolutely necessary, that it was their own fault and that she had done nothing wrong.

Their screams eventually died down until all she could hear was gurgled groans and shuffling.

She couldn't tell you why she did next what she did, maybe it was morbid curiosity, maybe it was to delude herself into thinking she had tried to do something, but she opened the doors and what she witnessed would scar her more than anything else she had seen or experienced today, as though that helicopter crash wasn't enough of a mental scar as it was.

Scattered across the floor were human remains laying in pools of blood everywhere, absolutely everywhere; belonging to the husband, the wife... the children.

She wanted to break down and cry, awash with shame and guilt. She had been many things throughout her life, but never had she thought herself capable of *this*. They were just an innocent terrified family, even if she couldn't save the adults, she could have convinced the rescue crew to save the children.

She began to hyperventilate, overwhelmed with self-loathing and guilt.

Ellie shut the door again and backed off from it, her heart racing, her mind a million miles away and her entire body trembling. At least they all died together, it would have been a crueller twist of fate for them all to perish alone, or at least that was morbidly the only comforting thought she had.

She glanced upwards, there were just a few flights of stairs to the top roof and she could already hear the helicopter. Tripping over herself in her desperation to get away, she clumsily clambered up the remaining flights of stairs.

With each step, she was reminded of the horrific screams and scenes of those she had left behind, the family, the pregnant woman, that old man and everyone else.

These steps felt like a mountain with this heavy burden of guilt weighing down on her, so it was only a relief to reach the top of the steps and step out into the open, greeted by a gentle breeze on her face.

She stood there for a second taking gulps of fresh air and thanking the heavens for keeping her alive, before making her way around to the roof helicopter pad, one of the few buildings in London to actually have one.

Exhausted and desperate to just be lifted to safety, eat, shower, sleep and be with her family, she stumbled up onto the helicopter pad as the helicopter hovered overhead.

Relieved that this would all soon be over, she waved for their attention and called out, but it didn't appear as though they could hear her over the loud roar of the propellers.

It wasn't long before she realised the tremendous error in judgement she had made, a cruel twist of fate, the bitchiness of karma returning to exact vengeance.

Her eyes opened wide, her arms dropped and she gasped as a red dot travelled across the ground and up her stomach to stop at her chest. Just before the gunshot, a thought passed through her mind, why the hell didn't she call off the text she had sent?

Bang!

End

Printed in Poland
by Amazon Fulfillment
Poland Sp. z o.o., Wrocław